Also by G.M. Malliet

The St. Just mysteries

DEATH OF A COZY WRITER
DEATH AND THE LIT CHICK
DEATH AT THE ALMA MATER
DEATH IN CORNWALL *

The Max Tudor series

WICKED AUTUMN
A FATAL WINTER
PAGAN SPRING
A DEMON SUMMER
THE HAUNTED SEASON
DEVIL'S BREATH
IN PRIOR'S WOOD

Novels

WEYCOMBE

* *available from Severn House*

AUGUSTA HAWKE

G.M. Malliet

SEVERN
HOUSE

First world edition published in Great Britain and the USA in 2022
by Severn House, an imprint of Canongate Books Ltd,
14 High Street, Edinburgh EH1 1TE.

Trade paperback edition first published in Great Britain and the USA in 2022
by Severn House, an imprint of Canongate Books Ltd.

severnhouse.com

British Library Cataloguing-in-Publication Data
A CIP catalogue record for this title is available from the British Library.

ISBN-13: 978-1-4483-0602-2 (cased)
ISBN-13: 978-1-4483-0604-6 (trade paper)
ISBN-13: 978-1-4483-0603-9 (e-book)

All Severn House titles are printed on acid-free paper.

Typeset by Palimpsest Book Production Ltd.,
Falkirk, Stirlingshire, Scotland.
Printed and bound in Great Britain by
TJ Books, Padstow, Cornwall.

For the Kara family

ACKNOWLEDGMENTS

Merci to Monica Rocchio for drawing on her Interpol experience to answer my questions regarding how murder investigations would be handled in small French villages. And to Susan Gurney, PhD, of the University of Cambridge, for her expert guidance in forensic science. All mistakes are my own.

To the Royals, for their weekly Zoom support, friendship, advice, and movie recommendations.

To Alison Steventon, forever awesome.

To the members of Sisters in Crime, Mystery Writers of America, and the Crime Writers' Association (UK). Many thanks for the camaraderie and the memories.

Special thanks to my agent, Mark Gottlieb of Trident Media Group, and Carl Smith, Natasha Bell, and Penny Isaac of Severn House for their excellent advice, calm guidance, and remarkable professionalism.

And above all, to Bob.

'A thing which has not been understood inevitably reappears; like an unlaid ghost, it cannot rest until the mystery has been solved and the spell broken.'

– Sigmund Freud

ONE

My father was bipolar, what they used to call manic-depressive – a better term, more descriptive of his self-destructive highs and lows.

When he was in his late twenties, he underwent electroconvulsive therapy. It did jolt him out of the manic phase he'd been circling in, at least temporarily. Just long enough to settle down and conceive me, if I'm doing the math right. ECT was what they did – what they still do. Centuries before, they'd have drilled a hole in his head to release the demons.

My mother, on the other hand, had borderline personality disorder. She was one of those people who didn't know where they stopped and others began, resembling Princess Di in looks and personality. In my father she found her own perfect mismatch.

Overall, our household could have done with a lot less drama.

When I was fifteen my father left, a final punch reinforcing my mother's already rampant fears of abandonment and igniting mine. Still I worshipped him from afar until the enormity of the damage he had done began to sink in. When finally I met the woman he had run off with (younger, goes without saying, and homely, with Ronald McDonald hair, harder to explain), I stopped adoring.

When my husband Marcus died, the finality actually helped. At least I knew he wasn't somewhere in the world, hiding his assets and being happy without me.

Strangely enough, I had a good if solitary childhood while my parents were preoccupied by their personal tragedies, but I suspect their marriage and its final unraveling are what turned me into a writer. If chaos and disorder are necessary ingredients, along with an abiding need to find a pattern and impose order, my upbringing certainly ticked all the boxes.

Possibly for related reasons, I avoided marriage and anything like a stable, well-paying profession like finance or IT. In college I dabbled in painting and, just as I was thinking I wasn't terrible at it, I sat next to a girl in class with real talent. It was like watching da Vinci at work on the *Mona Lisa*.

The next day I switched my major to journalism, suspecting my other interest, creative writing, was unlikely to pay the rent. I was right about that for quite a while. I never attended a writers' school like Iowa or a writers' colony like Yaddo or MacDowell (they rejected me, just so you know. I'm sure they still regret it). I wrote every day, trying to pin the world to the mood board in my head.

I was drawn to mysteries, of course. That imposing-order thing, although I wonder I didn't choose some angsty thing (something that might get me into MacDowell), some romance from a bygone age thing, even some dark serial killer thing. I tried, because according to *Writers' Digest* these books were what the public wanted, but I couldn't make it work. The angsty thing became a personal litany of grievances rather than a brave, heart-rending survey of the human spirit. The romance novel wouldn't get off the ground; it may have been a case of my being unable to write what I didn't know, but my attempt described two people so insipid I couldn't stand to be in the room with either of them for the year or more it takes to write a book.

The serial killer thing, I think we can agree, has been done to death. Despite my best attempts at creating a trophy-hunting psychopath with poor dental hygiene and serious mom issues, I couldn't make the guy scary. He was simply banal, which probably is true of most serial killers.

One day just before graduation, on a train from Maine to New York to interview for a job in journalism, I thought I'd pass the time by trying to write a detective story. I began sketching out an imaginary village on the pages of a shiny blue notebook I'd bought at the station bookstore, along with a guidebook to the south of France.

In my first draft I called the place Carrenac, a real village and a beautiful spot (I've since visited). If anyone living in Carrenac recognizes facets of their village and thinks I'm writing about them, let me say here that the people of Carrenac are too nice to commit any crimes. I did appropriate the village church and the personality of its priest and some real houses and shops, but I moved them around as needed for my plot, like pieces on a Monopoly board.

I had recently read a few of the Maigret books of Georges Simenon and been bowled over by the simplicity of the language, the stories which could only have been set in France, the characters who could exist nowhere else. He didn't have to tell the reader where he was; the giveaways were the trips to the boulangerie to buy baguettes, the travel by Paris Metro, the casual mention of the Arc de Triomphe. It didn't take a genius to throw those things into a story, of course, but unique to Simenon was the sophisticated, offhand way he described the world around him. Everything in his world was remarkable and yet it just *was*.

I didn't get the journalism job but I soon landed the ideal position for a crime novelist: an entry-level spot in DC, the low pay offering just enough struggle-to-survive to be incentivizing. The dullness of my duties freed up my headspace for what I saw as my real work.

The job consisted of thirty-five hours a week writing advertising and promotional copy for a newspaper that could have been written by a gifted six-year-old. Both the copy and the newspaper. My output consisted largely of documenting the paper's circulation numbers, and as those numbers rose and fell, I would be called upon to update the promo copy, in much the way a firefighter would be called to a blaze. 'Over 4 Million Readers' might have to be changed to 'Nearly 4 Million Readers', depending. If I got particularly bored, I might try changing it up to '4 Million Readers *Worldwide*', but that required approval from marketing so mostly I played it safe. It really was stupendously boring, and only my secret writing life, which began at 4 a.m. each day, saved me.

When the circulation figures fell to 3.7 million and most of my colleagues began openly updating their résumés, I doubled down on my pre-dawn mystery writing. As I had no savings this was a reckless gamble, but by the time the layoffs got started I had landed a three-book publishing contract. I quit the copywriting job and began writing all day in my local library.

This was in the early Internet days, when the library was still a quiet place to work, before programs like Toddler Rock N' Read had been invented, and Barnes & Noble was still a store stuffed with books rather than toys. I spent many hours there, too, or in Olsson's Books & Records, a now-defunct local chain. The word 'Records' in Olsson's title tells you how long ago this was.

By immersing myself in guides and photo books, I was able to create a village in the Dordogne – not too large, as it was necessary to keep the suspects to manageable numbers, and not too small, so there would be a variety of cruel or foolish or plain unlucky people to kill off. This setting gave me enormous pleasure, a place I could sink into, a place into which I could disappear.

The Dordogne, as you probably know, is in southwest France, in a region between the Loire Valley and the Pyrenees, and famous for its prehistoric cave paintings. That was good; I thought I might work that into a plot one day. Not an art theft mystery – for obvious reasons, stealing cave paintings would be tricky – but perhaps a crotchety misogynistic archeologist might meet his fate in one of the grottos there.

I decided to call my village Villeneuve-Sainte-Marie. Only much later did I realize Carrenac, on which it was based, was in the Lot, not the Dordogne, but no one ever called me on it, proving no one paid much attention to my first book. ('Diverting. *Je ne sais quoi.*' – *The New York Times*.) I corrected the error in subsequent books without making a deal of it, especially since imaginary villages can be in whatever department they choose. At least Carrenac is (misleadingly, if you ask me) on the Dordogne river, so I was in the ballpark.

Now I needed a Maigret for my village. I knew nothing of the ranks and hierarchies or even the uniforms of the French police; in fact, what little I knew about the police in France was based on reruns of an obscure, trashy crime drama of the seventies called *Crime of Passion*, where no one was ever given a long sentence for murdering their lover because everyone in France understood a *crime passionnel* is just one of those things. *Shrug*. I figured no one outside France knew much about how their murder squads operated, so it didn't matter. It did matter when my books started being translated into French, but I never thought that far ahead. Apparently, gendarmes are not simply promoted up the ranks to detective, as would happen in the US with patrol officers, but are two separate strands of law enforcement. Now you know.

I wanted a fictional detective who was smart or smart enough, without having to grant him supernatural powers. I wanted him to have a family – a large and warm and loving family, obviously the family I never had, and the sort of wife who would worry about him when he was out chasing villains, who would pack him a gourmet lunch and hand him a baguette on his return in the evenings. Or whenever he returned, generally late at night – it's a trope of crime stories that the detective is run ragged, that his office has a small budget and a sadistic supervisor, that one officer is a useless screwup, and so on and so forth.

I named my police detective Claude. I never got round to giving him a first name.

I was inspired not only by Simenon; I read all of Holmes and all the Agatha Christies, beginning with *The Mysterious Affair at Styles* and going straight through to *Sleeping Murder*.

I noticed Agatha rarely gave Poirot or Miss Marple a regular sidekick in the police force, apart from the ferret-faced Japp. Maybe she found it easier to make up new characters rather than be called out by eagle-eyed readers noticing changes from book to book. (I really am sorry about the Dordogne slip-up.) I wanted a sidekick who would stick around, in case the first book turned into a series. Series were what sold, said the gospel according to *Publishers Weekly*; series were sometimes made into TV shows.

So. Sidekick. I wanted it to be someone of low rank, a sort of junior detective, and I needed to decide whether the sidekick would be smarter than the boss. This is where the Caroline Bernard figure came into being. She was miles smarter than her supervisor, but so old-school she kept the fact hidden from him as best she could, feeding him clues and making discoveries he could claim as his own. This was getting harder and harder for me to pull off as the series progressed – most women at some point would have told Claude to go to hell. So I gave her a strict Catholic background, having her grow up in the sort of household where the man rules, or thinks he does, while the mother rules in fact.

Caroline would be approaching middle age, and while sharp-featured she would be attractive in the way of most Frenchwomen, who can turn a hazmat suit into a fashion statement with a scarf tied just so. She solved every single crime in the series – eighteen books and counting – and never once did Claude give her credit, although here and there someone in the department noticed and made sure she got mentioned in dispatches. Loyal to her clueless boss and to her husband, who was a ninny, this was how Caroline got by in life. Halfway through the series, she began having an affair with the man who owned the local boulangerie.

To be honest, I never saw it coming. Somewhere along the line, the fictional Caroline had taken on a life of her own and had gone from being a minor player in the series to sharing the spotlight with Claude, if not outshining him altogether. Reviewers and readers seemed to believe she was real. More than one fan letter carried a marriage proposal – for her, not for me.

I was writing book nineteen in the series when I was interrupted by a real-life crime in my neighborhood. My writing had stalled, anyway, so I was easily distractible.

Before long, happenings in the real world had eclipsed anything I could make up.

TWO

My true-crime story begins in Old Town, a place miles from the Dordogne, in spirit as well as geographically.

I've lived here twenty-two years, ever since I landed the one-note job in DC, although the success of the series allowed me to move from a one-bedroom apartment near the power plant to a four-story townhouse in the southeast quadrant.

I don't need four floors, especially with Marcus gone, and one day the stairs may be the literal death of me, but for now, living in lonely splendor in a well-preserved historic town is very pleasant indeed. Old Town is in northern Virginia, across the Potomac from Washington, and while it may be a veritable hotbed of political intrigue, sophisticated spycraft, and fine dining, it is also a quaint village – like St Mary Mead, like Villeneuve-Sainte-Marie – and in villages some people (people like me) are congenitally unable to mind their own business.

My neighbors may be busy, busy and often traveling out of town, or rather pointlessly going to and from their weekend homes, but there is little about the surface of their lives I don't know. What cars they drive, how many Amazon packages they have delivered, how often they have pizza delivered, which desperate housewife is having an affair. (I don't know whom Bettina thinks she's kidding. Why would the leaf-blower guy show up several times a week?)

I'm not particularly nosy. Honest. I just notice things because I'm home a lot staring out the windows and hoping for inspiration and trying to avoid the siren call of a bag of peanut M&Ms.

Which is why I knew before my neighbors vanished that their marriage was in a spot of trouble. I also knew (from watching *Investigation ID*) that Zora's husband would be blamed if anything bad had happened to her. Personally, I believed Niko Norman was not the kind of guy to snap out. That's not to say

I particularly liked him, but I didn't see him as the type to kill his wife, abandon his child, and flee the country. If that was what had happened.

At first, no one was quite sure how long they'd been missing. What lent urgency to their disappearance was the child, basically a newborn at one year old. That was what got the police's attention, not two adults possibly going on holiday and forgetting to ask anyone to water the plants.

My townhouse is part of a row of four connected homes on Fendall Street, each made to blend in with their historic surroundings, even though they're less than forty years old. My place is next to the big corner unit at Federal, the cross street. These four homes are part of a homeowners' association or HOA called Kildare Place – we call the HOA board the Tribe of Kildare – but they look like any of the other homes on Fendall erected in the 1800s.

The town itself is historic, without the inconvenience of outdoor plumbing, gaslight, malaria, and dysentery, and so it is much sought after by tourists. The upkeep on the older homes, strictly regulated by the city, makes them suitable to house only the wealthy.

Everywhere in Old Town are place names that invoke the town's Colonial and Scotch-Irish heritage, like Waterford Bend or Cork Mews or Stirling Docks. Kildare Place happens to have been built by a man who was an old friend of my husband's, Isaac Cohen. He and a few buddies put up money for the development, which quickly went bankrupt and was tied up in court for two years. I have no idea what became of Isaac, but I must admit – apart from managing finances – he knew what he was doing: The houses are attractive and mine is only just starting to spring a few leaks.

The people living to my left are the Ryans, practically the only people in the HOA who seem preordained to live in a place named Kildare. They have three red-haired kids who go to St Mary's. Their place squarely overlooks the Normans' in back, which is why their youngest, a set of five-year-old twins, came to play a role in the investigation into the Normans' disappearance.

*   *   *

My house at 11 Fendall backs upon twenty-eight townhouses facing a courtyard – Kildare Place proper. To the north of the courtyard is Duchess Street, where four townhouses reverse-mirror the ones on Fendall. There is huge snobbery at work among those who live in units that face proper streets instead of the courtyard, and a fair amount of feeling over the HOA budget, which always benefits the courtyard dwellers, who get the lion's share of mulch each spring.

From my first floor I basically have a view of the brick walls of my patio but, from the floor-to-ceiling windows in my second-floor living room, I can see straight into the backs of five other Kildare homes. It's like a stage set divided into parts, five sets of lives running simultaneously, all following their own plots. For whatever reason only one neighbor, the furthest from me in that row, has chosen to cover her windows. The rest of us don't get that much sunlight coming in as it is.

The quiet man directly in back was away when the Normans disappeared. He lived alone except for a woman who visited sometimes and who may or may not have been his sister. Occasionally he worked half-heartedly on various home-improvement projects, or played acoustical guitar. He only seemed to know how to play 'Classical Gas', but really, what other song do you need?

The house to the right, from my point of view, is shielded by an enormous magnolia tree (which really needs to be cut down) and is inhabited by another single man (I thought of him as Bachelor Number 1), former military, current advisor to one of the hundreds of government contractors in the area. He had lived in Kildare as long as I had and we'd probably spoken four times, twice when another of his trees fell into my patio after a heavy snowfall.

To the left of Bachelor Number 2 with the maybe-sister is Zora and Niko's place, the home from which they disappeared.

I still can't believe I didn't see it happen. I feel a crime writer should have a special radar for such things.

I don't stand at the window and stare out, mind. Anyone could see me and that would be weird, and besides, I have books to write. But if my lights are out, and if others have theirs switched on . . . well.

To all appearances Zora was a stay-at-home mom, although I later learned she spent at least part of the day at a computer doing some ill-defined marketing thing for an 'influencer'. Niko was a lawyer, of which the DC area and the world cannot have enough, apparently. He and I spoke at one of the HOA minglers, a Fourth of July barbecue in the courtyard. I wish I'd paid more attention, but I just had a vague impression of his being a together, successful, good-looking guy, who might be a snake in a courtroom but probably was a model citizen in his private life.

I knew her name was Zora Norman and his was Niko Norman and I only knew her first name, which I am sure Niko did not mention at the party, from seeing it with his in the HOA directory of contact information. I didn't know at first what the baby's name was, but it wore a lot of blue so in keeping with tradition I went with guessing it was a boy.

Their move-in was uneventful – so uneventful I was unaware the elderly couple living there had sold up and moved out. If the Hubbards had died and I hadn't heard I wouldn't be amazed, but I happen to have a spy in the courtyard who keeps me intermittently informed. The Hubbards had moved to one of those fifty-five-years-plus places.

It is like that around here, the way people don't know much about one another. To say anyone was unfriendly wouldn't be true, but the us-versus-them design of that courtyard contributes – if innocently – to the distance, not to mention to the mulch wars.

However, it is true everyone is consumed by their own lives, their own important jobs, and their LinkedIn profiles, and as soon as they finish gleaning what they can from among the sheaves of DC they tend to return to their real homes, wherever they may be: Iowa, Kansas, Montana. California is a popular choice but, generally, wherever the grandkids are. Holiday cards and letters are exchanged for a while with the Left Behinds, dispatches describing their new perfect lives in sunny retirement, cards with photos of grandkids of differing ages and degrees of cuteness. If one is unlucky, one will get a newsletter in the form of a poem, for example: 'We went to Baja / instead of Java, / then we went to France / where they looked askance.'

I'll just bet they did. Luckily no one's thought of setting this kind of thing to music, with the grandkids singing backup, but I'm sure that's coming.

Then the exchanges fall off, and sometimes there is a card announcing a death, which is sad, like hearing an already forgotten movie star or celebrity has overdosed. Sometimes, after a brief pause, a new wife or husband will step in to carry on the family's awful-poetry tradition.

Zora caught my eye out of this changing cast of Kildare dwellers because Zora was the type of woman made to catch the eye. There's no other way to put it: Some women command center stage without even trying. There's no point in envying people like Zora, these winners of the gene-pool lottery; one may as well envy a tornado or tsunami or another force of nature. They just are.

Even when Zora was unobserved, or thought she was, she had a way of slinking gracefully about or draping herself across a couch in a way that was so mesmerizing that you – I – couldn't wait to see what she might do next. Because her townhouse wasn't directly in back of mine, I could only see about three-quarters of her living room, where generally she would be reading or watching television or maybe eating a sandwich.

She was not tall, probably just over five feet. She was carrying extra baby weight when they first moved in, but with the help of exercise, which I witnessed but was not inspired to imitate, she soon lost enough bulk that you could see the Kardashian beneath, the difference between Zora and the reality star being that no part of her beauty looked particularly enhanced, waxed, shellacked, or rhinestoned. She just was. A curtain of silky jet-black hair fell down her back, sometimes held with a ribbon or scarf; the blinding sheen of it suggested frequent visits to the blow-dry bar. Her eyes were dark and slightly tilted; I couldn't tell what color they were, possibly brown. Sitting on the couch holding the baby, she looked like a twenty-first-century Madonna.

Niko Norman was not bad to look at, either. He resembled a beefed-up Jude Law, which is not a bad win in the gene lottery, either. The wonder was that Zora tended to outshine his beauty like the sun, making his blond good looks insipid by comparison, his cleft chin weak. This may be me reading things into his character which I only later came to question, but I think I'm right. Being around her probably drained him of self-confidence. In ordinary light, by himself, out on the street, he would have looked great.

He seemed like an OK father; at least he acknowledged the baby when he – Niko – came home. But you could see it plainly, at least I thought I could, the dynamic of that household – Niko moving towards his wife, drawn like the proverbial magnet, the baby forgotten, an accessory at best. If she happened to be holding the child, Niko would take it from her, give it a perfunctory kiss on the forehead, and deposit it in its playpen. The child seldom cried at this offhand neglect, not that I ever saw. Even at a tender age, perhaps it understood how people can easily be displaced by a shinier object.

They would settle onto the couch – one of those modular arrangements with outsized pillows, upholstered in a nubbly beige fabric, dotted with colorful boho throw pillows – and if the lighting was such that I might be noticed, I would discreetly withdraw. I wasn't keen on them staring directly into my place either, so I would go upstairs to my office to get some work done before dinner.

THREE

The night of the curious incident at the Normans' there was yet another documentary on TV about Keith Raniere and his NXIVM cult. The show was so engrossing it was pure chance I noticed anything else.

About halfway through I had come downstairs from the bedroom to pour myself a glass of wine. The kitchen is at the heart of the house, in between the living and dining rooms on the second floor. The stairwell and hallway occupy the rest of the space. The layout is the mirror image of Chez Norman.

I was in a hurry to get back to the TV, so ordinarily I wouldn't have paid much attention to what was going on out in back. Raniere was in the middle of explaining his theory of what constituted a successful life, and as avidly as I watched for any clue, I could not understand anyone's following this guy to Albany, New York. Tuscany, maybe, but Albany?

Like everyone else, I was particularly taken with the idea of anyone's submitting to being branded with anyone's initials, especially the initials of a guy who looked like he might work at installing HVAC systems. Even if George Clooney wanted to brand me with his initials, I'd refuse, although I might consider a small and tasteful tattoo.

But I do understand something of the psychology behind cults, and how easily one can be deceived by a charismatic and, to all appearances, benign figure. A highly respected pediatrician named Marcus, for example. It simply wrecks your head.

The fear of growing old alone is powerful and it takes a strong, integrated personality to resist the pull of anything that looks like love or a ready-made family, especially if your own family has gone out of business because of divorce or death or general craziness, especially if you've been alone in the world too long, and most especially (for Americans) during that dangerous time between Thanksgiving and New Year's Day.

That line about the phone never ringing? That was me before I met Marcus, who came bundled with lots of friends and family.

The night of the NXIVM show, as I was struggling with a stubborn cork in the wine bottle, I thought I heard a yelp coming from out in back. Not a dog – my place is surrounded by dogs and I know their individual operatic ranges – but a human making a sharp cry of pain. Not joy or ecstasy – pain. I never questioned that the sound was coming from the Normans' patio but, because it was summer, the large Japanese maple dominating my own patio mostly blocked the view. I thought it was a woman's voice, therefore Zora's. As if she'd stepped barefoot on a sharp object. Or someone had twisted her arm.

By the time I could cross the room to investigate, tripping over an ottoman in the dark room, there was nothing to see.

It would not be long before I had occasion to relate this to the police, and even over the phone I could tell they were rolling their eyes. It *was* a bit hazy, a smallish event from some weeks before, so I didn't mention it at first, even though I wanted so much to be the one holding the vital clue. I wanted to help.

I was pretty sure it was Zora, and that she was in some pain, if briefly. I offered to sign a statement to that effect, but the police demurred. Apparently, my best guess was mere hearsay.

I took my wine upstairs in case I could get a better angle on things from one of the two bedroom windows overlooking the back. If anything, there the foliage was thicker over the Norman patio and my own; I could see nothing. I turned down the TV volume but heard nothing more.

Under normal circumstances the incident might not have seemed sinister. Zora might have twisted her ankle on an uneven patio brick or stepped on a nail.

I quickly forgot about it. In fact, I saw her through the window the next day, playing with the baby, and all seemed well. No visible cuts or bruises.

I should have known that yelp was important. God knew I'd watched enough crime shows to have developed a sixth sense about such things. This was not the sort of neighborhood where women shriek in pain at ten at night. The detective who later interviewed me did ask if it could have been the husband, Niko, whose voice I'd heard. I said no, definitely not.

The detective who came to talk with me bore some resemblance to my series detective: tall and good-looking, with gray eyes and brown hair. That description could fit a lot of people, of course – I kept it deliberately vague so readers could fill in the blanks as they wished. But in my own mind Claude looked like Christopher Meloni, with more hair. As did this Old Town detective. The *Law & Order* jokes must have been constant. His abundant hair was salt-and-pepper, making me realize it was time to age my detective hero a bit. Claude had been forty-two forever.

The Old Town detective was married, to judge by the plain gold band on his left hand, which seemed a bit of a waste, but I hoped it was a happy marriage. Honestly, I did.

The night of that shriek – it was chilling, it really was – I returned to the machinations of cult-leader Keith, never realizing that the show at the back of my house was going to challenge the NXIVM story for ratings, and quite soon. It would be dramatized not just on *Investigation ID*, not just on *People Magazine Investigates*, but on dozens of shows documenting what seems to be a pandemic of violence in US homes. What happened at the Normans' put even Capitol Hill sex scandals on the back burner, if only – of course – temporarily.

It had everything writers and producers love: Beautiful young people crushed by tragedy, despite their wealth and education and their many, many opportunities.

This story didn't have the abduction of a child, sadly another common feature of these shows, but it did have a love triangle or two.

And for writers, it doesn't get much better than that.

FOUR

I wish I had kept a diary of happenings around the time of the murder, because dates and times would have helped a lot in my future chats with Chris Meloni, whose name turned out to be Detective Steve Narduzzi. I did keep a diary of sorts, but it was more a calendar of travel dates and book signings and writing deadlines, not a record of feelings or impressions or even the trivia of everyday life.

The online diary I kept when Marcus was alive I deleted shortly after his death. There was too much there I knew I'd never want to revisit. Besides, the more my fame grew, the more I worried someone would hack into my account and publish me on the dark web. Like anyone would care enough to do that, but still. It is a given they can.

Narduzzi and his partner turned up about a week after the Normans disappeared. When they asked me where I'd been the Tuesday that Zora and Niko went missing, I could only say I'd probably been in my office since ten o'clock, as that was my usual pattern. Or at least my stated daily goal. I'd try to work from ten to five every day with a short break for lunch when I wasn't traveling to some conference or book fair. Or commenting on Twitter posts.

I led the police upstairs from the hallway and settled them in my living room. I'd already put Roscoe in his dog bed in my office, with instructions to stay. He obeyed, but with bad grace, sensing something was up.

I offered coffee, which they declined.

'I thought they'd gone on vacation,' I told them. 'If I thought about it at all. They didn't leave any lights on for safety – to fool burglars, you know; they just left the place dark. You're sure they went missing on Tuesday?'

'So that was their usual routine?' he countered, establishing who was asking the questions. 'If they went away?'

'I guess so, but I really couldn't swear to it. They may just have forgotten. A lot of people around here go away routinely – many have second homes – but I don't think these two did.'

Narduzzi had brought with him a colleague in plain clothes, a woman who couldn't yet be twenty-five who was introduced to me as Sergeant Bernolak. She was wearing too much black mascara and liner and I wondered why she thought it looked attractive to appear as if you'd just emerged from a mineshaft, but at that age you can sort of get away with it. At my age, by the end of the day, I'd look like I'd stenciled tire tracks across my face. Bernolak looked bulgy and uncomfortable in a suit over a stretched-out T-shirt that made her resemble a flight attendant for a low-budget airline of a former Soviet-bloc country. Her role seemed to be to take notes of the conversation.

But it was to her I turned to ask, 'Who has the baby? Is it all right?'

'The baby is fine,' she said.

'It's with relatives?' I asked, ignoring Narduzzi's earlier claim to the question-asking role. 'Did they have relatives, the Normans? She had someone, right?'

'We're not at liberty to say.' This was Narduzzi. I would come to know it was a catchphrase of his, probably something they all were taught at police academy.

I'd been interviewed many times on TV and radio and, more recently, podcasts, so I knew something of the techniques. If I had shut up after the first question it would have been harder for him to ignore me. By muddying the waters with second and third questions, I'd given him license to disregard whichever questions he chose to ignore, since queries about the Normans' relatives were not particularly my business. None of it was, I suppose, but most people would worry first about the baby's welfare.

Speaking to Bernolak, thinking an all-girls-together approach might get me further, I said, 'But the baby is fine. Not harmed?'

She slid her smoky gaze over to Narduzzi before nodding in answer.

'Did they often go on vacation?' Narduzzi asked, even though I'd just answered a version of that question. It was disconcerting. Was he trying to trip me up?

'I wouldn't know,' I answered carefully. I knew so little of substance about my neighbors. Most of them simply watched TV at night rather than throwing Tupperware parties or playing Scrabble. And now, when it might be important to have paid more attention, to have gone against the cultural norms of Kildare – of the entire DC region, for that matter – and made an effort to get to know them—

'But when they were gone for a week, you did notice.'

I shrugged. 'It registered. More or less.'

'Any idea where they might go? Where they'd normally go?'

'I have to confess . . .' Wait a minute. That didn't sound right, considering my audience. 'I have to say I didn't know them that well. It's the layout of these townhouses, you see. The people with houses in the Kildare Place courtyard may know each other but I don't know most of them. I only tend to know the people who live on my street because I see them setting out their garbage bins on Monday or taking groceries out of their cars, and we might stop and chat. Fendall Street' – here I paused to wave in that general direction – 'leads straight to the river and that's generally the route I take on my daily walk. There's seldom a reason for me to make a U-turn into the courtyard. During the pandemic the river path became my sanity walk and I still do it. It became a habit.'

I was starting to blather and pad my story with extraneous details. If I were writing this in a novel, I definitely would cut at least the last two sentences. But I was nervous. Wanting to help but strangely worried about putting a foot wrong, saying something incomplete or misleading that might land someone in trouble, myself included.

Narduzzi shifted slightly in his seat. He and the flight attendant sat across from me in easy chairs I'd just had reupholstered. The couch I sat on was brand new. I know that's totally irrelevant but I was glad the place was looking spruced up. It seemed important to make a good impression. I wondered briefly if I were losing my mind from the stress of this. Something like a missing person's case doesn't happen every day in real life.

Now I waved an arm in the direction of the rear window, the catty-cornered view I had into Zora and Niko's house. It was broad daylight but the three tall windows at the Normans',

21 Kildare Place, were also brightly lit from within by what may have been Klieg lights set up by the police. It looked like a stage or movie set. Or a Restoration Hardware showroom.

'At night . . . well, you can see for yourselves, I can see into their living room if the lights are on. But it's not as if I stare over there, keeping a steady eye out. I don't use this room much, in fact; I'm generally on the other floors. It took me a day or two to realize their house had been dark for a while, and figure they must be gone.'

'So on . . . what, Thursday night you realized they had gone?'

'I suppose so, yes. Or Friday. I mean, it was no big deal, so I didn't really clock it. Not then.'

'When did you start to notice it?'

'Maybe by the weekend?' Bernolak scribbled that down as if it were a major clue. 'Fridays and Saturdays are different. A lot of times people go out or entertain on their patios if the weather's nice.'

'And you?'

'And me what?'

'Do you entertain? Go away at the weekends?'

'I don't have a weekend getaway place, if that's what you mean. I don't see the point in spending hours in traffic each way to drive to Orange or Middleburg only to turn round and come back Sunday night. I had a friend who used to drive from here to Pennsylvania every week for a job. I thought she was crazy. She was a psychologist, so maybe, yeah.'

That prompted a small smile from Narduzzi. It was a disarming smile, but I told myself not to be fooled. It was undoubtedly a smile technique used to soften up witnesses, to smile them to death until they gave up their secrets. Why I was acting like a guilty witness I still don't know. Well, I do know. Mark it down to Catholic school; you can never sand that paint off.

'She was your psychologist?'

Too late I saw my mistake. 'God, no, she wasn't *mine*. I wouldn't have let Jobelle analyze my cat. If I had a cat. *No*. She lived in one of the townhouses in the courtyard. When she wasn't in Pennsylvania, that is. I gathered it was the only job she could get at the time and didn't want to move there, so . . .'

'Ah,' he said, adding, 'I never saw the point in weekend homes, myself. I happen to like it here. Plenty to do around the house, anyway.'

'Right,' I said. 'You live in Old Town, do you?'

I thought this unlikely, to be honest. A detective's salary wouldn't generally stretch to Old Town. He ignored the question, pretty much verifying my guess.

'So you are here much of the time?'

I bridled at that. It made me sound agoraphobic, which would explain why I'd need a psychologist as cracked as Jobelle. I did have someone I talked with on occasion – several someones. A grief group we called the Desperados. I decided not to mention this to Narduzzi.

'I do travel to Europe here and there for long stretches,' I told him. 'For research, and for fun. Don't tell the IRS but sometimes I blend the two things.' I laughed nervously and when they both just stared at me, I realized this might not be the audience for that sort of joke. I cleared my throat and continued. 'But generally, if I travel it's to a conference or book signing. And that sort of thing is tied to when I have a new book out. Otherwise I'm here.'

'Book signing?'

'Yes,' I said. 'To – you know – sign books.' I gestured as if holding a pen. I don't know why but I thought as a matter of course they would run background on the people they interviewed as potential witnesses. Just as quickly I realized what an enormous taxpayer expense it would be if the police operated in an ideal investigative world like that. If I said something shady or suspicious, I supposed they'd look more closely at me. But for now they had to do what we all do, which was take me at face value.

'I write mystery novels,' I said. 'Crime novels,' I added, in case it added any weight to my testimony.

'Under your own name?'

'Yes.'

'Augusta Hawke?'

'Right.'

'My apologies. I haven't heard of your books.'

'I must tell my publicist what a great job she's doing,' I said, with a tight smile. It didn't matter if I had been on the *New York Times* bestseller list more than once. There were entire swathes of the population that didn't read fiction and, if they read it, they weren't reading me, and were fine with going to their graves having never read me. This fact no longer came as a surprise, even now that my publicist actually was making headway and reviews in the major outlets were a given. In fact, I had come to long for the days when I could write at Starbucks for three hours and not be recognized. It was why I wrote at home so much.

If I did venture out it was astonishing how many people I ran into who knew I wrote books for a living and – wouldn't you know it! – were writing a book or planned to write a book in their spare time. More often than not, it would be a memoir. The plan seemed to be that they would tell me their life story, I would turn it into a book, and my agent would run with it. The proceeds, sure to be enormous, would be split fifty-fifty.

This was the main reason I kept to a close circle of friends and colleagues. The average person on the street had little idea what was involved in writing a book and getting it published and how crazy-making the process was for all concerned, but every single aspiring writer I met was sure I could put in a word so they could cut to the head of the line. The business broke everyone's heart, routinely, but no one wanted to hear that.

'I always thought I might write a book, if I had the time,' said Narduzzi. He had inched a bit closer to the edge of his seat to show I had his full attention now.

My heart sank, even though members of the police often had compelling tales to tell. But those were precisely the sort of mean-street books I knew nothing about, and on which I had little advice to give. In a way, I dealt strictly in fantasy crime.

I glanced at Narduzzi's partner, on alert now for signs of literary ambition. She was twirling a lock of hair and looked as if she might be wondering whether it was time for a haircut. (It was.)

'I am sure you have some hair-raising stories to tell,' I said to Narduzzi, including Bernolak in my gaze, just in case, killing two potential novel-writing birds with one stone. 'But it really is a full-time job. Although I wrote my first book in the wee hours before work, I wouldn't recommend it for anyone who probably works all hours, as I'm sure both of you do.'

I hoped I hadn't said anything that might be construed as offering to write books for them since they were so busy. We were here to solve a murder, after all.

Notice the 'we'. I suppose my own dream had already become to move into their territory. The current book was going slowly, and I was starting to wonder if Claude and his wife should not think about retiring. Growing stale is a huge risk with any long-running series. Publishers want authors to crank out the tried-and-true formulas which made a series popular to begin with. But one can only go to that well so many times. Soon the identity of the killer becomes apparent from the third chapter, no one cares what the author ate for breakfast (Facebook Crime #1), and there are only so many ways to describe the weather in France, having cycled several times through all the different seasons.

'So anyway,' I said, 'I'm pretty much here at home a lot. But my face is in the computer screen and it's a large screen that blocks the view. Also it faces directly away from the Normans' – my office faces south onto Fendall, you see.'

Narduzzi nodded. He was with me so far. But his eyes had strayed to the bookshelves ranged behind me, and I was suddenly uncomfortably aware of how many murder books I owned, with an entire shelf devoted to poisons.

I said: 'As to Zora and Niko – I wish I could help more, but there was no reason their absence would send up alarms in my head. People around here have disposable income so they can travel for pleasure, and many travel for work. I couldn't possibly keep track of them all.'

I paused, thinking how to phrase this delicately, since we'd already established nothing was any of my business. In the end, I decided on the direct approach.

'What makes you think they're missing? That they won't just drive up and wonder what you're doing in their house with Klieg lights fading their carpets?'

'We do try to be careful,' said Bernolak.

'That's good,' I said vaguely. It was very hard to tell when this woman might be joking. Her generally gormless demeanor might be hiding a razor-sharp intellect, like that of my series heroine, Caroline. 'But I mean to say, they could reappear at any moment. Unless of course you know something I don't.'

I quickly realized how dumb that sounded; Narduzzi looked like he was trying not to smile. Of course the police knew a million things about the case I didn't, but I let it rest there, like some sort of found art on the coffee table between us. The silence grew. And finally Narduzzi said, 'We're not at liberty to discuss that.'

Fine.

As things turned out I didn't much need him, anyway. I soon had a direct line to the principals involved in the case and enviable access to insider knowledge.

They left soon after, handing me their cards on the way out. If I thought of anything, I was to call them.

'Day or night,' said Detective Narduzzi, scribbling a number on the back. 'Here's my cell number. Leave a message. I'll get back to you immediately if I can.'

Rather depending on the quality of my information. I got that.

The sergeant made no such empty promises. She simply tossed her pen and notebook into her faux-leather purse (chartreuse – a bold choice) and followed him out.

I locked the door behind them with exaggerated care.

The game was afoot.

FIVE

I was restless after they left, which was not surprising. I couldn't settle back into my pretend crime when a real one was unfolding across the way at 21 Kildare. But there wasn't a lot I could do except notice the Normans were waging the same losing battle I was with tufts of grass sprouting like hair plugs between the bricks of their patio. I had long noticed Zora was not one for gardening, that neither of them were.

They had a patio table with a furled umbrella surrounded by four chairs, but they never seemed to sit outside. Few Kildare residents did. We were right on the flight path into Reagan National Airport and some days the noise was noxious, not to mention the fumes those things gave off. But no number of petitions to City Hall or the FAA had made a dent. The airport had too big a role ferrying senators from their constituencies to the US Capitol.

I made myself some coffee in the French press and returned to the couch, revisiting what little I knew about the Normans.

There was one other incident apart from that overheard 'yelp' I hadn't mentioned to Narduzzi and Bernolak, and the fact I felt uneasy about the omission probably indicated I should have mentioned it. But it was guaranteed to cause trouble for Niko. Or Zora. Or both.

It was a simple thing. An argument. Was there a couple in the world that didn't argue occasionally? Since I felt my 'yelp' evidence was too minor to mention, I doubted the police would care I'd also witnessed an argument – albeit one in pantomime, since the Normans' windows were always closed, as were mine. That overhead plane noise again.

All I could say was I saw a lot of arm-waving on both sides to accompany the shouting, as in a televised Italian opera with the sound off; they were each bending towards the other in an almost choreographed way, hands on hips, to shout the other down. That leaning-in technique I used to avoid with Marcus

– just in case – since it gave him too much of an opening to take a swing. He did have a temper, this patron saint of children.

That was part of the reason I didn't tell Narduzzi what I'd seen: I couldn't tell who was winning or who won the fight, who had scored the most debate points. I certainly couldn't tell what it was about – perhaps he'd put the dishes in the dishwasher wrong again or he'd broken her grandmother's teapot. Marcus and I had had arguments like that, so I know how stupid these things can be, how the subtext is simply, We Have Been on Lockdown for One Hundred Years and I Need Some Space, Goddamit. During the pandemic, Zora and Niko's conversation was probably more typical of couples worldwide than not.

The other part of the reason I didn't want to tell Narduzzi was that I didn't want to solidify the impression I was up in my neighbors' stuff all the time, when I wasn't and clearly he thought I was.

I really was not. There is something creepy about a (nearly) middle-aged widow spying on her younger neighbors – there is something creepy about anyone spying on anyone, of course. Anyway, the number of times I had seen them in a prelude to lovemaking far outweighed the times I'd seen them quarrel.

Their operatic conversation went on for possibly five minutes, and then Zora stormed out and up the stairs. The baby must've been up there. I imagined their shouting had woken it up.

I'm quite certain neither of them had noticed me, but just as I was getting ready to head upstairs myself, Niko walked to the window to look out blindly over his dark patio. I feared a sudden movement would draw his eyes, and since that would have been especially awkward at that moment, I stayed put.

I wasn't sure he could see me in the dark, but I could see one thing clearly in the dim light from the ceiling lamp of his living room: there were tears in his eyes, rolling down his cheeks. Tears of rage or sorrow, I couldn't say.

On thinking it over, I felt I needed to let the police know what I'd seen. I could pretend I'd just remembered. Here I was sacrificing the truth to my own personal embarrassment, and it wasn't up to me to decide what was valuable knowledge and what wasn't. These were the professionals and I had to trust they knew what they were doing. Well, Sergeant Bernolak I wasn't sure about, but Narduzzi, probably.

I had retrieved his card from where I'd left it in a decorative bowl on one of the bookshelves, and I was reaching for my phone, mind made up, when it rang.

It was my editor. As tempted as I was to let it go to voice-mail, I needed to take the call. I'd only just submitted nearly three hundred pages of my new manuscript and it was a bit soon to be hearing from her. It was like in a jury trial, if the verdict came back too soon, it was bad news for the prosecution. Or the defense – I can't remember which. But either way, it is bad news, because it means the jurors made up their minds halfway through the trial and now wanted nothing more than their own freedom.

Had Julia read halfway through, decided it was awful, and not bothered to finish the second half (which I knew was far better)? Reviewers had pointed out I did have a bit of trouble getting to the action of a book – the murder – although like every other writer I struggled against arbitrary rules like, 'The murder has to take place on page one.' Life isn't like that and neither should death be. It's a long, slow, incremental process, this business of becoming angry enough to kill someone over whatever – a broken teapot, for example.

Julia had to be familiar with my style by now, but perhaps she was calling about something else. It was funny because, even though I'd written nearly twenty books for these people, I fully expected them to reject my most recent submission, every time. Every single time. Why I handed them this power over me, I don't know. But for this reason, among others, I had a healthy fear of Julia Swanson.

She had a reputation for being smart, tough, and for not suffering agents and their writers gladly. Also for barely clinging to sobriety after years of haunting the water holes of Manhattan, where she met her husband. Taking togetherness to the distance, before they married they made a pact to get sober together, and began attending daily meetings in the basement of the local church.

Her husband had died a few years ago, and everyone had held their breath, expecting Julia to resume her nightly bottle of wine, since it was clear they were a support team to beat all support teams, but it didn't happen. She got meaner and more unpredictable, but she never touched a drop. All the issues which may have fueled her addiction at the beginning were now just so much unpacked baggage she kept stored in the attic for deployment at a moment's notice.

It's astonishing how many people work in publishing who really do not like writers. Sometimes it's a case of those who can, do, and those who can't, edit. But I didn't feel that was true with Julia; I didn't think she liked anyone much since her husband passed.

Writers in general have a reputation for being high-strung, high-maintenance, or simply high, and the industry is larded with editors and agents who can't stand to be in the same room with them. Despite exceptions that prove the rule, editors who carry in their hearts a simple love of writing for its own sake and a similar love of their authors are so rare it is a wonder anything ever gets published.

I answered the phone tentatively, as if I thought it might be a telemarketer. If she hated the book, I figured I might as well get the news over with now and plan accordingly. I could rewrite it or my agent could shop it elsewhere, or both.

But that wasn't why she was calling. Somehow, she had put together from news accounts that I lived in the neighborhood where the police even now were seeking two missing people, one or the other of them presumed dead, possibly both of them.

She was calling to get the scoop. Of course she was. I'd forgotten she'd been a cub reporter for the *Washington Post* in a former life. Crime and scandal were in her blood.

I was glad to tell her what I knew, although it wasn't much. That came later in the day, by which time I was not sharing everything because I had come to appreciate not just the danger but the real people affected by this drama. I had been creating fictitious characters so long it was hard sometimes to pull myself into the real world where when people bled, the blood was red and the wound painful.

Besides, there was a chance Narduzzi had tapped my phone. I knew from my crime research it took longer than this, even if he'd – for some unknown reason – placed the wiretap order

the moment the crime was reported, but in any case I had to
be careful what I said to Julia. She might be subpoenaed one
day to testify. Why that would happen wasn't clear in my own
mind, but, better safe.

Besides, this was my story, and I was feeling the same way
about it I did with a novel in progress – I didn't want to unveil
it until the last possible minute.

Her call did make me wonder who had reported the situation
with the Normans in the first place. A neighbor? Some relative
of Niko or Zora's? Would Narduzzi have told me if I'd thought
to ask him? Certainly not.

'I don't know who reported them missing,' I said to Julia.
She had greeted me with a general invitation to spill, so I did,
not having to ask what or why. 'She had parents in the area; I
don't know about Niko. The mother – Zora's mother – owned
an art gallery in the District. In Georgetown. Still owns, I guess.
I only know that because for the longest time after they moved
in, their walls were bare white, just stark, and then one day I
happened to look over and the living room was decorated with
at least three or four large paintings. All artfully arranged and
lighted, as in a gallery. Some modern, mostly abstract, colorful.
I learned at a holiday party that Zora's mother had gifted them
from her gallery, tired of seeing blank walls every time she
visited. Is it a tax write-off to give expensive paintings to your
kid? Anyway, I don't know what her father did.'

'I guess they lived in DC to be near the daughter and
grandchild?'

'Or they were there already, and that's where Zora grew up.
Among the Cave Dwellers – you know, the bluebloods. But I
never met them – the grandparents on either side, I mean – so
I'm having to fill in the blanks from scattered conversations at
parties and neighborhood gatherings.'

I was slightly exaggerating the extent of my social life. OK,
exaggerating my practically non-existent social life, but it was
true I'd spoken with Niko on two occasions I could recall,
including a holiday party which had been thrown by another
neighbor a few blocks away. This neighbor, it so happened, had
taught Niko ethics in a law class at Georgetown, from where
he'd received his degree. He practiced family law.

I reported this to Julia. 'The husband did family law. He went to Georgetown.'

'Yes, that was in the news story I read online. The wife worked from home, but they didn't seem to know what sort of work she did.'

'I don't know, either – marketing, but marketing what, I'm not sure. They moved in when their baby was tiny. It still can barely be a year old.'

'Who has the child now? Not protective services?'

'Surely the grandparents—'

'Unless they're suspects.'

'Suspects in what, exactly?'

'In . . . I don't know what.'

'That is the million-dollar question, isn't it?' I said after a pause. The enormity of the thing was now weighing on me. That baby was missing its mother, at the very least. 'They both seem to be gone, the parents, and I'm quite certain they don't have a getaway home. They were usually here. If she left the house it was to stroll around with the baby – they didn't have a nanny. The occasional babysitter . . .' I paused, thinking that would be someone to talk with, someone who might know something. Another thing I should have mentioned to the police, I supposed, but surely that was something they'd realize for themselves. 'But they've been gone, neither hide nor hair seen, for a week,' I concluded.

'It's always the husband,' Julia said darkly. I heard the soft clatter of something hitting her desk, and imagined she was making her classic gesture of removing her thick dark glasses, the ones that made her look like Woody Allen, when she was concentrating on something. 'We know that.'

'We know that from reading too many mystery novels, perhaps.' Too many predictable ones, I might have added. Julia had some writers in her stable who had been phoning it in for years. So long as the public didn't seem to notice and the money continued to pour in, I guessed it didn't matter. The heavy lifting was done by the publisher's publicity department, trying to make every trope-laden book sound like it had been written by Shakespeare.

'And from real life as portrayed on *Investigation ID*,' she said. 'Always, *always* it's the husband. Sometimes the gold-digging wife. I don't know how they keep that show so fresh.'

'Lots of murders to choose from every day,' I said. 'It's a big country. Anyway, this couple seemed to have it all going for them, except for the usual waves. Every marriage has those.'

'Waves?'

'Um.' Why would I tell my editor what I had not told the police? Remembering just in time that possible wiretap, I rushed on. 'I was actually getting ready to phone the police about that when you rang. For one thing, they had a fight one night that I happened to witness. Not knock-down drag-out, just some shouting. I was wondering if it was even worth mentioning.'

'Jesus! Of course it's worth mentioning. You know yourself how every clue is essential in a case, especially early on. What is it – if the crime isn't solved in the first twenty-four hours, it might not be?'

'I think that's forty-eight hours.'

'Whatever. Look, you should call them right now. You don't want them to think you're an accessory.'

'Accessory? I—'

'*Now.*' She actually hung up, she really did, leaving me staring at the phone.

Julia was odd, no question about it.

I started to dial the number on Detective Narduzzi's card. Really, I did. But I ended up using it to mark my place in the book I was reading, instead.

Despite or because of the pressure from Julia, I needed time to think it through.

SIX

I once wrote a standalone novel called *The Nanny Beside Me*, when that sort of thing was at the height of its popularity. It's called domestic noir – the marketing people have a category for every type of book; it helps the salespeople when they're trying to get books on shelves. (Did you know 'Reverse Harem' was even a category of romance novel? Definitely a niche for the discriminating woman.)

Anyway. I don't think the appeal of domestic noir has ever faded. *Rebecca* is still the shining example of the genre. Most modern versions are set in the suburbs and have components of *Gaslight*. But the gaslighting is generally being done by the husband, not by Mrs Danvers. It varies.

My version of the story, told in first person, begins with the arrival of an interloper, who is younger and more beautiful than the wife. Although the wife has some very fine qualities, sexy is not one of them – motherhood has taken it out of her. Thus the couple's decision, a bad one as it turns out, to employ a nanny. The young interloper is cunning and with ambitions to be rich, none of which the heroine recognizes as a threat to the sacred family unit *until it's almost too late*.

I quite enjoyed writing that one, as it was a break from the series, even though my agent at the time wasn't happy about it. The nanny book was too far outside my usual range, he said; it might alienate my readers; the publisher would be angry, etc. He never referred to 'the publisher' using the name of a human being, so I never had a clue what he was talking about; he simply lived his life in fear of publishers, any publisher, mine in particular (Delamare, an imprint of Traitorsgate, both of New York). The people who worked for the company, if that is whom he meant, were always cordial to me, including the flesh-and-blood publisher, Ralph Guinness.

My new agent is so fearless she scares even me, which is

fine, so long as she scares Delamare into bigger and bigger advances. When I was interviewing her by phone, she said, 'Publishers are the dinosaurs of the modern world, and they know it. That's why they don't pay attention to any writer earning them less than a million a year. No matter, they'll all be working for Amazon in ten years.' I knew then she was the woman I wanted in my corner. She would not worry about being left off anyone's party list; she would work hard for me, her client.

If you are not an author, this must seem like a no-brainer, but believe me, it is not.

My domestic noir did well, and I realized some of the things that I learned writing it might serve me in looking into the disappearance of Zora and Niko. Surely a babysitter might fill the role just as well in the absence of a live-in nanny.

I decided to handle the investigation in the way I would write a book, jotting down ideas – potential leads – as they occurred to me.

Each of my novels had its own notebook, so grabbing a new one from the credenza in my office, I turned to the first clean, white page. I wrote *Missing: The Case of Zora and Niko* across the top, and on the first blue line I wrote:

- Find out who the babysitter was; talk with her.

I was stuck right there. Who would know how to reach her? The gallery-owning grandmother? But how to intrude on her grief at a time like this?

One of the neighbors?

More likely.

I tried to recall who else in the courtyard had children young enough to need a minder at night. It was not a child-friendly area, partly because of the real danger of one of them running out in traffic. The speed limit was 20 m.p.h., which many people ignored, particularly at night, particularly on leaving one of the many local bars.

There were families with children on Fendall Street, like Princess Prufrock across the way and two doors down, but she was seldom there. To my left was the family with three red-haired children who enjoyed running up and down and up and down and *UP AND DOWN* the stairs, but if they ever used a sitter, I wasn't aware. Their girl, Mary, looked to be about thirteen, and I assumed she was saddled with the job of watching her brothers on the occasions her parents went out.

The Princess and her husband were among those with a weekend mountain home somewhere to the south, where they lived for months during the pandemic while the husband worked remotely at the State Department. The nickname I have given her in place of her real name, which I have trouble remembering but I think is Angelique, probably demonstrates our lack of closeness.

Their house was falling into disrepair because of their frequent absences. In line with sexist thinking, we should have been annoyed with the husband, since fixing the place was 'a man's job'. But the truth was, the neighbors felt sorry for him. She was younger than he by about ten years but it was clear who ruled that roost.

I thought it just possible that Prufrock and Zora had met up for coffee and traded experiences about their pregnancy journeys or lactation issues or something. Their children were of similar age, so worth looking into. Reaching again for my notebook, I wrote:

• Confirm Prufrock's name; how to reach her?

Hers was a private home, not part of Kildare Place, so she and her husband weren't on the homeowner's roster. Too bad – putting pressure on them to get a new paint job and fix the roof would have been easier coming from behind the shield wall of the HOA. I had dropped a business card from 'Jerry's Handyman Services' through their mail slot a year before, with no evident result.

I sat thinking, tapping my pen against my cherry-wood desk. I was supposed to be getting four pages written on my next novel. The Rule of Four – a tip I'd picked up somewhere at a conference. The idea is to either write four pages or spend four hours at your desk working, but you'd be amazed how easy it is to fritter away four hours. I found a goal of four actual written pages to be manageable. At least it was until murder landed practically in my back yard.

Inspired by the reminder of the HOA, I picked up the phone to text Misaki, one of the priestesses of the Tribe of Kildare.

SEVEN

I knew Misaki Jones from planning parties for a group tour to Kildare, Ireland, a trip which had been cancelled because of the pandemic. The idea behind it was solid: Someone had finally realized it might be fun for us all to visit the town for which our environment was named. It was meant to be a great opportunity to bond, since we seldom bonded while we actually lived here.

We had all spent something like a year trying to get our deposits back from the airlines and hotels, a very minor inconvenience which of course far outweighed the stark terror of those times.

Misaki was a retired lawyer (yes, another lawyer, the area was stiff with them), divorced and with a son who lived out west in Colorado. Misaki tended to know things, and even though her days of needing a babysitter were in the past, I thought it possible she might know more than I did about what went on in the Normans' household. Her unit faced across the courtyard to theirs, giving her a head-on view. From her dining room I knew she could look into their dining area, and probably their kitchen, both of which were hidden from me.

I texted her, asking if she could meet me in the new coffee shop just down the street. I didn't mention the possible murder, since that was probably a word AT&T red-flagged for the FBI. I just made it sound as if I wanted to chat. She texted right back:

About the murder, right? See you at Beanery in half hour.

That gave me twenty minutes to get some 'real' writing done on my novel and five minutes to give Roscoe a quick walk. This eased the guilt just enough I could sprint out the door with my notebook to see Misaki, feeling lighter than air.

Misaki is the person I might have been if I had taken a more adult path in life. Even in retirement, she always looked polished and pressed. In the throes of divorce from an unfaithful husband, which I had helped see her through, she had remained calm and philosophical. It was, she told me, her own fault for choosing a man like Tom, so what had she expected would happen? She wished him well. Drawing on her skills in family law, she also took him to the cleaners, but she did so in a calm, polished, well-dressed, and totally unruffled way. If I had been Tom, I would have been terrified, and all reports were, he had been.

Maybe this was a bad thing, this untarnished polish in retirement, this constant pursuit of perfection, and she'd be dead of a heart attack inside ten years. But it was who Misaki was. Even if she lowered her standards to wearing jeans, she wore them below a tailored tucked-in shirt and belt, and they were pressed with a sharp crease. Her accessories were always bold and interesting without being silly. She looked a bit like a dialed-back Moira from *Schitt's Creek*, with less makeup.

It was a knack I didn't have. I understood fans expected me to look like something, or someone, creative but preferably not insane – to swoosh around in brocaded capes and embroidered jackets or in other ways alert the world it was in the presence of a great artiste. Inspired – nay, daunted – by the competition, I started to fuss about my appearance so much that I went to a personal shopper at Nordstrom's just before a yearly conference, and emerged with an expensive pile of clothing that looked like something the wife of a governor of Texas would wear. It all hung in the closet until one day I packed it up for Goodwill. I like to think there is a homeless lady living in Founder's Park who looks like Laura Bush, and that she and I will meet one day, and I can ask her if my wardrobe changed her life and increased her book sales.

I reverted to wearing mostly jeans, sweaters, jackets and boots. In summer I would switch it up to jeans, T-shirts and sneakers. I chose blue eyeglass frames such as a famous Scandinavian author might wear, but I decided that was all right. Europeans tend to be the best at designing that sort of thing, and it was, after all, my one vanity over my appearance. I didn't do $400 haircuts or spend half the day in salons – mostly I twisted my hair into a topknot – and the jeans were Levi's. This sartorial freedom was why I had shunned the corporate life. I could dress for comfort, and for speed, and work to my own timetable. That I could do so was down to saving, good planning, and Marcus's insurance policy.

Not everyone, I realize, has the financial cushion that allows them to do and dress pretty much as they please. If I never sell another book, I'm set for life, for which I am grateful. Samuel Johnson said, 'No man but a blockhead ever wrote except for money,' but he had all that wrong. No woman ever wrote except she was sick of being silenced.

Misaki had taken a corner table at the Beanery, away from the noise of the espresso machine and the dishwasher. It was our favorite table and tended to be free at mid-morning. Any later, by ten thirty, say, the mommies would arrive, fresh from a workout and shower at FitLife or the local Orangetheory. I belonged to the Y, although I seldom darkened their doors except for the tai chi classes.

I ordered a cappuccino at the counter and went to join her.

Misaki wore striped pants and a black top with chunky black-and-white earrings – like I said, a toned-down Moira. We greeted each other with air kisses. I don't really do air kisses, but I liked Misaki and I wanted to keep in her good graces. I had just put together, a bit slowly, the fact that not only did she live directly across from the Normans, but both she and Niko had practiced family law. She was twenty years older than he was, at a guess, but what were the chances she wouldn't know something?

'You've heard,' I said.

'From the police, no less,' she said, unable to hide her excitement.

'Me, too. They were in my house just a few hours ago.'

'*Oooooh*.' Clearly I had scored a hit, but Misaki was willing to be magnanimous in defeat. I told you she was philosophical. 'They only phoned me.'

I did my best not to smirk, even a little.

'A detective called Steve Narduzzi showed up with a Sergeant Bernolak. I have socks older than Bernolak. Narduzzi didn't say, but he must be a homicide detective. Or maybe he's part-time something else. This town doesn't get that many homicides.

I think there were two last year, both drug-deal-type things with
guns. I think Old Town tends to specialize in tourist muggings.'

'Wait a minute. Did they actually *say* homicide?'

'No. They were careful not to say anything, really. Totally
ignored my questioning look, which I'm sure was unmistakable.
But it's probably starting to look like . . . I don't know. A
kidnapping, at least. Maybe the Normans are being held for
ransom. They've been gone a week. It's not as if I spy on them
or anything, but it's looking like a week.' Even with Misaki,
this was a potentially touchy subject, though I knew she'd
understand. People do things; one happens to notice them doing
things. She was the same as me, which she proved with her
next statement.

'I happened to notice also they weren't there for about a
week,' she said. 'I'm kicking myself I couldn't pinpoint the
timeframe better for the police. I was just back from seeing
the kids. Anyway, the Norman place was dark when I got back
and it stayed dark, except for their outside motion detector.
Those things are a pain in the ass, especially at night. It's like
living in a prison yard. Every time a raccoon wanders by –
boom!' She threw up both arms, making her bracelets rattle.
'Like lights going up on an empty stage. When the Walters
put theirs in their patio garden, I finally installed blackout
drapes in back.'

Just then, the barista called my name. You wouldn't think
Augusta would be that hard to pronounce, but she put the accent
on the first syllable, and I didn't recognize myself at first.

'Hold that thought,' I said. 'Curtains.'

Resuming my seat, armed with the cappuccino and a sugar
cookie decorated as a yellow sunflower, I said, 'They didn't
have curtains in back. Neither do I.' It was my turn to be
magnanimous. 'It gives me an advantage, I know.'

'It's a strange choice,' she said.

'What? Them or me?'

'Well, having said that, I know you spend most of your time
on the third floor in either your office or in your bedroom,
watching TV. You've said. So "strange" depends on how much
time they spend in their living room on the second floor.'

I took a sip of my drink before answering.

'That's where they spend every evening. I can see them watching TV. Except I can't really see the TV from my angle, but it's either that or they're staring at the walls.'

'Unlikely.'

'Right. I sort of wish now I knew what they watched, although I doubt it matters. Sometimes one or the other of them is tapping at their phone screens.'

'A peaceful domestic scene, America in the 2020s. Where's the baby?'

'It has a sort of playpen in the living room but at some point they put the baby upstairs for the night. What is the office in my house is undoubtedly the nursery in the Normans'.'

'Did you ever see them fight?'

'Funny you should ask.'

'Oh, my God. You *did* see them fight?'

'Between us? Only once. And it was over so quickly – just a shouting match. Most of the time, if anything, they were very into each other. Once I thought I heard a sort of yelp of pain coming from the patio, but now I'm not sure.'

'Did you tell the police?'

'I meant to. Does that count?'

'As a lawyer, semi-retired, I can tell you it's not a good idea to lie to them, even by omission. It can come back to bite you in the most surprising ways.'

I nodded, sure she was right, even though she practiced family law, not criminal. Although the veil between those two worlds was growing thinner by the day. Which reminded me: 'Did you know Niko Norman in any capacity as a lawyer? He did family law, too, you know.'

'Sure I know, it's part of his email address on the HOA roster – mmdlaw.net. Stands for Masters, Milton, and Duckett.'

I jotted that in my notebook. I had to ask her how to spell Duckett. But of course, I'd heard of them.

'Sounds as if you looked him up,' I said.

'Sure I did. I'm as curious about what's going on as you are.'

'Am I that obvious?'

'Yes. It's a good firm, been around a hundred years. In fact, I attended their holiday party at the Metropolitan Club last year

– it was to celebrate the firm's anniversary and the holidays, all rolled into one. Big bash. He and Zora were there. Her looking smashing, as usual – dress cut down to there and up to here, tan from somewhere not out of a bottle. He was looking a bit "dragged to the party", as I recall. We spoke briefly just before they left, saying they'd promised the babysitter they'd be home early.'

'Ah. And?'

She shrugged. 'And nothing, really. It was a headache-inducer of a party if you don't like crowds, which I don't. A ton of people crammed into several small but elegant old rooms with high ceilings and flocked wallpaper but poor soundproofing. The food was great, though. No expense spared.'

'More about the babysitter, please.'

'I don't know anything about her. Or him. I think it's the same sitter Mellie Broeder uses, and that's a she.'

I made another note.

'You're treating this as a story?' she asked. She was familiar with my working methods.

'Not really. I don't know. Yes.'

'Just remember to name me in the acknowledgments.'

'Sure. You know, I'd forgotten she and Amir have young children.'

'You wouldn't forget if you lived in the courtyard. The boys like to play soccer out there. I nearly run over them on a weekly basis, and someone is always complaining to the board that they think their car has been dented by a stray ball. We've sent them a couple of notices, they're always apologetic, and things quiet down for a while, especially in winter. It doesn't last. We don't have a lot of options, short of threatening legal action, which we won't do and they know it.' She shrugged. 'It's not a neighborhood for kids. Kids need big grassy back yards. But they're from the Bronx, and that's how they grew up, apparently, so they don't see it.'

'There's a playground two blocks away,' I pointed out. But I wasn't really listening. I was considering how to explain to Mellie why I wanted to contact their babysitter. Especially since I didn't have kids.

'You think the babysitter might know something?'

'She would know them better than I do. She would know something of what went on in that house, at least during the brief times of child handoff. I've never set foot in the place and I barely know either of them.' I was using the present tense, I noticed, which was good. There was hope they would come back from an extended vacation in a place without access to news or the Internet, wondering why there was fingerprint dust all over their house.

'I see,' said Misaki, smoothing her hair behind her ears. 'And maybe the police would like to know about her, too.'

'I'm sure they're already on it. Known associates,' I added, to prove I knew the police jargon. The cable bill was starting to pay for itself. I deducted it on my taxes as research and here was the justification I was sometimes seeking.

'Augusta, again, you need to be careful about . . . you know, meddling.'

'Who's meddling? I'm conducting an enquiry into a serious local crime in my capacity as a writer.'

'I can't think of an excuse less likely to instill confidence in the police. They hate reporters, and you're not even officially working for a local paper like the *Gazette*. You're just a nosy neighbor.'

'Thanks.'

'What's he like, anyway, this Narduzzi?'

'Detective Narduzzi? He's like that guy from *Law and Order.*'

'Jerry Orbach?'

'No. One of the other ones. Chris Meloni.'

'I'd be looking for reasons to call Chris Meloni.' Misaki often took too large an interest in my widowed state. No use telling her I mostly liked me the way I was. Unencumbered. Roscoe was my only dependent.

'He's a *young* Meloni,' I said firmly. 'Maybe thirty-five. Thirty-eight, tops.'

'All the more reason. What exactly is your point?'

'My point is I'm forty-two. Almost.'

'No need to drop a hint. I got you a card already.'

'Thanks. I'm sure that'll help.'

'But you look forty.'

'It is customary to shave off five years when you're trying

to flatter someone, Misaki. Anyway, only in my author photo do I look forty. The publisher gave me a terrific photographer but that was a one-off, years ago, when they thought I was going to be the next Janet Evanovich or Sue Grafton.'

I wasn't going to go into the reasons I thought May–December marriages were a bad idea. I only had to look at my parents' example. And even though I began telling you my story with the sort of confessional gush I dislike coming from other authors, many of whom will do the dance of the seven veils if it sells copies, I'll probably take it out before it goes to print – if it goes to print. I really try not to manipulate readers.

And why was I even thinking about marriage? No wonder men freaked out.

'If you don't want him, can I have him?'

'Honestly, Misaki, he's busy right now with a possible murder investigation. Plus, he's married.'

That gave her pause, but not for long.

'OK. But people get divorced every day. And a policeman? Long hours, hazardous duty, crazy people showing up at the door with knives. That must be tough on a marriage. No need to dismiss him out of hand.'

Misaki always reminded me of Carrie Fisher with her Rolodex of eligible men in *When Harry Met Sally*. She didn't seem to notice she'd just listed more reasons no woman in her right mind would be interested in Steve Narduzzi.

'So,' I said, pen poised over my notepad, wanting to move right along in case she had any other bad suggestions. 'I have at least three avenues to explore.'

'We,' she said.

'OK,' I said. 'We.' In my notebook, I wrote:

3 AVENUES:

'There's the babysitter, whose name we can get via Mellie Broeder and Amir,' I said. 'What's Amir's last name?'

'Deniz.'

'Right. I seldom see him around; he's always on tour. Anyway, there's more than one family around here wanting a babysitter on occasion, but we can start with Mellie and Amir. Then there's Niko's law firm. There's the grandparents.'

These became bulleted items:

- Babysitter (Mellie Broeder, Amir Deniz – and others?)
- Niko (Masters, Milton, & Duckett)
- Zora's parents

'Tricky, that last one,' she said.

'I know,' I said, doodling as I thought about it, turning the bullets into daisies. 'And we can't forget, there are probably four grandparents to consider. But I've been thinking of buying some art for my first-floor library.'

'Since when?'

'And I might need some family law advice.'

'You have me. Ask away.'

'Pretend advice.'

'Oh.'

'Right, it's just an excuse to talk to someone who might know someone or something. Who do you know at Masters, Milton, and So On?'

'Duckett,' she filled in. 'Hmm. There's a guy there I used to date. He was the reason I got invited to the party. I'll try to find out what he knows, if anything, and get back to you. I don't even know what Niko's special area of family law was, and they all specialize. Family law has many paths, one goal, which is to line the firm's pockets by whatever means.'

''Course they do. Specialize. That way they can charge more, right? OK, you handle MM&D.' I adjusted my list to include Misaki's assignment. 'I'll drop by the art gallery.'

'Do you think it'll even be open?'

'In her shoes, I would be waiting for a ransom call at the store – don't you think?'

'I don't think that would be necessary. Not since they invented the cell phone.'

'Right. I know you're right.' I hesitated. 'At least I can get the lay of the land. It's a place to start; I don't think anyone's at home at Mellie's until the kids are out of school. But I'll try them first, just in case.'

'OK. What say we rendezvous for a drink about six? We can watch the evening news together. Surely they'll have caught wind of this by now.'

'My place?'

'See you there.'

EIGHT

I didn't often drive into DC and there was a reason for that: I valued my life. From Old Town the George Washington Parkway, which laces the edges of the Potomac River, is the best way into Georgetown, and it was not too terrible a trip outside of rush hour. The problem was, in or out of rush hour, no one in the area knew how to drive. It was never entirely clear if they had been issued licenses to do so. I preferred stop-and-go traffic to being pushed off the side of the road into the river.

Given a choice, I'd take the Metro, but Georgetown didn't have a Metro stop. The wealthy residents had quickly put a stop to that, if you'll excuse the pun. The Metro would attract riffraff, the type of people who didn't have a car. The poor, in other words.

I could take an Uber but the truth was my Jeep had sat in the garage so long I was afraid the battery would die if it didn't get a workout soon. I was getting a bit rusty about driving anywhere but to and from Trader Joe's, and I needed to stay in practice before I, too, became a hazard to others on the parkway.

For this special occasion, I put on high-heeled boots, but otherwise kept my ensemble intact. For an art gallery visit during daylight hours, I figured jeans were always in style. If all else failed, I could pass myself off as a starving artist.

I added some dangly earrings I'd bought from a friend who was a vendor at the local farmers' market. Now I could face Zora's mother looking more like someone she might expect to find in her store.

Which reminded me, I needed more of a name than 'Zora's mother' for the woman who owned the gallery. I opened a browser on my laptop to look up the gallery's website for the owner's name and address. I knew it was called Zora's and it was in Georgetown, information Niko had dropped in explaining why they suddenly owned artwork. I remember him saying, 'It breaks a mother's heart to see her child living without even so much as cave art on the walls – or so I'm told.' He said it with good humor, as a man might who long had accepted that marriage to a beautiful wife came at the price of a hovering mother-in-law who would never believe her daughter hadn't married beneath her. I'm sure he wasn't the first man to experience the universal truth about doting mothers-in-law, but he may have been the first to laugh it off easily.

Remembering that evening, I found it hard to reconcile the urbane lawyer with anyone who might have harmed his wife and then absconded somewhere to avoid prosecution, which was – I was certain – the police's working hypothesis. It was always the husband. An alternative scenario was all the above, followed by Niko's suicide in a fit of remorse. Again, I had the hardest time reconciling what I knew of him with anything out of such a sordid playbook. I supposed it was his education, his wealth, his handsomeness, and his general man-of-the-world demeanor that swayed me in his favor.

Plus, he practiced law. If he wanted rid of Zora, he had a million legal ways to extricate himself from the marriage, the sort of death by subpoena practiced with such abandon in the law courts when the wealthy parted ways. 'Drown them in paperwork' worked particularly well when you had the legal knowhow, the resources, and the time to do so.

I wanted to find out what the baby's name was, at some point. Baby Norman wouldn't cut it now he was a year old.

Suddenly I felt sad. Sad that I didn't know his name, and sad that, however this turned out, the kid might suffer once it was old enough to understand suffering went beyond needing a bottle and a nap.

I put Roscoe on his leash and took him to the dog park for a quick run. He'd been barking at shadows lately, forgetting his costly training at Old Town School for Dogs, but that may have been down to my own distraction.

I promised myself I'd walk him more often, and further. Just maybe not today.

I got the occasional raccoon out back, and one time, a

possum hanging upside down in a tree branch (which scared the living daylights out of me; those things are primeval) so Roscoe might not have been seeing things. I often wished he could talk.

As we walked, I put in a call to Mellie Broeder, which went to voicemail. At the command of her theater-trained voice, I left a message. A former actress married to actor Amir, she now worked as a director at Arena Stage.

I decided I really must call the art gallery, even though chances were good Zora's mom would hang up on me. I was torn: a surprise visit seemed intrusive and unnecessarily sneaky, like something a tabloid reporter would do.

But I got voicemail at the store's number, too. I hesitated only a moment. It could be a wasted trip, she might not be there, she might shut the door in my face.

In for a penny, I thought. She and her husband were the best sources of knowledge, far more than any babysitter.

NINE

Georgetown in Washington, DC, is famous mainly because John and Jackie Kennedy had lived there in various houses, separately and together. It's where they got engaged, at Billy Martin's Tavern, and where she briefly returned to live after the assassination before moving to the slightly greater anonymity of New York. All the homes associated with the famous pair are private residences now, but you can take a walking tour and stare at the curtained windows, which I have done.

I always wondered what sort of trace Jackie left behind of herself in these places. A book of etiquette, a recipe for Beef Wellington, a forgotten container of dental floss. Whatever it was, the people who lived there now were likely to preserve it in a shadow-box display case and hand it down to their heirs, Muffy and Scooter.

The art gallery was just off Wisconsin Avenue NW and, rather than try to get away with parking for an hour on one of the residential streets without getting towed, I pulled into an underground garage around the corner from Zora's Art Gallery.

I had been acting on a hunch Zora's mother might be in the gallery, in the hope her daughter would turn up there, but also wanting something to do that didn't include sitting at home wringing her hands and possibly getting into quarrels with her husband about whose fault it was their child had gone missing. I realized I was extrapolating a bit from my own childhood memories, but it would be a rare couple that wouldn't buckle under the stress of such a situation.

It was also possible the pair had divided responsibilities – he'd man the home front in case Zora turned up there, and she would guard the store. This proved to be the case.

Before setting off, I again tried the number on the gallery website, and this time Genevieve Garnier answered on the first ring, perhaps thinking it might be someone calling with good news. Instantly I felt awful I didn't have any. What I might have was information she might want to hear. But, softly, softly.

I was still torn about the quarrel I'd witnessed, and that yelp I'd heard in the night, and I thought I should play it by ear. If she seemed to want to throw Niko to the wolves over her daughter's disappearance, even without evidence, I might play it cool. If she seemed to think Zora and Niko were the type to just take off without notice, what I knew might be irrelevant.

There was no getting around the appearance they'd left their baby unattended in its crib. How in the world to explain that two people, to all appearances sane and loving parents, would do that? Had they phoned someone, like Zora's mother, to tell her to go pick up the child? To let her know something bad had happened? Was about to happen?

Genevieve's voice when she answered was husky from crying, I was sure. I introduced myself.

'Hello,' I said. 'I'm Augusta Hawke, a neighbor of Zora's.' I decided to leave Niko out of this, in case bad blood would spurt at the mention of his name.

I had been planning to apologize for the intrusion and yet to ask if I might speak with her in person. But before I could get that far, she said, 'You're that writer, yes?' She had a mild French accent I would learn came out more in her sentence structure than in her pronunciation. 'I know who you are, and I have been expecting you to call.'

I couldn't guess why she'd been expecting to hear from me, but it certainly made things easier.

'The name of my gallery is Zora's, if you didn't know. It is in Georgetown.' Despite her obvious distress, she was polite. 'Please be here within the hour. I'm closing today early.'

I backed the Jeep out of my single-car garage onto Fendall Street, heading west a few blocks to join Washington Street, which eventually opened up into the parkway. Every corner had a stop sign so it was slow going at first. The grid design and narrow streets of the city hadn't changed from colonial days.

Settling my sunglasses on my nose against the sunny day, tuning the radio to NPR, I set off to see what was up in the Nation's Capital.

TEN

The first thing I noticed at Zora's Gallery was the middle-of-the-road appeal of the artwork on offer. I am one of those 'I know what I like when I see it' types when it comes to modern art, but these were clearly in a category unto themselves. They were mainstream, so even I could appreciate them, but a dozen steps up from hotel room art, as reflected in the price tags. It wasn't necessary to seek to uncover their hidden meanings, or to fawn over the avant-garde-ness of their creators, or to otherwise struggle to make small talk about them. Colorful, and not trying too hard, and apart from the occasional depiction of a breast or other generally hidden body part, guaranteed not to offend. Washington hostesses were among the most conservative people in the world, and what they put in their dining rooms, if not a portrait of a sainted ancestor, must be neutral and, above all, inoffensive to both sides. Bipartisan artwork, as it were.

I imagined a lot of people in this part of the world, particularly in Georgetown, particularly visitors to Washington looking for a keepsake to ship home, found them as big a relief as I did. The capital wants to present itself as the center of the world, as being at the forefront of new ideas, particularly when it comes to social activism. It is not. For that, I'm sorry to say, look to New York.

The second thing I noticed at the gallery was the sound of a baby crying. It was coming from somewhere in the back of the store.

I turned to look questioningly at the patrician face of the gray-haired woman who was Zora's mother.

She nodded.

'Yes, it's Harry. Be with you in a minute. He wants his bottle.'

At last the baby-in-blue had a name. She turned to walk towards the back of the narrow store, which was separated from the front by a blue velvet curtain, returning about ten minutes later. As she didn't invite me to join her back there, I spent the time deciding whether or not I had $10,000 to spare for a painting in reds and browns that had caught my eye.

She returned carrying a now-sleeping bundle in a carrier, wrapped in a white blanket. I couldn't see what color his eyes were, but I did notice he'd inherited his mother's amazing dark eyelashes.

'Is it Henry, or Harry?' I asked.

'Harry. They wanted no ambiguity, no Henry the Eighth jokes. Harry James Norman. James is my husband's name.' After a pause, she added, 'He's an architect.' She seemed to feel that needed to be said to explain his absence, as if he might just then be hanging from the scaffolding of a newly renovated building. 'He used to be a lawyer,' she added.

I whispered the first question that came to mind – quietly, as if a one-year-old could understand me. 'He was there when . . . when they were gone?'

Which made no sense in any other context, but of course she knew what I meant. Nodding, she set the carrier down beside the semi-circular counter which served as her desk. Motioning me to follow her, one index finger to her lips in the universal sign for 'Don't wake the baby', we walked to the opposite side of the room.

'Zora rang me that morning, asking if I could come by and pick him up. She had never done that before, not so last-minute, and what made it a crazy request was the traffic that time of morning. It was eight o'clock and while most people would be heading into DC to work that time of day, it doesn't really matter any more: Traffic is *always* crazy.'

I nodded sympathetically. Traffic and parking were the universal ice-breaking topics in these parts.

'Anyway, I would have to make the return trip in the tail end of the traffic jam, and I would be late opening the gallery.'

'Right. But she didn't care? I mean, your daughter insisted?'

'She did insist. She said if she took the time to drive into DC to drop Harry off with me, she'd be late for her doctor's appointment. And she couldn't take the baby with her – the doctor had strict waiting-room rules about kids – rules that were never loosened after the pandemic. I asked her why she didn't think of that before.' She paused and on a small, gasping intake of breath, said, 'I am afraid I was a bit sharp with her. Zora could be . . . like that. A wonderful girl, but a bit . . .'

I didn't rush to fill in the blank, an unusual bit of self-control for me. Normally, when we see someone struggling, especially someone speaking what was clearly not their first language, the human tendency is to rush in, to help them out, as if providing the right word would ease their discomfort.

Still, the silence lingered until finally she said, 'When you are a young woman who looks like Zora, you have got the world at your feet, and it only gets worse. Or better, depending on how you look at it. She merely had to bat those eyes, especially with men, to have people falling all over themselves.'

I nodded. Zora dressed for a party had been a sight to behold. Men stared as if they couldn't believe their luck being in the same room. It was probably something they relived and fantasized about for years to come.

How Niko handled it, I did wonder, but he seemed to have been gifted with a remarkable detachment, a sophisticated aplomb. If that cool manner had been hiding an evil killer, he wore it well. But while most of the killer husbands on *Investigation ID* were easy to spot, those in my novels were not. Mine were urbane, successful, and upstanding, unlike the real-life killers on TV, who by and large were just losers.

Still, I never could quite figure out what Zora was doing with Niko. The head cheerleader always dates the captain of the football team. It is one of those rules mandated by the gods.

'I don't know what Zora was doing married to Niko,' Genevieve said, echoing the thought. 'They were chalk and cheese. He was well off and well educated and good-looking if you like that sort of thing, yes, but she could have had her pick. She had the boys running at the snap of her little fingers from the time she was playing in a sandbox. I asked her why, what the attraction was. I really tried to talk her out of marrying him, but I didn't dare press too hard, you know?'

I nodded solemnly. Parenting 101 teaches that offspring will do the opposite of what they're being pressured to do, particularly in choosing a mate. I supposed I was a living example. My mother had disliked Marcus on sight.

'I suppose it was love at first sight. She said he made her laugh. About what, she didn't say. If he had a sense of humor, he didn't waste a lot of it being witty around me. Or her father. I would have said he was driven, all about making money, humorless. And now . . .'

'You think Niko had something to do with this?' I was still trying to gauge how useful my information about the couple could be. Or how needlessly destructive, sending everyone off course. Most couples, as I have said, fight about something, at some time.

'I don't know, do I?' She pushed her hand through her short, springy gray hair, blowing out her lips in what I thought of as a typically Gallic way. 'My mind has been all over the map, trying to figure it out. When Zora didn't turn up for her doctor's appointment, it was a sign something had gone wrong, I knew that, but it was worse than we could have imagined. Her father and I thought the car had broken down.' She hesitated, perhaps wondering why she was giving me so much insider knowledge of the case. I was wondering the same thing. I chalked it up to a major case of frayed nerves.

'"Worse"?' I prompted gently.

'She didn't have an appointment at all. When the police called the doctor's office, tracing her movements for the day, they said they hadn't been expecting her.'

'I see.'

'She was lying about it – whatever she was doing, she was lying to me, to get me to come take care of Harry. *Why?* She was not dishonest, my girl. Stubborn, but not dishonest.'

I took a moment to absorb that, running through all the possible reasons why. Mother–daughter relationships can be fraught. My own was no exception. But why did Zora not just tell her mother she had something to do she couldn't talk about? Because it was expedient to lie? I suppose lying always saves time in the short run.

But I answered my own question: Because Genevieve wasn't the type of mother to just say 'OK' and roll with it, not without a good explanation from her daughter. She was undoubtedly a doting grandmother, but she was also a businesswoman, to all appearances a successful one. And success like that, in what I suspected was a tricky business, doesn't happen by accident. It certainly doesn't happen unless you open your doors on schedule.

Zora must have felt she had to have an unassailable excuse, especially since whatever she was up to, time was of the essence. She didn't have time to talk about it, to answer questions, or to be dragged into making a complicated explanation. Or to hear 'no'.

An Uber would have been the answer, but not with a doctor who didn't offer daycare – and what doctor did?

But I was already forgetting, there was no doctor's appointment. Whatever Zora was up to, and wherever she was going, she had to go baby-free.

'What about the babysitter? I mean, why not ask her?'

'I asked the same thing and was reminded she'd be in school that time of day.'

'Do you know who they used as a sitter?'

'Trixie something.'

'Trixie?'

'Short for Beatrix. Trixie. I don't know her last name, which now seems hugely irresponsible of me. Who would ever have thought it would matter?'

It was a step closer, but a talk with Mellie Broeder would still be in order. If I had talked with her or her husband right away, I could have saved myself a lot of trouble. But I wasn't to know that for a while, until it was almost too late. Instead I made a mental note of the first name. Although the chances I would forget anyone probably named after the famed children's author were slim.

The baby chose that moment to make that grizzling sound they make when they're just about to wake up and demand something. Genevieve rushed to see what was wrong, soothing Harry back to sleep in a few minutes. That was one good thing. Zora had left the baby in safe hands. As of course she had known she was doing.

When Genevieve returned, I asked the question that had been bothering me.

'Why me? I mean, you've let me into your confidence here, and while I'm flattered, you don't really know me.'

'Oh, but I do. I've read every single one of your books. You could say I'm your biggest fan.'

Both flattering and ominous, that. I of course immediately thought of Stephen King's number-one lunatic fan. We all had one or two. He probably had hundreds.

'But, I . . .' I began, and stopped. I hardly knew what to say.

'Anyone who can write the detective novels you do must have some special abilities,' she said. 'To take clues that make no sense and make them make sense. If that makes sense. Your Caroline is some sort of genius who hides her genius under a basket.'

Bushel, I corrected automatically. 'Well, that's very flattering but *I'm* hardly a detecting genius. And this is a case for professionals, anyway.'

'The professionals don't have a clue, that's obvious.' She sneered on the word 'professionals'. 'And besides, they don't live in the back of my daughter's house, with insider knowledge of what went on behind closed doors.'

'Now, hold on, I really don't—'

'They used to see you, you know. Looking into their living room. Watching them. I don't mean they were bothered by it. It was just something Niko mentioned in passing.'

No doubt as part of his famous charm offensive in which he deployed humor. *Crap*. I knew my face must be flaming red. I sounded like some Miss Marple of the village, my lace curtains twitching as I spied on the neighbors. God, had I been that obvious?

Genevieve was quick to notice.

'I can see I have offended you,' she said. 'And I am sorry, but I have lost my daughter to God knows what sort of horror. I'm being blunt and using plain words because I don't have time to coat things with sugar. I need to know what's in your head, what *you* know or may have seen. I wish I had time for the niceties. I don't. I need you to tell me what you know – now. What you saw going on in that house.'

'But I—'

'Whatever it is, I won't hold it against you. I can't promise to keep you out of this, though. If it's something the police should know and can help me with, I will pass it along. But more likely I will use it to help find my daughter myself, by any means available. And if helping find my daughter includes keeping the police in the dark, I will do that.'

'I understand. I do. I think I do. But Niko is missing, too.'

'Is he? Or is he in hiding? I don't know. I don't know what to think about that.'

'Do you really think he would have put Zora in danger?' I asked.

'You tell me.'

ELEVEN

There was a small kitchen at the back with a built-in breakfast nook for four. The art gallery clearly had been a home once, one of those Civil War-era dwellings now fought over by the wealthy of both political parties although, because of the Kennedy associations, Democrats tended to overbid.

Over a cup of Earl Gray, I told Genevieve Garnier, sitting opposite, what I knew. It wasn't much, so I had to resist any temptation to embellish. It was still more than I had told the police.

Baby Harry napped in his carrier, now on the floor between us. His little hands emerged from the top of his blanket as he slept on his back; two pink feet poked out the bottom, pointing in opposite directions. I was mesmerized by how small and plump and beautifully formed they were, like something from the paintbrush of Botticelli. He looked so completely vulnerable and trusting it twisted my heart.

Where is your mommy? Silently I asked the sleeping form. *She would never just leave – you know that, don't you?*

Genevieve had put the 'Closed' sign on the front door of the gallery and pulled down the shades. Returning to the kitchen, she offered me cinnamon oatmeal and raisin cookies.

The police could not come to know I was the source for information, I told her, since I had said nothing to them apart from my having gradually realized over the course of several days that Niko and Zora were not at home. If she said otherwise, I could be in trouble.

I was trying to swear her to secrecy without sounding like someone no sane person would ever confide in.

'I hope you understand,' I concluded, delicately wiping bits of oatmeal from my lips. The cookies were homemade. 'They probably also would not be thrilled to know I'm here talking with you. But it might look as if I had been less than

forthcoming with them, which is bound to look suspicious.'
Actually, the police would probably think of it as 'withholding
information' as they asked a judge for a warrant.

'Why were you,' she asked, 'less than forthcoming?'

It was certainly a reasonable question.

'It's difficult,' I said slowly. 'A difficult place to be in. People
in your house, writing down every word you say.' Looking like
they don't believe you, I might have added. Sizing up your
possessions, particularly your large collection of murder
mysteries, like they were a clue to your character.

What kind of job was policing anyway that made you think
everyone you met was a liar?

She nodded understandingly. 'And I hate to put you in that
difficult place, but for my daughter's sake I will insist.'

It sounded so reasonable when she said it. It also sounded
vaguely like a threat.

'Right. Of course. But I didn't see anything really important,
like Zora being attacked or behaving as if she was in any trouble.
Naturally I'd have said something right away. Especially if Niko
– if anyone – had hit her or acted menacingly.' Or *vice versa*, I
thought, but I didn't want to explore in front of her mother all the
ways this whole thing might be Zora's fault and Niko the victim.

Something else I didn't want to look at too closely was how
likely it was I would have called the police on Niko for 'acting
menacingly'. If he'd hauled off and punched his wife, certainly
I'd have intervened. Wouldn't I? Who wouldn't? It would have
been the end of life in Kildare's Happy Valley as I knew it, but
surely I'd have had the courage to really stick my oar in if the
situation called for it.

She dangled a way out of my dilemma in front of me.

'Your place is one of three with a good view into Zora and
Niko's living room and their downstairs library,' she said.
'Whatever you tell me, the police won't have to know who told
me. It could be any one of three neighbors across the back from
their place, since, for whatever reason, those two never bothered
to put up drapes or blinds. They wanted, she said, "to live
authentically and openly".'

So all I'd have to do would be to drag the other neighbors
into it. Right.

'The lack of curtains is pretty much a matter of practicality,' I told her. 'There are several trees back there that block the daylight. They also block big parts of the view into your daughter's house. I can't speak for the others but, once I'm looking down over the foliage on the third floor, the view is obscured. Even in winter – partially.'

'But there are things only you or one of the neighbors could know. I can't help that but, if you're worried, tell the police you forgot when you spoke with them initially. That you didn't mean to stare – something caught your eye. Zora might be being held hostage as we speak, a knife to her throat, unspeakable things being done to her.' She was playing her trump card – I had already imagined for myself the terror Zora might be going through. 'The police won't be bothered by anything you say or don't say, if it brings her home safely. You have an obligation to—'

'All right, all right,' I said quietly, palms up. I was beginning to see how this saleswoman could afford to take a lease on premises at one of the priciest zip codes in America. 'Here is what I know, but it doesn't amount to much.'

'Shoot,' she said.

'I saw them quarrelling, Zora and Niko.' I'd decided against telling her about the yelp. That was vague. The quarrel was not.

Quickly, she leaned in. 'When was this?'

'I've been trying to pinpoint it. A month ago? My days are much the same some weeks, so without highs and lows it's hard to pinpoint. I believe I had just come back . . .' As I spoke the memory grew clearer. 'That's right, I'd just come back from seeing my editor in London. Sorry, I completely forgot – the brain fog is terrible when I fly from east to west. I'd been unpacking my bag piecemeal downstairs rather than haul all that weight upstairs to the bedroom.' I reached for my phone to check my calendar. 'It was the fifteenth of last month, then. I returned from Dulles exhausted and put off dealing with the luggage while I sorted through the mail and had a bite to eat. By the time I turned my attention to unpacking, it was dark out. Zora and Niko had their art lights on in their living room – you know, lights that illuminate their artwork; well, of course you know – and when I walked into my own living room, I could see clearly into their place.'

'Saw them fighting.'

I nodded, reaching for another cookie. 'Do you mind?'

She nodded, waving away the interruption.

'There was clearly something going on over there and it stopped me in my tracks. I didn't turn my own lights on. They were shouting at each other, back and forth, give and take, arms waving. It was definitely what I would call a heated argument. It went on about five minutes, then Zora stomped out – she went upstairs. I assumed they'd wakened the baby' – I nodded to the still-sleeping Harry – 'and your daughter went to check on him.'

'That's all?'

'That's all.' I took another bite of the second cookie. Immediately I wanted a third and felt that would be warranted only if I had important information to impart. This was old, somewhat feeble news; whatever was going on between Zora and Niko, it hadn't amounted to much. 'You can see why I didn't mention it.'

'Did she come back? Into the room, I mean?'

I shook my head. 'Not that I saw.'

'What did he do?'

'He watched TV, as near as I could tell. The screen wasn't visible from where I stood. He may have been staring at the wall.'

'He has the TV on a lot. Watching sports. She complained about that once. But jokingly, you know.'

'They got along OK, then.'

It was clear she didn't want to admit this.

She shrugged. 'I would have said they got along for the most part. Yes. I guess.'

'You just didn't like him. Your son-in-law.'

'I did not.'

I said nothing, just quietly munched on my third cookie, which I had decided to go for after all. I didn't think she would notice and homemade doesn't come my way often. I tried to look wise and interested, letting that space grow where she might decide it was safe to confide in me. I knew I had a quality that made people confide – a quality that could yield a mixed result, believe me. I was that person on the plane who would never be left alone to read the novel she'd been dying to read, the woman waiting in the train station whose obvious interest in her email would be ruthlessly ignored. I clearly didn't know how to say no, or to turn away a person in need. I didn't mind once the initial irritation passed. People ended up talking about their grandchild, who was headed down a bad path, or about their grandmother who had Alzheimer's and how pointless it seemed to be traveling to visit someone who never knew who you were, or who thought you were their high-school sweetheart. I heard a lot about ungrateful children and, more than once, straying husbands. Much of the fodder for my books came from these random confessions by strangers, and much of my value as a person, I supposed, was being the one person on that day, in their lives, willing to listen.

I never saw these people again or exchanged contact information with them or even mentioned I was a writer as I shoved a promotional bookmark in their hands. There are some levels to which I will not stoop in selling a book – not many, but a few – and taking advantage of someone else's pain was high on the list. From their questions, I gathered some mistook me for a therapist. Probably it was the glasses or the tweed jacket with elbow patches I wore in the fall. I thought of myself as the masked woman of Amtrak and Southwest Airlines.

Genevieve sat back in her chair, fiddling with the handle of her teacup, the tea long grown cold. She didn't look at me as she began to speak but at the baby, whose little chest rose and fell under the blanket. Surely he would wake up soon and break the spell.

'I didn't like him, no,' she began, speaking softly. 'To me at first he seemed like just another of these lawyer types you meet around here. The area draws them, fresh out of school, because this is where the law is made, in a manner of speaking. Made and broken. Here in Washington, DC.

'Not all of them are bad, of course. My husband used to be a lawyer and he's even retained some of his youthful belief in the justice system. But all of them are ambitious. And when it came to Niko, my dislike was irrational – even I thought so.

Instantaneous dislike. Zora brought him to our place for dinner, the classic "meet the potential in-laws" scenario, and I could see him sizing up the furniture, like he was an appraiser, for god's sake. I knew he wanted Zora as his trophy wife, something – some *thing* – he felt entitled to have on his arm as a reward for being at the top of his class at law school. With her looks, that was to be expected. But he was also very taken with where she came from – not to brag, but my husband and I are very well off. Niko proposed within days of their meeting – romantic, right? Supposed to be. But in fact it was dangerous. She knew nothing about him. Her father and I soon changed that.'

She hesitated and I went with my hunch. 'You ran a background on him?'

'We did. And not just a Google search, either. We hired a pro. That's how alarmed we were.'

I scooted in closer to the table.

'A private investigator? What did she find out?'

'He. He found nothing that would stop Zora or frighten her off. Nothing at all, really. Niko had led a blameless life, to all appearances. Small-town boy from Pennsylvania, University of Pennsylvania, Harvard Law School, Georgetown, winner of the most billable hours competition at Masters, Milton, and Duckett. He worked at home during the pandemic, like many people with desk jobs, and I think that's where the problems started.'

I nodded. 'The divorce rates sky-rocketed once people were vaccinated, I read somewhere. Togetherness has its limits.'

'Don't I know it. Watching my husband eat his granola was more than I could bear some mornings. I just wanted to push his face in the bowl, you know? But we've been together many years, and—'

Her phone buzzed and she leaned forward to pull it from her back pocket. I'd been right – she wouldn't be separated from that lifeline for a moment.

'I have to take this.'

She left the table and went back into the gallery. I could hear her talking in hushed tones. 'She's here now' and 'I'll tell you later.'

She returned a few minutes later.

'I'd ask you to stay but my husband needs me. He's sounding

hysterical. Men, sometimes they are not strong. Besides, if Zora is going to show up anywhere, the chances are good this time of day she'd show up at home. I'm going to leave a note on the door, just in case.'

I knew this was my cue to leave. I didn't have business cards, only bookmarks. I asked if I could put my contact information in her phone.

We exchanged information, and I stood to leave.

'I hate to ask,' I said, 'but do you have any enemies?' I knew the art business was a flashpoint where fraud and money-laundering often met. Looking around me as if for hidden Picassos disguised as living-room art, it seemed ridiculous, but you never know.

'No,' she said flatly. 'If you think of anything else . . .' she began.

I nodded. 'I'd like to talk to the guy who investigated Niko.'

She hesitated.

'He won't talk with you without my permission.'

'I know,' I said, holding her gaze. She was trying to find a reason this would be a bad idea and could think of none.

'No stone unturned,' I said. 'He may have found things he didn't think worth sharing with you. And those are the things which could help us find Zora.'

She shrugged. 'I guess. I don't see what harm it could do. I gave a copy of his report on Niko to the police, for what it was worth. I could tell they didn't think much of it.'

'Could I see a copy, do you think?' But this was clearly an ask too far.

'I'll have to think about it,' she said.

Interesting. How many prospective in-laws do a background on their prospective sons-in-law? Around these parts, probably a lot. There are a lot of assets to protect. I wondered if the police thought it odd.

I didn't want to jeopardize my chances of seeing the report for myself by pushing her too hard, so I settled for her sharing the name and contact information of the private investigator they'd hired. She sent his phone number and address to my email.

'He's supposed to be the best. Kent Haworth.'

'Uh huh,' I said. I recognized the name from a writers' association I belonged to. 'I know him. He's a writer.'

'I didn't know. I didn't recognize his name.'

'I didn't say he was a well-known writer.' I gave her a tiny insider smile. 'Actually, he'd probably be open to hearing from me. I know he has a new book coming out in a few months.' That was always 'all hands on deck' time for any writer. *'Buy my book! Give it five stars!'*

I didn't think it would be a good time to tell Genevieve that Kent Haworth specialized in writing about true crime. He'd covered the Laci Peterson murder before anyone realized what a national obsession it was going to become. Unfortunately for Kent, he had a huge amount of competition – at least twenty books were written about Laci's convicted killer, her husband Scott Peterson, one of which became an instant classic like *Fatal Vision*. Kent's offering had drowned in all the chatter and reporting on that case. I saw the remainders of his book at Barnes and Noble going for 99 cents soon after it came out and I was sad – truly, I was. No one likes to see that sort of author graveyard, even when it's an author as full of himself as Kent Haworth.

It was going to be tricky to navigate these shoals. I did not want Zora – or Niko – to simply become fodder for the next *Investigation ID*.

'Leave it with me,' I told her, gathering my belongings and standing to leave. 'Meanwhile, any time, day or night, don't hesitate.' I didn't know what to say that would in any way help her through her nightmare, and we weren't on hugging terms. I gave her a little wave and a grimace meant to convey she had my full sympathy.

I noticed Harry was awake now, watching us wide-eyed but not making a sound. What a good child.

I waved goodbye and he smiled. That did it. That was all it took. Come hell or high water, I would find out what had happened to his mother.

TWELVE

The phenomenal recent success of true crime has never successfully been explained. It became popular in the eighties but was probably launched as a genre by Truman Capote's *In Cold Blood*. Ann Rule began her career in 1980 with *The Stranger Beside Me*, the tale of über-creep Ted Bundy. The list goes on, but no TV producer has seen anything like it in terms of a money-making enterprise since the Military Channel began replaying every modern-day and historic war for the American male audience over fifty.

The audience for true crime is largely women, not surprising since they are usually the victims of a particular type of crime – the intimate partner crime. What is surprising is that – even though so often the perpetrator is a male partner or husband of the victim – we still never tire of the descriptions of how these poor victims became victims.

Kent Haworth's success in this genre was not hard to understand once you met him, which I set out to do on leaving the gallery. I rang the office number provided by Google and he answered on the first ring. Probably a case of a writer with writer's block hoping to be interrupted. Also, I suspected Kent didn't run to having a secretary in his outer office to run interference, like Mike Hammer's Velda. The address for Kent's business – The Yard, 700 Pennsylvania Avenue SE – was, I suspected, one of those coworking office spaces freelance types could rent by the month so they could have a photocopier, a phone/fax line and, most critically, an important-sounding address for their business cards.

I asked him if I could drop in to discuss something, choosing my words carefully in case I was making it sound like I was going to pay him for his time or expected him to track down a deadbeat dad for me. Also, I did not refer to Genevieve Garnier by name, worried it might make him skittish.

Intrigued and probably dying for company, Kent agreed to see me at two p.m. at a coffee shop near his place.

Weighing my travel options, none of them good since they all involved getting myself across town in traffic, I decided to leave the Jeep in the garage and take an Uber to Foggy Bottom to catch the Orange Line Metro to Eastern Market. Washington, DC, for all its faults, can hold its own against any European country when it comes to its Metro system, if you are willing to ignore the times it is down for repair. It was clean, the announcer's voice was soothing, and it ran mostly on time.

We'd agreed to meet at Jasper's Espresso and, by the time I arrived, Kent had established a beachhead, surrounded by books and pens and papers, his laptop open to his latest manuscript. I suspected he spent most of his time in Jasper's and that he had set his Pennsylvania Avenue office number to forward to his cell phone.

He stood and greeted me with a bear hug, then cleared his books off the chair he'd saved for me. Like many male authors of a certain age, he had cultivated a Papa Hemingway persona – trimmed salt-and-pepper beard (which I think Hemingway didn't adopt until he was much older than Kent), steel-rimmed glasses (ditto), chambray shirt or fisherman sweater. It all made him stand out in largely buttoned-down DC.

'Thanks for coming out,' he said. 'What can I get you?'

'A cappuccino with almond milk would be grand. Thanks.'

I settled myself in a wooden chair and looked around at the decidedly artistic ambience. Local artists of various shades of talent had their wares displayed on the walls of Jasper's, all with touchingly ambitious price tags. I wondered how long they had hung there. It was a far cry from Genevieve's place with its offerings so carefully curated, so aimed at its target audience of tourists and policy wonks with money who were insecure about their taste in art and furnishings.

One thing that could be said for Jasper's display, it would take real courage to hang any one of these in a living room in Georgetown. Avant-garde didn't approach it. The painting hanging just across from me was of a blue frog with three breasts, to give you one example. There were worse.

Kent returned and put my drink in front of me, along with

one of those five-hundred-calorie cookies. My dismay must have shown.

'I simply cannot. I'm still working off my pandemic weight gain.' I might have mentioned Genevieve's cookies of less than an hour before, but did not.

'No problem,' he said. 'We'll share.'

I took a sip of the excellent coffee and asked him what he was working on.

'My book? I'm stuck at the everlasting research stage for my next one, to be honest. Every famous crime out there has been written about or filmed already. I have to wait for something new to come along.' Off my expression, he said, 'I know – ghoulish. We're in a strange profession, aren't we?'

'I was related by marriage to a pathologist – my husband's brother. You know, a guy who cuts open dead bodies for a living. And he thought *my* job was strange. I could tell he was worried I might do him in in his sleep whenever we stayed at his place. I should have been worried he'd take out my liver and put it in a jar. There really is no explaining it to people, no matter how you try.'

'I know! We're the normal ones. Anyway, it's a matter of time before some idiot thinks he's going to kill his wife and get away with it. I won't have long to wait.'

'You have to wonder how many do,' I said. 'Get away with it, I mean. And not just the men.'

'Uh huh. Women killers are far more interesting because they work against the stereotype. I'm talking about on paper. I'm certain in person they're as stupid as their male counterparts. But what I wouldn't give for a good black-widow murder. I'm sure there is one out there being committed right now. It's a matter of waiting.'

'Like a spider,' I said, smiling. I leaned in, folding my hands. Down to business. 'But books are not what I wanted to talk about. I understand Genevieve Garnier and her husband hired you once to investigate their son-in-law, Niko. Before he became their son-in-law.'

I waited for him to ask why I thought this was my business but, as it turned out, he was saving this for later. Unperturbed, he said: 'Niko Norman. Right. It sounds like they may have called that one right.'

'You got something on him?' I'll admit I was surprised.

He smoothed back his hair, a luxuriant mane threaded with gray that he must have a paid a barber a lot to keep in such perfect trim. Resemblance to Hemingway aside, Kent looked the part of the successful author – his clothes only slightly worn to indicate a preoccupation with higher thoughts.

Or perhaps the private-eye business wasn't paying as well as he'd hoped.

'It was more that when I meet a perfect specimen of human being, I'm skeptical. I went a little further digging into his background because I couldn't believe what was on the surface. No one is that blameless. And head of the lacrosse team? Give me a break. No one is that WASP-y, either.'

'Tell me,' I said. 'How did you get the job of looking into Niko's background? Did you know the father – Mr Garnier?'

'Garnier? Oh, I see, you're thinking of the mother, Genevieve Garnier. She uses her maiden name professionally, for the gallery. Their last name is Barbieri. James Barbieri is the father. Barbieri was Zora's maiden name before she married Norman.'

Funny, I hadn't thought of the name business, but it helped explain why I wasn't a PI. Genevieve may have owned the place before she married.

'OK. Did you know either of them before they hired you?'

'Yes, as a matter of fact. I knew him, not her. I used to do a lot of work for his firm before he gave it up to become an architect. It became my bread and butter when they had a big legal case coming up. Jury selection, that sort of thing.'

'Sounds fun, in a way.'

'It is. The psychology of what a potential juror might do is a whole other specialty, of course. I look at what they have done in the past and let the shrinks extrapolate.'

'Lucrative?' I was never above the crass question, but no one ever answered with specific numbers. That would be un-American. Kent was no exception.

'Between that and vetting job candidates for corporations, I do all right. It's better money than writing books. Just not as enjoyable. But needs must.'

'When the devil drives.' I nodded, digging my notebook out of my bag. As soon as I'd left the art gallery, I'd jotted down notes from my conversation with Genevieve before I could forget, leaning against a nearby brick garden wall to do it. I hadn't wanted to be writing as she spoke. Our relationship seemed too tenuous for that.

Flipping to the relevant page, I read aloud: 'From Pennsylvania, University of Pennsylvania, Harvard Law School, big shot at Masters, Milton, and Duckett.'

'That about sums it up.'

'Is that the only place Niko's worked?'

'In a manner of speaking. He did an internship at Bob Barnett's office.'

'The literary agent.' It wasn't a question. Everyone in our little writing world knew who Bob Barnett was.

'I wouldn't say literary, necessarily. He represents a lot of TV types, journalists mainly. And politicians – most famously the Clintons.'

'I know,' I said. 'Wow.'

'Indeed, wow,' he said, grinning. 'Don't tell my agent, but I'd kill to have Barnett in my corner. Sadly, I am not a politician with a wicked past I'm trying to whitewash for the public. A true-crime hack, that's me. Anyway, that's where Niko learned to sharpen his incisors, in the offices on Twelfth Street. After that he went to MM&D. Where he stayed.'

'No problems there, one presumes.'

'MM&D don't pay you if you cause problems. You're supposed to be the problem-solver.'

'So, who did you talk to there? A senior partner, something like that?'

'Are you kidding? That's about the last person who would know something personal about Niko or who would tell me if he did. No. I cultivated what used to be called the typing pool. The people, mostly young women, who keep the place ticking over. Who not only do the lion's share of work in that sort of high-pressure place, but are good at listening at doors.'

'Good thinking,' I said. Seriously, I was impressed. 'And?'

'I found two of them on dating apps and I took those two out to dinner – on four separate occasions, of course. Maybe

it was six. They were great women. And since I wasn't paying
for the meals – Barbieri was – I thought I'd take the slow
approach.'

'You're kidding. And you just . . . what? Asked them what
they knew about Niko?'

'More or less, but I was way suaver – more suave? – anyway,
I was extremely roundabout and subtle. And at my absolute
charming best.' He gave me the benefit of his finest Papa
Hemingway smile. 'Seriously, I just got them talking about their
work – people love that, men and women both. I could look
like Boris Yeltsin and people would still talk my head off about
their jobs, so long as I make them feel they are particularly
good at their jobs, which these two clearly were. Are. I still see
one of them now and then.'

He paused to break off a chunk of cookie and wash it down
with coffee. I caved, breaking off a bit of cookie for myself.

'I told them I had an aunt going through a particularly sticky
divorce, which happens to have been true. After years of Aunt
Becky being the major breadwinner, her thug of a husband
decides he's leaving her for someone he met "playing bridge"'
– he inserted air quotes here – 'all day and night long while
she worked to pay the bills. So naturally he decides he's entitled
to spousal support.'

I nodded uncomfortably, having flashbacks to Marcus's
increasing fondness for bridge, his determination to master its
many byzantine layers. To me, it was just a stupid game, particularly when he described the way people nearly came to blows
if their partner bid wrong. I thought the challenge and novelty
were keeping him alive but, as I came to know, there were other
motivators.

'That game can be a bit of a magnet for a certain personality
type, I'll grant you,' I said.

'Or a happy hunting ground for a spouse on the prowl.'

Again, uncomfortably close to my experience of the game.
I changed the subject.

'Anyway, you told your dates about your aunt, and they said
what?'

'They both mentioned a few different people at their firm
who were specialists, whose names I dutifully jotted down, but

they also both said the best at their firm, in all areas, was Niko. And that he was hard to get and expensive as a result. "Oh!" said I. "Money is no object." In which case, they proceeded to sing his praises. Bringing in a well-paying client would only boost their status, you know. They both were studying law at night, with plans to move up.'

'Sure.' I looked resolutely away from that cookie, holding Kent's gaze instead.

'There was only one odd moment, but it didn't seem worth mentioning to Genevieve and James. Now you're asking, though, and given what's happened, I wonder if I should have mentioned it.'

'Yes?' Again I leaned forward, hands folded on the table to show he had my fullest attention. Clearly, we had reached the part of Kent's revelations where Niko would turn out to have feet of clay.

'They both skirted around their real point,' he said, 'but they both asked how old Aunt Becky was.'

'How old?'

'Yeah. And when I said sixty-five, they visibly relaxed. I mean, it was subtle, but it was there. The firm doesn't hire blabbermouths, but body language is hard for anyone to control. After three glasses of very expensive wine one evening, one of them came closer to saying what she meant.'

'Which was?'

'She'll be fine,' she said. 'He specializes in thirty- to forty-year-olds.' Then she put her fingers to her mouth, like this' – he mimed a person who'd said more than they'd intended, eyes wide – 'and she tried to backtrack, but we both knew what she meant.'

'Young women going through a divorce. Vulnerable and possibly looking for a savior or a place to land. Or simply a diversion from their woes.'

'Right.'

'Did you tell this to Zora's parents?'

'I did, sort of. I told them he had a reputation for being flirtatious.'

'Is that what it's called?'

He opened his hands in a sort of helpless gesture. 'He was

a single guy at the time, so why not? I didn't want to overstate it, to make it sound like he drugged women so he could have his way with them.'

'Kent,' I said. 'He took advantage of what was supposed to be a professional relationship. Women came to him for help. They were *paying* him for help.'

Kent shrugged. 'Genevieve and James could draw their own conclusions. I told them what I knew, but rumors are not facts.'

'Did you tell them about his age requirement? Thirty- to forty-year-olds only need apply?'

'I don't know that I got that specific. Look, the guy was clean otherwise, and, as I say, he was a single guy in DC. I imagined marriage would slow him down.'

A thought struck me. 'You say you're still seeing one of these dating-app women?'

'Um,' he said. 'Off and on. Like I said.'

'Did either of them realize you were for hire? That you were there not because of their desirability but because of where they worked?'

'We never had that conversation. No.'

He said it with such confidence, as if of course this was normal behavior for a PI, leaving me to ponder the ethics of the entire profession. Which, from my reading of crime novels of the 1940s, doesn't have a whole lot going on in the ethics department.

He wiped a crumb or two off his beard and said, 'Now, fair is fair. Why are you so interested? Why are you even talking with Genevieve about all this? Why did she give you my name? Are you somehow friends?'

'I'm her daughter's neighbor. She and Niko have a townhouse behind mine.'

His eyes lit up. 'You were friends with them?'

'I wouldn't say that. There isn't a lot of socializing where I live – at least, not what I was used to where I grew up, where everyone was up in everyone's shit.'

'Where was that?'

'Maine. Besides, there's an age difference of about twenty years – *plus* she had a very young child to care for. It's not as if we had so much in common that we hung out together swapping recipes and referrals for roof-repair guys . . .' I paused, realizing there was something I'd missed before. 'Come to think of it, if she belonged to some sort of mommy play group, I saw no evidence of it. The women with young kids hang out at Windmill Hill – it's a park nearby with a sandbox and play-ground equipment. Although most of the babies in that group can barely walk, let alone navigate the slides and swings. But the women take over one of the picnic tables or, in nice weather, spread out blankets on the grass. Zora always seemed to be indoors with the child, and if she ever felt the need for sunshine for herself or for Harry, I never saw her outside enjoying herself.'

'Who's Harry?'

'The baby.'

'Ah. You'd have to trail her pretty closely to know she avoided the outdoors,' Kent said. 'And why would you?'

Trail her? 'If I'd known what was going to happen, I would have,' I said, miffed. 'When I walk the dog, I do notice things.'

'So you and Niko and Zora are near neighbors who never talk or see much of each other. Sounds more like New York.' I noticed he wasn't using the past tense to describe the Normans. They still were my neighbors, out there in the world, living and breathing, until we knew otherwise.

Where, I wondered, could they be? They'd been gone a week.

'Does it?' I asked. 'Around Old Town, it's the norm. We're all busy working, or off traveling somewhere for work – rarely socializing. I'm guilty of it, too.'

'I do know what you mean. Even birthday parties in DC are less about socializing than they are about networking. Heads swivel to and fro trying to see who else is in the room – who else more important that they should be chatting with. Even when the party is a fund-raiser – or perhaps, especially when it is, especially if it's a political fund-raiser. Everything must be purpose-driven, on the meter, not a minute wasted. And no one seems to know how to just have a good time, not after a certain age.'

'I wonder sometimes why I don't just pack up and leave for Montana,' I said. 'Or go back to Maine. In theory, I could work from anywhere.'

'All writers have that daydream, don't they? But wouldn't

Montana be even more isolating? Anyway, I can't leave yet, since for me this is still where the work is. When I strike it rich, it's California, here I come.'

The last of the cookie had disappeared so I sat back.

'Anyway, Niko and Zora were always friendly. Just, always in a rush. And not in my age group or my work group – whatever you want to call it. They weren't crime writers, or we'd have had more to talk about. That makes a big difference.'

He nodded. 'So . . . Based on your practically non-existent relationship with Zora, you end up speaking with her mother.'

'Something like that.' Put that way, it was very hard to explain, so I added, 'It turns out she's a fan – that helped. She *wanted* to talk.' I'd been going on instinct, knowing something was very wrong and wanting to help. Plus, I was on deadline for my book and trying to ignore that fact with any distraction – and this, I had to admit, was the best distraction I'd ever come up with. It beat Facebook and Twitter all to hell, but this was a distraction with a purpose.

However I framed it, it all added up to a compulsive need to, well, snoop.

To get to the bottom of things, I amended. To find out what happened to that young woman and bring her home. Her and Niko. And if her husband was involved in her disappearance, to make sure he paid for it. To make whoever was involved pay for it.

'Have you talked with the police?' Kent asked.

'I have. This morning. A detective and his sergeant.'

'No kidding. Homicide?'

'I didn't ask. He gave me his card. It just said Old Town Police Department with his email and phone number.'

'They transfer those guys around a lot. Probably saves on printing costs to issue generic cards. Anyway, what did he say?'

'He didn't drop by to confide or go over the case with me. He asked me how well I knew them, all that sort of thing. He could see from my living room I had a view into their place, so he wondered, you know.'

'If you'd been doing a reprise of *Rear Window*.'

'Minus the leg in a cast. Right.'

'And did you see anything?'

'Niko with a large trunk tied up with rope, you mean?'

'And cleaning a handsaw?'

'*God*,' I said. 'No. If he'd been doing anything like that, I'd imagine he'd do it in the downstairs room – the library – rather than have to haul a heavy trunk around. It's what I do when I travel – take the suitcase apart downstairs, so I don't have to carry it up. I do a lot of packing down there, as well.'

'I see you've given this some thought,' said Kent.

'I have.'

'And have you decided Niko killed her?'

'Of course not. It's the simplest explanation, or the most common – the husband did it – but there are others.'

'For example?'

'They ran off together.'

'Leaving the baby.'

I stirred what was left of my cold coffee and drank it down. 'That right there's the problem. Zora had her mother come and collect Harry.'

'Her mother told you this?'

I nodded. 'That's in confidence, all right?'

'The news outlets aren't saying anything like that.'

'That's what I mean. You can't ever repeat what I just said.' I lowered my voice. 'Nothing can get out that would jeopardize the investigation.' Or make Genevieve stop confiding in me. Or get me in trouble with Narduzzi. Or get me doing hard time in some women's prison in Central Virginia. I was kicking myself for having told Kent, but he did have a way of drawing people out. Or in, depending. The wining and dining of the two women from the law office on someone else's dime, pretty clearly turning one of those encounters into a private romance, was probably off the chart, ethically speaking. If he never got round to telling the woman what was really going on – wouldn't I, in her shoes, be completely ticked off if I found out?

To be honest, I wasn't sure. Kent was a charmer.

Still, I couldn't see what harm it would do to tell him about the baby. Maybe he'd think of some reason for Zora's behavior – and Niko's – that had escaped me. True crime was his arena, after all.

'Nothing I ever saw led me to think they were neglectful parents,' I said. 'And obviously Zora's recruiting her mom into daycare, of which the police are aware, dispels that notion. So we're left with . . . what? Zora running from her abusive husband but making sure the baby is taken care of?'

'That would make sense. But only if he showed up later that night and reported her missing. Which I gather he did not.'

'Not that I'm aware,' I said. 'The police seem to be looking for both of them.'

'Guilty or innocent, that's what he'd do. Call in the experts.'

Unless, I thought, it was a kidnapping for ransom, and Niko had been told by the kidnappers not to call anyone. But if so, where was he now?

'So where is he?' I said aloud.

'Is his car parked at home or is it missing?'

Crap. 'I never thought of that,' I admitted. 'Their place is a carbon copy of mine, flipped in reverse, so they'll have a one-car garage. I don't know if it's empty now or if she has a car parked in there. Most couples in the neighborhood have two cars, and whoever draws the short straw has to park on the street. Which is a battle to the death among residents, tourists, and restaurant workers looking to park their cars at night. The streets are mobbed with waiters and chefs running around in aprons to move their cars every two hours to avoid a ticket.'

'Why don't they park in a garage?'

'Because it costs more than most of them take home.'

'Oh. Got it. Anyway, the police must be on the lookout for his car – or hers. That would be elemental – they'd start from there. I used to date a cop who worked the criminal investigation unit of Old Town. I wonder if she's still around.'

He pulled out his phone and opened it to his address book. He put a cursor in the search bar, then hesitated.

'You don't remember her name, do you?' I asked, knowing the answer.

'Just give me a minute. She had red hair and blue eyes, and she was really a fiery type. I'm thinking Irish extraction. Was it Colleen? *Damn.* With that temper, not everything you'd want in law enforcement. She was angry with me when last seen, so one has to make allowances. Bernadette?' He sighed. 'I'll have to think about it.'

'I hate to ask, but what makes you think Colleen or whatever her name is would be willing to talk with you about Zora and Niko's cars?'

'Why wouldn't she? Oh, because she was angry.' He waved a hand at that. 'She'll be over it by now.'

The arrogance was breathtaking. I did so envy people with that level of insouciance. 'Remembering her name would be a good start towards making amends.'

'Right. We have to start there. Now, if Niko kidnapped Zora, something like that, it's as if she knew something was going to happen and that's why she had her mom pick up the kid, ahead of time.'

'Like Niko announced his intentions? That makes zero sense. And, who is this "we"?'

'Two heads are better than one. Wasn't I just saying I've been waiting for the right true-crime story to come along? And this just falls in my lap. Well, you just fell in my lap.'

'I most certainly did not.'

'Figure of speech.'

'You're not suggesting we collaborate or something, are you?'

'Do you want to know what Shannon or Siobhan tells me about the cars, or not?'

I was pretty sure my face displayed an unbecoming pout by this point. Inwardly, I sighed. A contact within APD who could tell me everything Narduzzi no doubt would refuse to tell me, even if I dared ask? Priceless.

The thing was, I had almost as much confidence in Kent's charm as Kent did. If what's-her-Irish-name was still around, I had no doubt he could worm out of her whatever he wanted. It might take time, but he'd get there.

Echoing my thoughts, he said, 'Just leave it with me. I'll have her on file at home and I'll find her one way or another but, once I do, I'll need time to, you know . . .'

'Soften her up.' I was not going to ask what this file of his might consist of. Did he file her under 'R' for redhead or 'I' for Irish? Did he cross-index? I wouldn't let my mind wander into the other filing possibilities. Kent was, let's face it, exactly the kind of predator mothers warn their daughters about.

'OK, fine,' I said. 'But what exactly do you mean by collaborate?'

'You tell me what you learn; I tell you what I learn. Fifty-fifty.'

'You're talking about writing a book? I don't know. For a start I'd have to ask my agent.'

'That's not what I meant. I meant share information, not profits.'

I paused to consider the imaginary profits. There were all sorts of reasons to back out of this discussion. For one thing, any book would involve writing about living people, always tricky. At least one of them a lawyer – Niko himself. And James, Zora's father, whose firm Kent had called his bread and butter in his work with jury selection. Talk about biting the hand that fed you.

Even with dead people, authors could find themselves dealing with disgruntled heirs.

Besides, publishers were always shy about lawsuit-happy people who thought they'd been wronged somehow by what you'd written or implied. I worried about that myself when I was writing fiction. That someone with blonde hair and brown eyes would decide she was my murder victim – and usually my victims, more than most people, deserved to die, they were such complete asshats. It was always easier, more interesting, and safer to make up characters, if only to knock them off. Still, I paid exorbitant insurance premiums for an umbrella policy, which in theory shielded me from the nutcases.

Writing a non-fiction book would be a whole other minefield.

With true crime, saying you made it all up wasn't an option. Those standard-issue disclaimers at the front of books – the legal verbiage that stated any relation to persons living or dead was unintentional, and no one was harmed in the creation of the book – wouldn't apply.

'Well,' I said. 'But I—'

'Great,' he said. 'When can I come over?'

'What?'

'To your place. I need to see the scene, get a feel for things.'

I'd meant to repeat – firmly, like the businesswoman I was not – that I would talk with my agent, but this threw me off. It's probably some inherited genetic tendency, but I can too easily be talked into things. An Author Without Borders, that's me.

I convinced myself it made sense. Kent might see something unusual I'd missed, since I'd been looking at the same scene for years.

'I guess tomorrow. Afternoon.' There was no real reason to specify afternoon, except I felt I had to seize back control somehow. 'I work in the mornings,' I added.

At least, I was *supposed* to work in the mornings. I was already formulating other plans.

'Done,' he said. 'I'll see you around four.'

THIRTEEN

K ent left for his rent-a-room office while I hailed an Uber to take me back to my car. I avoided going into DC for this very reason, the tortuous and expensive routes you ended up taking to get from Point A to Point B. As it was, I'd talked with Kent just long enough to be unable to avoid the rush-hour traffic headed south on George Washington Parkway, the nation's speedway for Lexuses and Beamers.

It was past five thirty by the time I got home, pulled into my garage (thinking of the Normans' car – could Kent's redheaded friend help us with that?), and thought about what was for dinner. A freezer full of Trader Joe's entrées revealed three cartons of my standby, Reduced Guilt Mac & Cheese (270 calories, decent source of calcium). With a fork I punched holes in the covering, put the tray in the microwave for four minutes, and poured myself a glass of pinot noir while I waited. Usually, I rounded out the meal with microwaved broccoli, but on this night I couldn't be bothered. There was too much to think about.

I decided to eat in the living room in front of the TV, enjoying my Reduced Guilt in the privacy afforded by the darkened windows of the Normans' place and mine and the summer lushness of the trees. The Klieg lights appeared to have been taken away or turned off for the moment. Forensics people had to eat, too, I imagined.

Bachelors Number 1 and 2 seemed to be out, as their windows were dark. I realized how much privacy I often was sacrificing to be where the 'action' was. Especially since I so seldom took advantage of my trendy location. Today's foray into DC was rare enough to mark on the calendar.

I put my feet up on the coffee table and punched the remote to CNN while I waited for Misaki to show up. Channel Eight was more likely to have news of the Normans, but for that the DC area had to wait until six.

Misaki arrived at precisely 5.55. I opened the door to her and, without preliminary, she said, 'Have you seen the courtyard?'

I closed and locked the door behind her. 'Why, what's it doing?'

'It's got news trucks all over. We had to shoo them out of the courtyard proper – no one could get to their parking spaces – but between them and the police vehicles, no one could park, anyway. No one is happy, particularly Jeff Barnstable. His place is right in the thick of it all. I don't dare open my email until I've had a drink.'

'I've got a bottle open in the living room and another glass waiting. Help yourself.'

By Jeff Barnstable, Misaki was referring to the man who lived directly behind me, the presumed Bachelor Number 2 who lives alone except for occasional visits from a woman who may or may not be his sister. She appears so rarely I have come to assume 'sister here on vacation' rather than Jeff's having some amorous liaison. I have seen the two of them dine outdoors in summer at his little round table, serenaded by the roar of the overhead planes. I prefer to take my meals without jet fumes and stroke-inducing heatwaves. The airlines are killing us all, but we sit on our patios and take it, apart from an occasional angry letter to Old Town City Hall, which I'm sure goes straight into a special file labeled CRACKPOT.

Anyway, Jeff Barnstable was the neighbor immediately to the right of the Normans' place, from my perspective out the back. I couldn't see (and didn't know) who was on the Normans' other side. I may have mentioned that person had had draperies installed and was thus useless for my purposes. For the purposes of what I was already thinking of as 'my investigation', I mean.

If those draperies were ever pulled back, I never saw it happen. Certainly not at night, which was the only time we could all see in and catch up on what everyone else was doing. I liked to think of it as an advanced form of Neighborhood Watch. Personally, I felt a bit safer knowing that if I failed to appear for a month, and was never seen walking through the living room or putting out my garbage bins in front, someone might eventually think to come and check on me.

I wondered if that person would be Misaki. Probably.

I chased away the morbid thought. But wasn't this exactly what had happened with the Normans? The Neighborhood Watch, Kildare Place version, had swung into action. Eventually.

'Which news people are out there?'

'Channels Four, Five and Eight. But, once the police technicians stopped trooping in and out of the Normans' front door, there wasn't much for the reporters to do, and the neighbors who were home refused to talk with them. Being on the board, I thought it was my job to have a word with them. Turn to Channel Eight, just in case.'

I did, and came in right at the top of the news hour, where the story of 'a missing couple from Old Town' was the highlight of the evening, alongside a new resolution for safeguarding the downtown mall in DC. We were promised details, right after the commercial break, which gave me time to run into the kitchen to pour some mixed nuts into a bowl.

Returning, I saw Belle Natala, the anchorwoman for Channel Eight. She sported a chopped-off haircut with ombré streaks that looked trendy on her but would have made me look deranged and, moreover, like a woman who did indeed run with scissors.

She was leading with the story of the absent Normans. 'Police Baffled by Disappearance of Wealthy Old Town Couple', read the chyron scrolling beneath her. She had adopted a serious, concerned look for the occasion, her journalist's empathy on full display. Her demeanor would change into something more flirtations when she began interviewing Detective Steve Narduzzi of the Old Town Police Department. I couldn't blame her, but really, there is a time and a place for everything, Belle.

She began speaking to him from the left side of the split screen.

'Detective Narduzzi, what can you tell us about the disappearance of this popular young couple?'

He looked completely comfortable in the role of spokesman, as if he'd done this sort of interview many times before. 'The Normans have not been seen by neighbors in Old Town since last Tuesday, meaning they've now been missing for just over a week.'

A video of the front of the Normans' house appeared on the screen, the camera panning over the façade from top to bottom. It was indeed a copy of mine, except their place was painted white with black shutters. (Mine, FYI, was a pale apricot with rust-red shutters.) Two windows on the second and third floors faced the front; a little gable window graced the fourth floor. When I'd bought the place, the real-estate listing had described that area as a nanny flat, since it had its own attached bathroom. Marcus had used it as his office. No one in their right mind would use it as a nursery since that would require too many trips up and down the stairs at night. I assumed the Normans housed baby Harry on the third level, down a short hallway from the master bedroom.

'The couple had a young child, is that right?'

Narduzzi nodded. 'He is completely safe and was never in any danger.'

'Where is he now?'

He dodged that one deftly. 'The question for your viewers is, where are his parents? It is urgent that we find them.'

His face was replaced by a photo of Zora and Niko on their wedding day. She was resplendent in a classic Grace Kelly gown with a silk cummerbund accentuating her hourglass figure; a crown sat on her dark-haired updo, securing a lace veil. She held a white Bible instead of flowers.

Next to her and slightly behind, almost an afterthought, was Niko, wearing a tux, pride writ large on his face. They made a stunning couple.

Did I only imagine the slight apprehension in her expression? She wasn't smiling, at any rate. Maybe she was just acknowledging the solemnity of the occasion.

The wedding photo was replaced by a casual snapshot of the couple on a picnic with Harry. I even recognized the location, further down the parkway near Dyke Marsh. The baby's face had been blurred, possibly at the request of Genevieve and James. Or it may simply have been the station's policy to protect children.

'Are there any clues for the police to go on?' Belle asked as the still photos were replaced with Narduzzi's visage. 'Their car, for example?'

I sat forward. This was exactly the question I wanted answered, among others.

'They had two cars. One is still in the garage. The other – the car most often driven by Niko Norman – appears to be missing. We'd like to show your viewers a photo and a close-up of the license plate. This information was of course immediately shared with all law enforcement in the area.'

I scrabbled to get a piece of paper and pen from my desk to write down the information as Misaki calmly snapped a photo of the television screen with her phone.

It was a black late-model Mercedes with a non-personalized plate. Misaki read the numbers aloud for me as I wrote them down.

'Good luck finding a particular black late-model Mercedes in this town,' she said.

I knew what she meant. It was the uniform car of Old Towners.

'So are the police thinking it might be a carjacking?' Belle wanted to know. 'I know there's been a rash of that sort of thing, ever since the pandemic.'

'We are not ruling out anything at this point,' he told her. 'Although by now there should have been some trace of them or the car.'

'The fact that Zora's car is still in the garage – what do you make of that?'

'The assumption is they left together in his car. We are screening video footage taken by parking enforcement of all the cars parked on the street that day. Once we locate where the car was parked, we'll be canvassing the near neighbors to see if they saw either Niko or Zora entering the car or driving through the area.'

'And you've spoken with their near neighbors?'

Again I sat to attention, although the chances Narduzzi would repeat anything from our largely useless interview were small.

'We have and they've been most helpful.'

Some of them have, he might have said. I never did get around to mentioning that fight, and the more my silence on that topic went on, the worse it was going to look.

Belle thanked Narduzzi for being there and cut to a commercial for car insurance. His five minutes of fame were up. Belle had apparently left the interview with Misaki, spokesperson for the Tribe of Kildare, on the cutting-room floor.

'I'm recording Channel Four at my place,' said Misaki, 'in case they have anything to add. Only Channel Eight seems to have landed an interview with the cop. You didn't tell me how dishy he was.'

'Yes, I did,' I answered distractedly. 'I told you he looked like a young Chris Meloni. But I also told you he's married, remember?'

She flung herself back against the sofa, shielding her stomach with a throw pillow, a teenager in full sulk.

'What did you find out about MM&D?' I asked her. 'Anything from the guy you used to date?'

'Really not much, except that he's married now with a kid on the way.'

'I meant, about Niko.'

'Oh. He told me Niko's specialty was a sub-sub-category of family law. Parental abduction of children.'

'You're kidding.'

'I know. Crazy.'

I was deeply surprised, certain she was going to say he was a genius at getting blood from turnips in nasty divorce fights. For one thing, Niko hadn't struck me as some great humanitarian, the kind of guy who wears his heart on his sleeve, a male Mother Teresa. Surely that special field of law called for a good line in empathy and compassion.

Or perhaps not. If you wanted your child back from a partner you'd grown to loathe, I'd be willing to bet you'd hire a lawyer who could fight dirty.

'I mean, yeah, how weird is that?' said Misaki, reaching for the spoon I'd provided in the bowl of salted nuts. 'Now he's been abducted himself, in a way.' Pouring a scoop of nuts into her palm, she added, 'Do you think there's a connection?'

Belle had returned and – after the downtown mall update – was moving on to a wreck on the parkway. Technically, a fender bender on the parkway wasn't news so, apart from the disappearance of the Normans, it must have been a slow news day. After muting the TV with the remote I sat back, staring at the pattern of lights dancing on the ceiling. Many of my neighbors had begun lighting their back patio areas to deter criminals, I was sure in response to the events at the Normans'. The light pollution was going to destroy all our circadian rhythms. I already had trouble sleeping at night.

'It certainly is weird,' I said. 'I wonder what the police are making of it?'

'Why don't you call Narduzzi and ask?'

'I'm going to call him later. I never mentioned to him the sort-of fight – rather, quarrel – I saw them have. The animated conversation, let's say, between Niko and Zora.'

'*Augusta*,' she said. 'What did I tell you? You could be on thin—'

'I know, I know. I've been busy. Anyway, I did learn something today about Niko Norman. It might have some bearing.'

'Yes? From whom?'

'A friend of mine,' I said. 'Not really a friend so much as a guy I know from one of my writers' groups. He's a private eye who did work for Zora's dad.'

'That sounds very promising,' she said. 'What led you to think of talking to him?'

'Zora's mom led me to him, actually. Look, it's a long story, but basically, she and her husband didn't trust Niko, and they had my writer friend look into his background. Before he and Zora were married.'

'*Ooooh*,' Misaki breathed, suitably impressed. 'OK, you have been busy.'

'Want to know what he told me?'

'Yep.' She kicked off her shoes and put her feet on the coffee table, a practice I would have discouraged had it been anyone else. I was still the tiniest bit germophobic since the pandemic.

'He told me Niko on paper was pretty much godlike, but in person he had a bit of a reputation. He had a roaming eye and roaming hands to match. If that even makes sense. But you know what I mean.'

She shook her head. 'I don't get it. Good-looking guy but next to Zora he looked like one of those Neanderthal-man computer reconstructions by *National Geographic* or whatever. Beauty and the Beast.'

'I know. Apparently, he was lousy with charm. I never saw

it, myself. Maybe it's a generational thing. But Zora must have.'

'Jesus Christ,' said Misaki. 'Are you saying he was cheating on Zora? *Zora?* All his late billable hours were a front?'

'I guess. For cheating on her or trying to. My . . . friend . . . seemed to think his Lothario reputation dated to his single days, though. There's nothing then or now that's concrete to go on, just rumors. Scuttlebutt among the paralegals, who noticed the sultry glances across the tops of filing cabinets, the sudden hushed conversations when anyone walked into the photocopy room unannounced, all that sort of thing. I'm guessing but, when I worked in an office, that's how we figured out what was going on between my boss and the new hire in marketing.'

'Do the police know?'

'I assume you're asking about Niko's wandering everything and not about my old boss. So, I guess so. Maybe. How would I know?'

'Fair enough. How do we find out more?'

'Let me think.' I decided not to mention Kent's redhaired police source in case nothing came of it, and because it was so borderline sleazy I wouldn't be able to hold my head up around anyone campaigning for women's rights. I had decided with Kent to adopt a wait-and-see approach. When and if he learned something, he and I could pool our resources. Or not. I still wasn't crazy about getting sucked into a collaboration on his book. Not without something in writing that had been vetted by my agent and maybe a lawyer or two. Idly, I wondered if super-agent Bob Barnett was busy. I merely said, 'My friend might have an avenue to more information, but I'm not counting on it.'

'Why not?'

'Basically, because I'm not sure how much of his blarney is true.' Misaki nodded. She knew my well-earned trust issues too well. 'There must be a way to worm our own way into Duckett whatever's confidences. You're a lawyer, Misaki. Family law, no less. Think of something.'

'I can't think of anything ethical.'

'The situation doesn't require anything ethical,' I said.

'Oh. Well. OK, you could call pretending to be a prospective client wanting a free consultation.'

'Me.' Somehow, I knew that was coming.

'Gus, *I* can't do it. I practice family law myself, remember, or I used to. I might be recognized. Chances are good I would be. Even if I weren't a lawyer, too – their competition, no less – someone might recognize me from that holiday party. Or from some ad my company ran with my photo when they were trying to drum up business and prove how diverse they were. No, it has to be you.'

'But I'm Niko's neighbor. There's no way.' I paused, trying to think it through. Would anyone at Niko's firm know my place and the Normans' were so close, and put my address together with his? And from there, figure out I was there to snoop?

'Would they know you were neighbors?' Misaki echoed my thought.

'I don't know, Misaki. They'll want my name and contact information, just to make an appointment. Someone might notice my address is near the Normans', even though the two street names are different: Fendall Street and Kildare Place.'

'So you tell them, if they notice – and honestly, what are the chances? But if they google-map you, simply say it's a coincidence about the Normans, you've been planning to come in for ages. Just say they come highly recommended by . . . I don't know. By someone. Or you could just make up a name and address. Why not?'

'I could wear a disguise,' I said. 'Maybe a wig and glasses.'

'Yes! That would work. A blonde wig, I think, with your pink coloring.'

'I'm kidding, Misaki.' Thinking of the million ways I could be caught out and have no way to explain myself, I really did not want to do this. It was borderline unethical. And across-the-board strange. They might call security on me.

I shook my head. 'I think we should wait to hear from my private-eye writer guy.'

'I don't know why it only struck me just now. I'm telling you, blonde hair would really work on you. Meloni wouldn't stand a chance.'

'Narduzzi. And knock it off.'

FOURTEEN

After Misaki left, I surfed different channels for news, but they had all moved on to their regular programming, which seemed to involve a lot of true-crime shows. Had the entire world gone mad?

Who needed true crime? I was living it. And getting nowhere trying to solve it.

When I stood to take the empty wine glasses out to the kitchen, Steve Narduzzi's business card caught my eye, protruding from the bestselling book where I had been using it as a bookmark. I had been asked to endorse the paperback edition and had been grappling to find the right words. 'Gripping' for a book which had lost my attention on page ten didn't seem fitting, but I owed the author's editor a favor, so I was determined to plow ahead until I could find something to praise. There was always the good old standby 'page-turning', if the best I could manage was to flip through the pages to read the end.

Misaki's parting advice was – again – to call Narduzzi, and I knew she was right. With any luck he wouldn't be in the office by now and I could leave a message.

He picked up on the second ring.

'Detective Narduzzi.'

'Oh! Hi. Yes, hi. This is Augusta Hawke. I'm the neighbor – one of the neighbors – across the back from the Normans' place. We spoke earlier. With your sergeant. In my townhouse.'

'Right. Sure.' I heard the sound of paper crinkling and guessed I'd interrupted him in the middle of a Big Mac dinner at his desk.

'You said I should call if I remembered anything.'

Definitely the sound of a hamburger wrapper being crumpled. I heard a soft 'ding', and pictured him tossing it into a wastebasket across the room.

'I'm sorry to interrupt your dinner,' I said. 'I don't even think this is important.'

'Everything is important, at this stage.'

I braced myself in case I was going to be scolded for not saying anything before. I began babbling, weirdly overcompensating with word salad.

'It's just that, well, we are all living cheek by jowl here, you know. Worse than Japan, where they've learned all these social rules so they don't just go crazy, you know. They rarely look each other in the eye or stare at people and so on. They have women-only train cars, did you know that?'

'I'm sorry, but I'm really—'

'Yes, yes, you're busy! OK. Anyway, so here in Kildare we've likewise learned to ignore everyone's little peccadilloes. Unless they involve parking in someone else's space. There is no social rule that covers that, and it's the sort of outrage that can never be forgiven, really. God help you if you block someone's driveway. Seriously.'

'You're calling to tell me about the Normans' car?' he asked.

'No! No, of course not. I don't know anything about the car.' Yet. I hadn't heard from Kent about what his police source might know, which was not exactly information I could drop into this conversation, anyway. 'It was just an example I was giving you. In case you wondered why I didn't mention it before. Actually, I forgot. Sort of. I just, you know . . .' I wondered if they recorded calls to the station as a matter of course. Naturally, they would. I had to get a grip. At this rate he'd think I'd kidnapped everyone in the courtyard.

'What,' he said flatly. Just the thin edge of rudeness creeping into his voice. It had no doubt been a long day at HQ.

'OK. Here's the thing. I saw them fighting. Quarreling. Words, not fists. In case you were getting the idea it was one hundred percent bliss over there . . . But it was just the once. All couples quarrel. I don't think they were any worse than most. My husband and I used to quarrel sometimes, you know. And I really regret it now he's gone, even though he was . . . But I thought I should tell you.'

'Uh huh.' He didn't sound particularly interested, which was good. It meant I hadn't wrecked the investigation by keeping things to myself.

At the same time, I felt he should be treating my eyewitness testimony with a bit more respect. Maybe telling him about the yelp I overheard would do it.

'There's more,' I said. 'I think I heard Zora cry out in pain once.'

'Really?' Again that blasé attitude. I could picture him scrolling through his phone or something when he should have been paying attention to me.

'Yes, really. They were on the back patio one night and I heard this, like, yelp.'

'Uh huh. You're sure it wasn't Niko?'

I tried to think back to the moment.

'No,' I said with more certainty than I felt. 'It was higher pitched.'

'You're sure it was Zora?'

'Well, no. I'm only sure it was coming from their patio.' To be honest, I wasn't even sure of *that* now, but I felt I'd lost quite enough ground with him already. He was probably thinking some smart-aleck attorney would make mincemeat of me on the witness stand.

He was probably right.

Since we had inched into a slightly new phase of our relationship, however, I thought I'd chance a question or two.

'So . . .' I said. 'Any leads? I mean, does anyone have any idea what happened?'

'I can't tell you more than what you've heard on the news. Niko's car has been found.'

What? 'That was on the news?'

'Channel Four,' he said.

Damn. 'I was watching Channel Eight. You were good, by the way.' I reached for the remote. Channel Four was doing another true-crime show. I'd have to wait for the real news at ten.

'Channel Four has better turnaround,' he said. 'They've got a bigger staff and they can send out a scrum of reporters for a story like this.'

'Apparently. I'll remember that next time. We were only watching Channel Eight because a friend of mine thought they'd show the interview they'd done with her.'

'Who's your friend?'

It sounded like an idle question, but I wasn't sure why he would ask. 'Well, sort of a friend. She's a member of the Kildare HOA board so the reporters thought she might know something. Which she doesn't, I'm sure. I mean, the entire focus of the board tends to be on what wattage of bulbs to use in the court-yard streetlamps.' I was hoping to discourage him from asking for Misaki's name. I already felt like I was ratting her out. Besides, I wanted to be free to discuss the case with her, my own neutral sounding board.

'What's her name?'

'Oh. Well, It's Misaki. Jones. Misaki Jones.'

'Right, we've already spoken with her. You're right, she doesn't know anything.'

That sounded vaguely insulting, so I said, 'She knows a whole lot but not about this. I mean, you must understand, this has upset the entire community. And that's basically, I'm sure, what she told the reporter. That she was upset. Naturally.'

'Of course. Do you have something more to add to what you've told me about the quarrel you witnessed?'

'Not really, no.' I could feel I was losing him – his French fries or whatever were undoubtedly getting cold – so I rushed on: 'So you found Niko's car. But not Niko.'

Silence.

'And not Zora? No trace of Zora?'

'Mrs Hawke, you know I'm not at liberty to—'

'Yeah, I know. And it's *Ms* Hawke. Hawke is my maiden name. Can you at least tell me where it was found? The car?'

'Since this was on the news, sure. Someone had driven it into Dyke Marsh. It was found buried up to its hubcaps in mud, we've had so much rain this year.'

'You're kidding. That's, what, only seven miles from here.'

'Less.'

'Wow.'

'Tell me more about this verbal altercation,' he said. 'What was said?'

I shook my head, even though he couldn't see me.

'I couldn't hear them. I could just see gestures. Facial expressions. You know.'

I proceeded to tell him basically the same story I had told

Zora's mother, with a heavy emphasis on how much jetlag had impaired my memory.

He listened to the end, perhaps taking notes. For whatever reason, he seemed to be less dismissive than he'd been at the start of the call. He said, 'And that's all? That's all you saw, just the one time?'

This gave me the opening I needed to establish I wasn't the sort of woman who would snoop on her neighbors just for something to do. I parsed his question literally – he was asking what I *saw*.

'That was the only time I saw anything for sure amiss over there,' I said. 'I'm almost always in my office, which faces the other way. South. I think I told you that already, you and your sergeant. I'm really too busy to keep tabs, even if I were inclined.'

'That's too bad,' he said. 'In an investigation like this, ears on the ground and eyes on the prize are extremely valuable.'

'Well,' I said. 'Of course, if I can be of any help.' Part of me knew he was bullshitting me, and part of me knew I really could be of help. *If* I saw anything.

Like what? I wondered. Like Niko sneaking back into the house late at night because he'd forgotten his toothbrush? Even if that weren't unlikely, the police must have a watch on the place.

Overall, this did not seem the moment to tell Narduzzi I was thinking of going to Niko's office under false pretenses. In my own defense, let me just say I hadn't fully decided I was going to go that route. I wasn't at all convinced I wouldn't get caught. I could probably portray an outraged wife well enough, but there was every chance in the heat of the moment I'd forget what my name was supposed to be unless I wrote it on my inner wrist. And whatever Misaki said, I wasn't sure about that blonde wig. Perhaps hair extensions?

'Of course,' I repeated. 'I wish I could tell you more. It really is awful, this happening. *Here*.'

'You don't seem to have been Facebook friends,' he said. 'You and Zora.'

It was at that moment I realized how bad I was at this investigative thing. It was one thing to dream up preposterous plots for my books but here, in real life, I had fallen at the first hurdle. Not once had it occurred to me to look the Normans up on Facebook. The most basic step in law enforcement these days, I'm sure. All those hours of watching *Investigation ID* had been wasted time, with nothing learned except, 'Don't ever let the bad guy get you into his car.'

And obviously, the obverse was true as well. Narduzzi had been checking up on my friend status. Surely inconclusive, whether or not he'd found a bond there between me and Zora, but it did make my skin crawl a bit. I was as under investigation as anyone else who happened to be in the Normans' orbit, intentionally or not.

'No, we weren't. There's rather a large generation gap. We don't – didn't – do lunch. It was just not that sort of relationship. Around here you're grateful if people are friendly, and mostly, they are. She was. *Is*.

'Hopefully, still is.'

FIFTEEN

As soon as I got off the phone with Narduzzi, I pulled up Zora's Facebook page. There wasn't a lot to see, since we weren't friends, and she seemed to have had her settings locked up tight to avoid random gawkers.

Or maybe the police had shut her page down partially – would that be possible? Through the power of the subpoena, I supposed it was, maybe to keep the press out. That seemed doubtful, what with First Amendment rights and all, although I'd never considered before how useful Facebook might be to an investigator. In my novels I just avoid the whole social thing, letting my French detectives wear out their shoe leather the old-fashioned way. Narduzzi even now was probably watching me log in, tracking my digital footprints.

For whatever reason I could see Zora's photos if not her posts, and photos were always the good stuff – the interesting bits of a person's life, even if carefully curated to show only the good times and hide the double chins. Both the photos and the biographical information were helpful. She had attended Georgetown (she didn't list whether she'd graduated, or in what), and before that she'd been at Sidwell Friends in Washington, DC, the same fancy prep school the Nixon and Obama daughters had attended. Nice. *Mucho dinero*, but then I knew that already from meeting Zora's mom and visiting her gallery. My stepson had spent many of his school years in rehab, paid for by his education savings. For which he never forgave Marcus or me, when he realized we'd drained the account on his behalf. By the time he was straightened out and ready to go back to school, he realized he'd have to take out a student loan to do so, and he never bothered. After his father died, he moved to Vancouver, where he got married and somehow ended up owning a pig farm, settling himself somewhere on the Prepper spectrum with all the other doomsayers. I often picture him, sitting in the wilderness, surrounded by trees and stockpiles of toilet paper and hand sanitizer.

He claimed to be happy. I hoped it was true. My visit to his pig farm had not been a happy time for me or his wife or the pigs and I'd not made a return visit.

Anyway. As I clicked through Zora's photos, I thought about my visit to her mom. I no doubt might have mentioned that visit to Narduzzi, along with a few other things. But Genevieve had invited me to her gallery. Well, she had welcomed me once I had invited myself. And she'd only told me her suspicions about her son-in-law Niko, suspicions I had no doubt she'd shared with the police. I told myself it wasn't withholding evidence if everyone knew already.

The few photos visible on Zora's page were the usual thing and included the wedding photo I'd seen on the news. Clearly the press had been there before me. There were a few links and shares to museum and art gallery showings – she seemed to have inherited or acquired her mother's tastes, then, although her preference seemed to be for nothing more modern than the Impressionists. There weren't many photos of a personal nature – a couple of selfie-type things showing her having lunch with girlfriends. I had no idea who those women were, but I recognized the restaurant as Ada's on the River. It was just steps away from Kildare Place, but the wait list for a table in good weather was always months into the future.

There were zero photos of Niko, but I knew sometimes people felt they should shield their loved ones from the limelight. Also there were zero baby pictures, which was more interesting – what mother doesn't want to show off her kid? But maybe Zora was a little more sensible, a little more aware of kidnappers.

Not that, in the end, kidnapping danger awareness had helped her much – not if both she and Niko had been kidnapped.

It was all frustratingly slim pickings as far as information went. No job information, no follows or likes of a business page. I wondered if she'd friended her mother, who would as a result have fuller access to the account than a passing stranger like me. I wasn't sure how often I could in good conscience bug Genevieve, though, given the circumstances.

Before I logged off, to make it look good for the police's IT forensics team – like I was just there idly scrolling about the site and not reading up on my neighbors – I searched for the local bakery and sent a message asking about their opening hours. Surely that would throw Narduzzi off the track. Then I checked my own newsfeed and liked a few animal photos and pithy words to live by. My feed tended to be full of fellow authors, and it was understood in rather a Masonic code way that you would show your 'likes' for them in public even if somehow you never got around to reading their books.

Niko didn't even have a Facebook presence.

Next I went to Instagram to see if Zora had an account there – no luck, and with a name like Zora Norman, I figured she'd be easy to find unless she'd opened an account under some other name. Twitter, same thing – nothing for either her or Niko. I supposed I wasn't by this point fooling Narduzzi or anyone else, so I had a brazen look around Pinterest while I was at it.

Nothing doing there, either. I cleared my search history and called it a night, investigation-wise.

I knew I was getting a bit paranoid already. It was what I'd call anticipatory paranoia. Frustrated by the dearth of information, I'd already decided I would go to Niko's office and learn what I could learn. I was so determined to uncover more, I actually convinced myself it was a good idea.

Meanwhile, my manuscript sat untouched. I promised myself I'd double down on my quota the next day.

But first things first.

The next day I went over to Misaki's, carrying a folder so it looked as if I was there on HOA business, in case anyone was watching. I thought about drawing up an official complaint about the mulch distribution inequality, but realized how unlikely it was Narduzzi would ask for documentation.

She must have seen me crossing the courtyard, because the door flew open before I could knock and she hustled me inside, giving a decidedly dodgy look left and right and up and down the courtyard. All very subtle. She and I might as well be wearing signs saying we were up to something, but we weren't – at least not yet. The news vans had cleared out, otherwise we'd likely have found ourselves featured on that evening's news.

Without bothering to ask if I wanted coffee, she poured me a fresh cup. Clearly, in her mind and mine, there was no time to waste.

'I'm going to do it,' I told her.

We were seated in her upholstered breakfast nook, overlooking the courtyard. I couldn't help but stare in the direction of the Normans' place. Someone had closed the curtains over the dining room and what was probably the baby's room, giving the house a bland, blind look. Had the police done that to keep the newshounds out, or had Zora, or Niko, before they vanished? The little garret window had only a decorative swathe of white cloth across the top, but in this light and at this distance, there was no way to see inside.

'You're going to Niko's?' She looked impressed, as well she might.

'Yes.'

'What's your cover going to be?'

'What you suggested. I'm going to pretend to be a potential client needing a divorce lawyer, quickly.'

'Was that my idea?'

'It was if it turns out to be a terrible mistake.'

'Got it. Shared blame. How can I help?'

'I'm going to dig through my attic and see what I have that will work as a disguise. All you have to do is tell me I don't look like myself. And help me rehearse my lines.'

'I'm in. So you're going with the disguise, after all? Remind me why that's necessary.'

'It was your idea if you'll recall. While no one from the firm should be able to recognize me, it occurred to me that the place might be lousy with police right about now. Maybe they put someone in there working undercover as a pretend paralegal or water-cooler attendant. I really don't want them coming back to bite me over this.'

'Yeah, OK. You're using a phony name, too?'

'May as well. In for a penny . . .'

'That's the spirit.'

'As soon as they open, I'm going to call and make an appointment with my phony name. Hopefully they can fit me in today if they realize I'm loaded for bear. And loaded with money to pay for an extended hostile takeover of my imaginary husband's life with his truck-stop floozy.'

'Shouldn't you use a real name? I mean a real name that isn't yours? In case they check your net worth or something.'

'Hmm. OK. Let me think about that.' I took a sip of coffee but no helpful thoughts percolated in my brain. The people I would drag into this willy-nilly without asking permission were few, and asking permission for such a caper seemed doomed from the start.

'I think overall a made-up name and address,' I said. 'If they ask – why would they, seriously? – but if anyone asks about the address, I'm staying with friends during the awful breakup from my brute of a husband. And surely they won't bother to run my finances for a simple get-acquainted interview. I might not even hire them. What am I saying? Of course I'm not hiring them.'

'You've gotten into character already. Fantastic. Anyway, I agree it's unlikely they'll do more than chat with you. Then you tell them you want to think about what they've said. Then disappear down a dark alley, never to be seen again. You know, I'm really kind of thrilled you're doing this.'

'Be thrilled when it's over. First I have to talk them into an appointment for today.'

'No worries. They'll clear the calendar for a new client like you, fizzing with righteous anger and clanging from all the coins in your pockets. Just let me know when you need me to come over for the dress rehearsal.'

'OK. I'll text you. Something innocuous, like, "Thanks for roofer reccy."'

'Wait here a minute while I get my jewelry box out of the safe. I'll loan you my pearls.'

SIXTEEN

I had experience in amateur dramatics, as Misaki knew. The Little Theatre was seven blocks from my door, making it easy to walk to rehearsals. Acting was generally a cleanse-the-palate exercise in between finishing one book and starting another. With Marcus gone, performances and rehearsals came more and more to fill my evening hours.

In the past few years I'd done *Shakespeare in Love*; I'd done *To Kill a Mockingbird*; I'd done *Steel Magnolias*. Supporting or walk-on parts only, of course. In *Agnes of God*, in which the director took great liberties with the script, I was in a chorus of nuns chanting 'Shame! Shame!' and 'God is watching!' It really was terrific fun and one hundred percent cathartic.

I didn't have time to do more and, while I thought I was good, rather depending on the director, I knew I wasn't great – it really was very small theater, catering mostly to Old Town locals and elderly people bussed in from retirement communities like Godwin House. But I loved it. I loved it enough to wish I were better at it than I was, good enough to make a living at it. But, as with art classes, I knew my place, and it wasn't hanging in the Louvre and it wasn't taking center stage, even in community theater.

But here was my chance to put all my training and experience to use. It was as if all the rehearsals, all the practice, all the sacrificed nights and weekends, all the love that one brings to amateur dramatics had brought me to this moment. I was going to play a deranged almost-divorcée out for blood on a cheating husband. This I could do.

This I had sort of lived, after all.

This may be the point in my story to bring you up to date on Marcus, and me, and what I came to learn was the sad state of our marriage.

*   *   *

I met Marcus when I'd been in DC ten years. It was love at first sight. It really was.

How many love stories start that way but end badly? Millions, I'm sure. Maybe all of them. But I'm a bit cynical on this subject.

We met through a dating app. I told myself it was research for my writing, but by this point I'd exhausted all the traditional ways of meeting men, and I was ready not to be alone every night. The problem was aggravated by my profession – if I saw an unattached male, he was usually attending a crime writers' conference, where everyone was sort of out for blood, if you'll pardon the expression. It was not the tender setting you'd want for a romantic meeting, even though I did return from these things clutching business cards by the handful. Everyone there was in marketing mode and, while it was not unheard of for writers to meet across a crowded Hilton ballroom, the last thing I wanted, really, was another crime writer in the house. One was bad enough.

I'd heard all the warnings about the apps, of course, but it worked well for me and Marcus. For a while, it worked great. We were married almost six months to the day from our first date.

We'd decided to meet in person after an extended email exchange, by which time I'd done my due diligence. When he told me his profession, I googled him and, to be honest, I couldn't believe my luck when I saw he hadn't been lying or exaggerating. He had a private practice and privileges with the INOVA healthcare system. Born in Pennsylvania, he attended college and medical school in Rhode Island and did a three-year residency at Children's National in DC, which is what brought him to the area. Since he was older than me by thirteen years, I sort of knew the deal going in. I was thirty-two going on ninety, and his forty-five years seemed very close in age to mine. Men in their thirties were always either too needy or too hung up on their careers. Marcus was established and, if a bit preoccupied with his career, at least it was because he was serving a worthy cause. The fact that he was saving children's lives was impossible to complain about.

Misaki, who is into chakras and candles and things, tells me

I'm an old soul. Perhaps it's true. Perhaps I prefer my men already trained by some hapless girlfriend or wife in the past – Marcus had had a brief first marriage that only left scars in the form of a son he didn't know what to do with and a sister-in-law he couldn't seem to shake off. We were invited to Bertra's house for dinner a few times; it was one of the oddest post-divorce situations imaginable. I thought she was interested in Marcus's money but wisely kept that thought to myself. When she found she wasn't in his will, she certainly disappeared fast enough. If she'd factored in the bills for medical school, she'd have known it had taken years for Marcus's practice to thrive. In fact, it was my royalties that helped pay the bills more than once. He died about the time the ledger for his practice was starting to move solidly into the black.

Was thirteen years too big a gap? A twenty-year difference I tell myself I would have had the sense to worry about. And in the end his age really had nothing to do with it. I guess you could say a lack of character had everything to do with it. Certainly I would say that was true.

Marcus was not handsome, but he had the kind of strong Roman features which once seen could not easily be forgotten – masses of dark hair springing from a high forehead, hooded dark eyes, a sharp bridge of a nose, the works. His kids loved him. By that I mean the kids who came to his practice.

I'm not sure he liked his own son, even when William was small, but that happens, right? It was not Marcus's fault his son started adult life as a ne'er-do-well – he had been raised by his mother, so let's blame her – but Will liked to play that card as often as he could.

Anyway, by way of contrast, other people's children are charming even when they're ill, or at least it's possible to feel some sympathy for them even if they're bad-tempered. Best of all, at least from Marcus's perspective, at the end of the appointment they are taken away by other people.

If they're seriously ill – well, that was when Marcus came into his own. No child was going to die on his watch. Not one child, not ever. It slowly began to dawn on me that what looked like saintliness on a grand scale was a case of colossal ego. Marcus always had to be right.

Of course, it came to pass some of the children did die. No matter how many hours he spent at their bedsides, no matter how many tests he ordered, how many reports of new medical theories and treatments he read well into the night, sometimes the germ or the virus or the defective gene took over and they died.

It is not an exaggeration to say a bit of Marcus died with them.

And that, right there, was the trouble. The downside of living with a miracle worker when the miracles stopped working.

He tried alcohol, he tried drugs, he tried 'hobbies' like bridge, which of course led to hobbies like other women, one in particular. Obviously, I found out. The 'sick child in the hospital' excuse for being out late was really about visits to his girlfriend's place downriver near Mount Vernon. I never suspected and he'd probably never have been caught out if he hadn't hit a deer on the GW Parkway, driving too fast on an empty highway at three a.m., miles away from where he was supposed to be.

His girlfriend, knowing the jig was up, showed up at the funeral service, dressed in black. With a heavy veil, no less. All very Jackie Kennedy.

I came to feel the deer was as big a loss to the world as Marcus.

Bigger.

SEVENTEEN

The offices of Masters, Milton, and Duckett were on I Street (often written as Eye Street, to save the sanity of post office employees). DC is unique in being at the epicenter of take-no-hostages legal wars and, as I've probably mentioned already, there are more lawyers per square foot here than anywhere else on earth. It's where laws are made to be broken, even with a disbelieving country watching, clutching its tattered copies of the US Constitution.

How much do these lawyers make? I don't know. How deep is the ocean? For family law, the going rate for a middle-class split was probably anywhere from $200 to $400 an hour, and up. I don't know what the working classes did, whether they stayed in bad or dangerous unions or simply disappeared. It's not as if they could ask for court-appointed attorneys.

MM&D was a large firm handling all manner of cases, not just divorce and custody, and they were famous enough even I had heard of them. The polished-brass sign on the front of the building proclaimed the firm had been established in 1929. The year of the stock-market crash had not been a good year for everyone, but apparently it had been for some.

I wondered how long Niko's specialty had been a thing. Parental child abductions surely had their place in the annals of history but, as a legal specialty, I thought it might be rare. I was as curious to learn more about it as I was to learn what Niko had got up to in the office. I had to assume his services were only called upon when the police had given up trying, or even pretending to try. I once heard a writer at a conference speak about his background in law enforcement; I remember him saying an abduction even by a parent was still an abduction, because the parent was ready to flout the law to get what he or she wanted.

The woman who had answered the phone at MM&D briskly identified herself as Valentina and asked – rather warily, I thought

– how she could help. While she sounded professional and sympathetic to my plight with 'the big selfish brute', she did not sound *too* sympathetic, because people would be sure to waste her time when all she wanted to do was slot their names into her computer calendar and connect them with the right associate. Or get rid of the too-crazy ones, as needed. I felt sure this was an acquired listening skill, added to which, not all people wanting a divorce or child custody or even help in finding an abducted child could afford such things. It was a given that MM&D's receptionist would have a nose for the desperately poor and send them packing.

Or worse, take them on as a client and soak them in fees they couldn't afford to pay. Somehow, I doubted MM&D needed to stoop to that, but one never knew.

Perhaps I judged too harshly: Surely some of their work was pro bono? While I back-burnered the question, I did think it one worth asking.

Valentina – an unfortunately romance-laden name for a woman whose job it was to defend the ramparts of a divorce shop – had a slight accent I could only place as Russian or originating from somewhere in Eastern Europe. In the sort of weighted but disinterested English one might use to commit a prisoner to hard labor in a gulag, she had explained my wish to make an appointment could be granted, but it would be a matter of stupendous good luck on my part and cunning on hers. Mindy Goodacre, just returned early from vacation, had an opening, and Valentina was sure she could fit me in that afternoon for a consultation.

Mindy being the former or current paramour of Kent Haworth, PI – a name I had pried out of him that morning. Actually, it took no prying, Kent definitely being the type to kiss and tell, but I did have to dodge his questions as to why I wanted to know.

In making the appointment, I had of course said that Mindy had come highly recommended (in a way, I guess, she had), but I was only interested in consulting with her.

I didn't have a Plan B. I wasn't sure whether just anyone working in a good-size law firm like MM&D would have the insight or knowledge into Niko that I wanted. How much did lawyers hang around the water cooler trading gossip? Really, I had no idea. It was just fortunate Mindy was available so quickly.

Valentina set the time for my meeting at two p.m. and did not ask if it was convenient for me; it was assumed I was just sitting around a friend's house sobbing and plotting revenge. Valentina's long experience with aggrieved spouses was evident.

At the appointed time – actually ten minutes early – near the offices of MM&D, an Uber deposited an exquisitely turned out and evidently wealthy woman in her forties. A blonde with impeccably shellacked hair, dark glasses designed to hide any escaping tears, and a slash of cherry red lipstick to match the tailored suit and the soles of her high heels. The woman wore a three-tier pearl choker with matching earrings, a gift on loan from her friend and potentially indicted co-conspirator, Misaki.

Yes, as you've guessed, the shellacked woman was me, and if I do say so myself, the disguise was a success. I had used Callista Gingrich as my role model for the sort of woman I was trying to portray – fabulously wealthy and destined to become one day an ambassadress to the Vatican from the USA. (I am not making up that last bit.) It was all part and parcel of the social connectivity and power I wanted to exude, not to mention the steely iciness I felt the role required. My soon-to-be ex, whom I had decided to call Ralph, had better watch his imaginary back, is all I can say. I really did look primed for a long fight and not willing to put up with a moment's more shit from Ralph, who had been caught sleeping, in a stunning lack of originality, with his PA. By me, Patrice-Louise Nelson, returning from feeding the homeless.

Seriously, that was part of my cover story. Patrice was lying, of course, but she wanted to put on her best face before showing it in court.

I was so totally into Patrice that I was already entering the dangerous yet interesting territory where I wasn't sure where I left off and my character began. How much all this made me like my borders-challenged mother, I tried not to think about.

For the occasion I had brought out my own wedding band and engagement ring, which had a sizable diamond bound to further establish my rich credentials. Marcus had insisted on buying me the biggest and the best; blushingly I will tell you I did see the size of that rock as a token of his esteem. I had fully intended to sell it rather than let it sit unworn in my jewelry box but, as it was proving useful suddenly, I thought perhaps not.

It didn't deter men from giving me the once-over as I sashayed down the street. Really, it was amazing what blonde hair, a low-cut bandage dress, and a ton of makeup could do. The Augusta Hawke who schlepped around Old Town in brown hair, green eyes and blue jeans seldom drew the longing male gaze. I supposed I liked it that way or I would have dressed as Patrice, a hot soon-to-be divorcée, more often.

Patrice. Patrice-Louise Nelson. My new stage name, as I had to keep constantly reminding myself. It had been a full year since I'd played Mrs Soames in *Our Town*, as obligations connected with the series but having nothing to do with writing the series commanded more and more of my time. Rather thrillingly, the local reporter for the *Gazette-Packet* had singled out my 'spirited' performance. I always meant to ask him if, since Mrs Soames was a spirit, the pun was intentional.

But acting is like writing. You really have to do it every day or you get rusty.

That morning, after planning my Patrice costume and character, I had put in as much time writing about Claude and Caroline as I could. My goal, as I've mentioned, was to write four good pages a day, come what may. That's about a thousand words, which doesn't sound like much, but they do add up over time to a satisfying heap. Hopefully, if I weren't rushed or distracted – or caught up in a real-life murder investigation – each page would turn out to be a gem not requiring a lot of polishing.

I sincerely hoped my little detour into deception with MM&D wouldn't derail my writing process entirely. I vowed to get back to work on the manuscript before nightfall – I had one more page to go. Right now, my focus had to remain on the part I was playing.

Patrice. Patrice. Patrice. I chanted the name as I walked through the revolving door into the Greco-Roman premises of MM&D. I had tried to practice my accent – Southern belle out of Georgia – on the Uber driver. He was listening to what sounded like an incitement to riot on the car radio, so I'm not sure how much of what I said registered.

The majestic offices of MM&D were erected at the turn of the nineteenth century in a style meant to remind the visitor of the historic foundation of the laws the firm was paid to uphold or exploit, depending.

I was duly awestruck. After Old Town, with its relentlessly twee charm, its painted clapboards and red-brick walls covered in ivy, this vast space made me feel I was being weighed for admission into heaven. Indeed, the scales of justice figured heavily in the assorted gold-leaf-edged carvings which decorated the various pillars and pilasters. I wondered whose job it was to use a Q-tip swab to prevent any dust collecting in the ornate crevices.

The lobby was basically marble top to bottom, and walking into the cool interior was, I would imagine, like walking into a very large sarcophagus. Directly ahead of me and covering nearly the entire wall was a painting depicting four men wearing clothing of different generations, who looked vaguely similar and were presumably the founders of the establishment – great-grandfather on down to current-day son. The grandfather had a wild-eyed, stressed-out look that suggested a chemical imbalance, which luckily he had not passed on to his son and grandson. From my online homework, I recognized the Duckett clan, who now rode at third place on the masthead: The firm had initially been called Duckett, Masters, and Milton.

I hadn't been able to find a reason for the Duckett fall from grace, or learn what sort of coup d'état had left Masters in first place and slid Milton into second, but perhaps – in the spirit of compromise – the extremely large Duckett family portrait in its gold-leaf frame had been given pride of place in the foyer. No doubt at the time the painting had been commissioned, Duckett the Fourth (they were all named Roger) was still ruling the place by gift of birthright.

He had that expression; I'm sure you know the one I mean.

To the right of this display of responsibility and privilege, handed down generation to generation via the male line with no one, apparently, screwing things up by having a girl baby, was a vast swathe of walnut, marble-topped reception desk. Behind this fortress sat a severe-looking young woman, presumably Valentina, she of the ill-chosen name or, rather, profession. Her last name, going by her nameplate, was Pavlova. Nice. It was as if she were rebelling against all the amiability suggested by her name.

Indeed, she seemed to guard the place like a dragon, despite her relative youth. I imagined that whenever confronted by a new visitor she kept her finger on an alarm beneath the desktop to alert security to any problem. I was a bit surprised not to be greeted by a uniformed security guard, in fact, but perhaps Valentina preferred civvies. I was sure she had been trained to repel all players. She looked as if trouble had found her once in her brief life and she would do whatever it took not to let it bother her again.

Her coal-black hair fell straight from a center part, which precisely divided the point of her heart-shaped hairline. She'd accented her eyes with black winged eyeliner and the effect was very much of a cat watching its prey. Behind my sunglasses, I had also gone in for the cat's-eye look, dated though it was. It gave us girls something in common, anyway.

If you wear too much makeup, it's all people notice or remember about you. Not your eyes but your makeup. That was my rationale for the Petula Clark sixties guise, since I was technically in camouflage. I had no idea what Valentina's reason was. Perhaps she was in hiding from the CIA. Somehow it wouldn't surprise me.

I nearly lost my footing on the shiny marble floor, being unused to wearing high heels in even the best of circumstances and the gravelliest of floors. It was literally my first misstep.

Valentina lifted her head from her computer screen long enough to say, 'They just polished the floors.'

I held the pose of a tightrope walker, arms outstretched, until I regained my equilibrium.

'Thanks,' I said. 'I'm here to see Mindy Goodacre.'

'I'll let her know you're here. I just need to see a photo ID.'

*   *   *

Crap. I should have thought of this. Security in downtown office buildings is crazy tight ever since 9/11, ever since the 6 January storming of the Capitol Building, ever since – you name it. With one calamity and bomb threat after another, people could no longer wander off the street into places of business without their bona fides being documented. Whether it kept out the crazies is anyone's guess, but at least they knew who the crazies were, barring someone's using a fake ID. Which was, according to my research, dead easy to buy on the dark web.

I was kicking myself, wondering why I hadn't just borrowed someone else's name, but really – even if they resembled me, who would just hand over their drivers' license for an afternoon so I could impersonate them? Misaki probably wouldn't have hesitated, but the situation called for someone with at least a passing resemblance to me.

Crap.

I pretended to root around in my handbag for my driver's license, growing more frustrated by the moment. I didn't even have to act that frustrated part; I was truly annoyed with myself. What further proof did I need I was already in over my head with this detecting thing? Finally, I dumped the bag's contents by the handful onto Valentina's polished marble top, keeping my wits about me enough to make sure my wallet wasn't visible.

She did not like this one bit. I also suspected this had happened with more than one client. People wanting anonymity for a high-profile divorce probably used made-up names all the time, just to get an appointment and stave off media interest as long as possible.

'I can't let you in,' she said. A slow, sly blink from those heavily painted eyes.

I did not imagine it. The small power this woman wielded had gone straight to her head. Clearly Valentina loved her work.

'I just . . .' I began. 'Can't you, just this once?'

She ignored that, of course, and looked disappointed in me. I suppose this was where I should have slid a hundred-dollar bill across her desk. 'I can ask Ms Goodacre if she would be willing to meet you at the coffee shop down the street.'

'Oh,' I said. 'Sure. I guess. I'll wait.'

She picked up a space-agey silver phone, dialed an extension, and tapped her red-tipped fingernails against the desk as she waited for someone to pick up. Without preamble she ratted me out to the person on the other end of the line, presumably Mindy Goodacre.

'She forgot her ID.' She listened a moment, said, 'Right, will do,' and hung up. Resuming whatever fascinating thing she had been doing on her computer she told me, 'The coffee shop is down the street to your left as you leave the building. It's called The Grind. Ms Goodacre will join you in a few minutes.'

EIGHTEEN

T en minutes later I was cooling my high heels and a cup
of coffee at a table for two at The Grind. Naturally Mindy
Goodacre would be late, to establish her basic superiority
and to reinforce her being the type of person who never forgets
to carry her driver's license. Possibly her driver's license and
her passport and a small overnight bag.

I hadn't asked Ken Haworth for a physical description of the
woman he had used to obtain his insider information on Niko
Norman, but I had seen Mindy's headshot on the law firm's
website. The woman who (finally) walked in was a surprise.
She was one of those forty-year-olds who could pass for thirty,
no problem, and she really needed to switch out that web photo
to reflect the fact. No doubt she'd run with it because it made
her look *au courant* on torts and contracts, as well as hard as
nails – both definitely selling points in her profession.

But the woman who unhesitatingly sat across from me – I
assumed Valentina had passed along my physical description,
a conversation I would love to have heard – looked more as
if she had just come from milking the cows. She had one of
those pleasant round faces, pink cheeked and merry eyed,
and within moments I had decided she was the kind of person
I would definitely want at my side, at least in the first round
of negotiations with an unruly, stingy, ungrateful spouse. I
imagined her technique was to divert the opposition with tales
of her background, perhaps regale them with stories of a poor
childhood spent raising chickens on a remote farm in
Wisconsin with her five sisters and deeply religious parents.
And then get them in a headlock before they knew what was
happening.

Pity the soon-to-be ex-spouses. I would have felt sorry for
my Ralph had he ever existed.

She asked if I'd like a new coffee and I accepted. I felt this
was very much a good way to get on my good side, having

kept me – an important new client with vast resources of wealth, mind – waiting for so long.

She went to place the order with the barista, returning with two coffees. The shop used real cups and saucers rather than cardboard, for which I gave them bonus points in the ecologically sound column. Tucked under Mindy's arm was a thin, exquisitely detailed leather portfolio, presumably holding a blank agreement for me to sign should I agree to use the services of MM&D. I felt a tinge of guilt about wasting her time but, remembering why I was there, tamped it back down. There are causes bigger than ourselves, I told myself firmly. And helping puzzle out the whereabouts of Baby Harry's parents certainly counted among those causes. Hopefully before the child was old enough to register something was amiss in his small universe of sleep/food/sleep/cry.

I sat up a bit straighter and, allowing my gaze to drift around the room, aimed a lightly flirtatious look at a man sitting at a high-top by the window. I was rewarded with a wink and a smile. I smiled back just long enough to make sure Mindy had noticed the exchange.

Having establish my bona fides as a newly single woman back on the market and undoubtedly out for revenge against my spouse, I aimed the smile at her next.

'Now,' she said, 'Mrs Nelson.'

'It's Patrice. Patrice-Louise Nelson. I dropped the "Louise" ages ago. My family called me Patty-Lou and I do feel at a certain age you need to let that go. Besides, no one could figure out what to do about the hyphen, so I decided to make things simple.' I felt it was much the best approach to emphasize I was who I said I was. Mindy was looking a tad uninterested so, rather than go on in this down-home vein, I asked, 'May I call you Mindy?'

She nodded. 'Patrice it is. So, Patrice, you wanted to discuss a possible separation or divorce from . . .' She looked around, a moment too late, for eavesdroppers. Fortunately, our table was socially distanced from the others, possibly a holdover from the pandemic. It allowed for our conversation to remain private in the semi-empty room, so long as we kept our voices down. It was the time of day everyone who wanted coffee had filled up

hours before, and the pastries in the glass display counter were
starting to look stale. I was personally wondering how much I
would pay with insomnia for drinking afternoon coffee, but
I wanted to appear sociable.

Nonetheless, given our now-public location for this discussion, I downgraded my earlier plan to break into compulsive
sobs at some point in the conversation, probably when I got to
the part where Ralph had desecrated the sanctity of our marital
bed, like a Viking invader sacking the church at Lindisfarne,
by sharing it during 'lunch hours' with his PA. My story, again,
was that I'd returned early from my volunteer work at a soup
kitchen to find Ralph and Brandy entwined, not a care in the
world nor a fig leaf to cover their nakedness.

It was a shame, really – a lost opportunity to win Mindy to
my side. Although I did wonder about using the reference
to Lindisfarne – how much history of the British Isles would
Patty-Lou have absorbed during her cheerleading days in, I had
decided, Atlanta, Georgia, that location being the best way to
account for Patrice's sugary Southern accent.

I realized Mindy was waiting for me to fill in some basic
blanks for her.

'His name is Ralph,' I said. 'Ralph Horace Nelson. And he
works in the export-import business. Ex-Im, as it's called.'

'Yes, I'm aware,' said Mindy. 'And would you say his
business is successful?'

Cutting right to the chase, I thought. What a pro. Best to
establish the stakes up front.

'Extremely. We live in McLean.'

One need say no more around these parts. While Old Town
is both trendy and pricey, McLean was where the old money
went to play tennis and die. Vast and green, the mansions there
had the acreage for pools and cricket pitches generally lacking
in Old Town.

Mindy nodded somberly. I was speaking her language.

'And, how long have you and Mr Nelson been separated? I
assume you *are* separated?'

'Oh, yes indeed. Can't stand the sight of him. And I wasn't
staying in that house another second once he had defiled the
place with his hussy. That's what my mother calls Brandy and,

while it's a good old-fashioned word and a nicer one than she deserves, I'd say it fits the case here.'

'I see. And how long . . .?'

'About a month.' This seemed a good time to root around in my bag and produce a packet of tissues. 'Those were my brand-new Egyptian cotton sheets, too, with a six hundred thread count. He can keep the sheets in the settlement. I want everything else.'

Mindy beamed. I was clearly the type of client she lived for. She said, 'I am licensed to practice in Virginia, but their laws, I have to warn you, are rather arcane. You and your spouse have to have been separated for at least six months to a year, depending on whether you have minor children. How long were you married to Mr Nelson?'

'Twenty years, and I *thought* they were the best years of my life. I was a Miss Teen Georgia Peach, you know, and I could have had my pick in those days. That was how Ralph and I met. I came to Washington with my Baptist gospel group, and I was wearing my winner's sash – showing off, you know. I also brought the crown with me but only wore it when we went out to dinner at night. Anyway, we toured the Capitol, and he was there lobbying someone or other and the rest is history.' I assumed she would pick up on the fact Patrice had probably been underage when Ralph took up with her, adding to the long list of his perfidies, but just in case: 'I was only seventeen.'

'Uh huh.' I was hoping for more of a 'Wow, what a creep!' reaction, but perhaps she'd heard worse. 'And did you have children with Mr Nelson?'

'God did not choose to bless us with children.' Here was my cue. I pulled out a tissue and dabbed at my eyes, being mindful of the eyeliner. 'That was not part of the Creator's design.'

'I see.' She did see, and I was fairly certain she did not care. These factoids I was giving her were being entered on some internal spreadsheet, set to calculate how much Ralph was worth, how much I could have nailed him for child support (a missed chance, there, but inventing a child of the union seemed a lie too far), how much for alimony, and the exact date when the party could get started, in terms of filing papers at the court-house. None of this mattered, of course, in the real world, but it was fascinating to watch Mindy's gears churn over. I imagined her mindscape looked like something out of one of da Vinci's engineering sketches. From her bio on the MM&D website, Mindy Goodacre had graduated *magna cum laude* from Georgetown School of Law. There was no grass growing under Mindy's well-shod little feet. I was irrationally pleased I'd chosen the best to rake fucking Ralph over the coals.

She said, 'I'm sure I can help you,' which was gratifying, as if I'd passed a test.

She added, 'It's too bad you've left the house already.'

'Why?'

'I don't suppose you stopped to take a video of the house's interior – your possessions, I mean?'

'No, why – oh. I get it. There wasn't time.'

'He might try to hide certain movable assets. In fact, he's sure to. You need to be able to show what possessions were in the marital home, at least at one time.'

I thought a moment, then snapped my fingers. 'The insurance company sent someone out to make a video when we had structural damage caused by some nearby construction. I'm sure I have it on a disk somewhere.' It helped that I'd lived through something similar in my own neighborhood, where new condo projects on ever-decreasing pockets of available land had proliferated in recent years.

'Good. That'll help. I'll also need whatever financial documentation you can provide.' She smiled, showing nice white even teeth. 'We will want to maintain you in the style to which you are accustomed. It's only right. Never forget, you are the injured party.'

I gave her a teary-eyed thumbs up at that.

She asked a few more questions of a similar nature, and when she began closing the sale by reciting the history of the MM&D firm, I decided it was time to bring the conversation round to her esteemed colleague, Niko Norman.

This was going to be the tricky part, but it helped that the whole town was talking about his disappearance by now.

'I actually feel I know quite a bit about your firm,' I told her. 'It's been so much in the news lately.'

I had caught her mid-sip on her coffee drink. 'Excuse me?'

Surprised at her surprise, I said 'Yes. What's his name? Niko. Niko Norman. He's with your firm, right?'

Cautiously: 'Yes.'

'He's gone missing. He and his wife, they've gone missing.' How could she not have known this?

She stared at me, dumbstruck. 'Niko and Zora? When did this happen?'

'Last week sometime. Really, it was in all the local news. You didn't know?'

'I'm just back from vacation. I have a little hay farm in West Virginia where I go to chill. I haven't seen the news and that is a deliberate choice. When I go off the grid, I mean off the grid.'

I thought about showing her the news clips on my own phone, but then wondered if my real name or a message at odds with my Georgia-peach persona might pop up. Misaki might choose that moment to text me or something.

It didn't matter. Mindy was collecting her gear, clearly minded to bring the interview to an end. I had touched a nerve.

'I'm so sorry. I didn't mean to shock you.'

'I'm not shocked, I just need to get back. If you have any questions, feel free to call me.'

I could not let her get away. Quickly I said, 'My friend, the one I'm staying with in Old Town. She did mention Niko had a bit of a reputation – I guess a friend of a friend, a drunken Halloween party, you know the sort of thing goes on in Old Town. You don't . . .? Well, my friend says it's like the last days of Versailles. I don't care about any of that, but if it's true his disappearance isn't all that surprising, now is it?'

'I don't follow.' She was a terrible actress, probably worse than me in my early improv classes. She followed me, all right.

'He had a reputation as a bit of a philanderer,' I said bluntly. That hit home.

'People think that? I mean, people outside the firm?'

Leading me nearer the very topic I had come to discuss, which was what people *within* the firm thought of Niko.

'So he did have a reputation, even at work,' I said. 'Well, that's very interesting.'

She didn't take the bait. 'Are the police involved?'

'I'm *sure* they are. It could be a murder – or two, a kidnapping, grand larceny – any number of things.'

'What? Where are you getting this?'

'Online.'

I needed to say no more. Online was the petri dish for all conspiracy theories. I had in fact seen a few blogs where people were acting on the assumption that they could say with impunity whatever they wanted to about Niko and Zora, since (they reasoned) the couple had gone to ground after having been up to something nefarious. I don't think blog writers worry overmuch about being sued for libel.

'What about the child?' she asked. 'He had a child.'

'So I understand. I haven't heard anything, except one blogger hinted the child had been secreted away and was being taken care of. It didn't go missing along with its parents, in other words.'

Seemingly satisfied with my nebulous and unsubstantiated answer, she had stopped listening. I could see her trying to absorb the first wave of this sonic boom in her life. The second and third waves were taking a while longer.

Meanwhile, her already hectic milkmaid complexion was glowing a fiery red. There was no doubting I'd hit a nerve. How best to exploit it, I wasn't sure. I was new at this.

But suddenly I realized I wasn't new at this at all. I had been writing about interrogation techniques for years in my Claude and Caroline books. Caroline, naturally, was better at breaking down a suspect using the old iron hand/velvet glove technique, and undoing much of the damage inflicted by Claude, who tended to go into an interrogation room with guns blazing, figuratively speaking. It wasn't so much that they played good cop/bad cop. It was that they were working at cross purposes most of the time, rather than working as a team. The only way anything got done was, as I have said, via Caroline's letting Claude take the credit for her efforts.

Anyway, during the split-second pause as Mindy grappled with the news, I had to decide how to proceed. Really my only option – she was definitely ready to bolt, taking her unsigned contract with her, and open a web browser ASAP – was to get to the obvious as quickly as possible.

'Did you really not know?' I said gently. 'I would've thought the entire office was talking of nothing else.' From her look I could answer my own question. The entire office of course had heard the news, and some might know of her close relationship with Niko, but it was possible they were just standing quietly by and waiting for her to be hauled off to a police interrogation room not unlike the one used by Claude and Caroline, which definitely needed a coat of paint and other amenities.

I gazed at her knowingly, sympathetically, one wronged woman to another, a technique Caroline had honed to perfection. Amplifying my honeysuckle accent, I said, 'Honey, I get it. Believe me I get it. I've seen the photos of the handsome Mr Norman in the news, and I'm going to make a guess here. Now first of all,' I touched her hand lightly, then withdrew. She pulled back her own hand a notch – not repelled but also not willing to breach the lawyer/client divide just yet. 'First of all, this client confidentiality thing goes both ways, doesn't it? Well, it should and I'm telling you, with me, it does. I'll be telling you all my secrets and I know nothing goes further than this table. Now, I can see from your expression this news hits a bit closer to home than you'd like it to. Am I right?'

'No. It's just that when you've worked with someone for years—'

'Now you must pardon my French, but you are talking what my granddaddy used to call hogwash, only he didn't say "wash", he said another word that rhymes with knit. My granddaddy, he held with speaking the truth and shaming the devil. Ms Goodacre, you should see your face. Now, I wouldn't be surprised if you had a visit from the police soon and it will help very much if, by the time they get around to you, you've taken time to think through the whole thing calmly and have your responses prepared. You don't want to just blurt things out. Well, I don't have to tell you this – you're the lawyer! You wouldn't go into a court of law without knowing what was going on and what you were going to say, now would you?'

She shook her head very slightly. She was with me so far.

'So first let me tell you what I know from the television news and newspapers. And from the chatter in the fleshpots of Old Town.'

'They're not talking about me, are they?' She looked so alarmed I almost felt sorry for her. None of this was her fault – or was it? How did I know she had been chilling out at a hay farm? I remembered my mission: Baby Harry needed me to be ruthless in the pursuit of truth. Maybe the police needed to broaden their search to include that hay farm.

'No. I only know there was talk that he got around, and folk wondered out loud if the women in his office were safe. Of course, none of this crossed my mind when I made the appointment with your firm. It's news to me you even knew the man. It's such a large firm and frankly the last thing I've been thinking about has been Niko Norman and his whereabouts. No. This . . . relationship . . . with you comes as much as a shock to me as it will to the police. Not that it changes anything. I am ninety percent convinced you are the best woman to represent me in taking Ralph Nelson down.'

'Police?' she said weakly.

I guessed she thought I was threatening her, so I rushed to say, 'I'm certainly not going to tell them anything. What do I know? I don't know anything and why would they ask me, anyway? I'm just a prospective client.'

I could see her exhale a sigh of relief. I could also see tears forming in the corners of her eyes. Luckily, I had lots more tissues in my bag. We sat together in sorrowful companionship, two women muffling their sobs and dabbing carefully at their makeup. She wore a gorgeous shade of bronze eyeshadow that I was dying to ask her about but couldn't figure a way to insert the question into the conversation. Besides, before long, most of it had disappeared onto the tissue.

The guy I'd been flirting with earlier stood up and left, no doubt having decided this sort of emotional drama was more than he had bargained for.

'This is just crazy,' Mindy said, having regained some of her composure. 'Niko adored his wife. *Adored* her, I tell you. He told me so himself, he would never leave her.' Having veered dangerously close to what was undoubtedly a real conversation she'd had with Niko, possibly a breakup conversation, she abruptly stopped speaking.

'I understand,' I said. And I did.

'So, from what you're telling me,' she continued after a moment, 'this means that they're both being held somewhere. Or they're . . . oh my God!'

'I think the possibility they're deceased has occurred to the police,' I said. 'According to the evening news, they found Niko's car hidden in park service land on the way to Mount Vernon. The car was empty, so . . .'

'Oh my God,' she said again. 'This is . . . Look, I really have to . . . if you have any questions, I can email you the contract if you decide you want to . . . Just . . . don't return to the house for any reason. If you absolutely must go for something important like medications, something of that nature, take the police with you.'

For a split second I didn't know what she was talking about. Then I silently awarded her bonus points for keeping her wits and professionalism about her long enough to warn me. The most dangerous thing I could do – Patrice could do, I mean – would be to return to her house to retrieve her possessions. That is where the oftentimes deadly mischief started when couples split up.

'Thank you,' I said, meaning it. 'Believe me, I won't go near the place.' It was an easy promise to make. 'Look, it's obvious that this is a personal loss to you. And no judgment – really truly. I hope they find them both and find them alive and well.'

'There must be a sensible explanation,' she said, again rising to leave. 'There must.'

I could think of a few explanations, none of them sensible.

NINETEEN

Shortly after that I headed for home, taking off my wig, makeup, heels, and – when the driver was preoccupied with a tricky left turn – the push-up pads in my bra in the backseat of the Uber. I shoved everything into my big carry tote and extracted my Superga sneakers.

This time I was piloted by a silent young man who greeted me by saying his radio was broken and did I mind. Not only did I not mind, I decided on the spot to give him a bigger tip. Silence really is golden when you're being subjected to someone else's idea of music.

From the Uber, I texted Kent:

You were right about M.

No reply, so I tried his voicemail. The 'leave-a-message' message was classic Kent, managing to convey his importance and busyness in brusque, Philip Marlowe-esque tones: 'You've reached the voicemail for Kent Haworth. I'm working on another case but leave a message and I'll get back.'

Then I texted Misaki:

Babysitter news?

She texted back straightaway.

Still on it.

As I was putting the phone away it rang, the screen announcing an unknown caller. I normally ignore this kind of thing because, in this politically highly charged area, especially, it's always someone calling on behalf of someone running for office. Someone whom I have blocked repeatedly to no avail and whom I have asked never to text, email, or phone me again. Someone who always, always wins at the polls, despite my determination to oust him.

It might've been a good idea not to answer the phone in this case, but I wasn't doing anything except sitting in the back of a luxuriously silent Uber cab and staring out the window. And besides, as things turned out, I would merely have been delaying the inevitable.

To my surprise, Detective Narduzzi of the Old Town Police was on the line.

Well, this is awkward, I thought. I probably should tell him about Mindy Goodacre but a) I don't want to and b) I know he'll ask how come I know so much.

'Hey,' he said. 'Are you at home?'

'I'm in an Uber headed home. Why?'

'I have something I want you to look at for me.'

'Me? Really?'

'Well, yes, I thought you might be right there, at home. Most of your neighbors are still at work or I'd ask them.'

'Oh, I see,' I said, slightly disappointed he wasn't calling me because of my evidently keen investigative intelligence. 'I *do* work at home. It may not look like work since I don't use a concrete mixer or anything, but it's really work.'

Aware he'd hit a sore spot, he said, 'I think you could be invaluable to us because you are clearly a detail person. I'm reading one of your books now.'

I don't know what I expected him to say but it certainly wasn't that. Little did he know he had uttered the magic words for any writer. Actually, the even more magical words were, 'I can't put it down.'

I had to ask. 'Which book are you reading?'

'The one where Caroline keeps running into the guy who runs the boulangerie. When will you be home?'

I peered over the driver's shoulder and saw it was clear water all the way. 'Give me forty minutes.' I built in extra time so I could make sure all the makeup was wiped off, that there weren't any stray false eyelashes sticking to my ears, and that I had time to throw on some real clothes and walk Roscoe.

'OK. See you then.' He rang off.

Less than an hour later, Narduzzi was seated in my breakfast nook, tap-tapping away across the table from me at something on his laptop. He was alone; I figured Sergeant Bernolak was either working on another facet of the case or out shopping for eyeliner.

'I'm so glad you liked my book,' I said. 'It sounds as if the one you're reading is *Dies the Swan*.'

'Umph. Yeah, I think that's the title. Here's what I want to show you.'

I really wanted to ask him if I had got the forensics right in that book – it had been a tricky case involving a drowning – but I tamped down the urge. Clearly, whatever he wanted to talk about was more important, at least for the moment.

If I got the forensic science wrong in my books, there was no one to tell me so – scientists tended to scorn my sort of writing in favor of Michael Connolly's stuff. Fair play to Michael, but the people I heard from most often were librarians, and their concerns tended towards the literary or taking issue with my use of the semi-colon. In either case I always blamed the copyeditor.

A few more taps and Narduzzi turned his laptop screen towards me, then came over to my side of the table so he could maneuver the controls as I watched. The rattan chair squawked under his weight as he sat down. I felt a little too aware of his presence. The guy exuded masculinity of the non-toxic brand.

On the screen I saw what looked like typical surveillance footage from a crime show, dark and grainy and – to anyone who wasn't an expert – essentially useless.

'What is this?'

'It's security video from one of your neighbors. They have a camera aimed at the courtyard and it picks up the front of the Normans' townhouse.'

'This is from the night they went missing?' I asked.

'From the night they must have gone missing, yes. It looks as if they had a late-night visitor, someone who has not come forward.' He hit 'play' and I leaned in closer to watch, pulling my reading glasses down from atop my head.

The video showed a hooded figure in black being ushered into the Normans' home. Door opens, some kind of greeting, door closes.

He looked at me. 'Ring any bells?'

I shook my head. 'Nah.'

He fiddled with the playback settings, moving the cursor through more than half the length of the video before stopping it again.

'Here is where they leave. Watch closely.'

'They?'

'Look.'

I did. The same hooded figure emerged from the house, followed by a man who from his general build resembled Niko Norman. But it was hard to say, because he also was wearing a hoodie and sweatpants. He could've been very fit or slightly overweight; it was hard to tell from the baggy clothing. I'd probably seen him many times, if briefly – not long enough to give me a lingering sense of his style or presence, of how he carried himself.

'Is that Niko?' I asked.

'We think so. The height is right. The in-laws think so, but . . .'

Little did he know, he didn't need to complete the sentence – at least, not for me. Judging by my conversation with Genevieve, she would be looking for any tiny resemblance to Niko if she thought it would throw him in it.

'What about the other person, the visitor who comes to the door? Any ideas?'

I shook my head. 'Absolutely no idea. I would guess it's a young person because young people tend to have that kind of sloping, athletic gait but apart from that . . .'

'It's not anyone you've seen in the area either.'

'Really, it's hard to say. Old Town is a popular place, tons of people, especially on the weekends. Mostly when I venture out, I'm trying not to get run over by a scooter or a bicyclist and I'm not really watching how people walk. And I guess you know the black hoodie with matching sweatpants look is *de rigueur* for people of a certain age.'

'Right you are,' he said.

'I can't say I've ever seen Niko dress like that, come to think of it. It's a bit young for him. But I wouldn't be the expert on what he wore. I'd guess usually a suit and tie.'

'For his job, right.'

'If you don't mind my saying so, it's almost as if the

people in the videocam footage knew they were being photographed.'

'Interesting,' he said. 'We thought the same thing. You noticed how the faces were turned away and tucked well inside the hood.'

'It looked deliberate to me.'

'Well, if you think of anything more . . .' He made moves as if to leave.

I couldn't let him go so fast, not before I got out of him as much as I could. I supposed he couldn't drink a glass of wine or whiskey on the job, and the offer might be misinterpreted, anyway. I was trying to hide my attraction to him and wasn't sure how far I was succeeding.

'I don't suppose you can tell me anything about the case,' I ventured. 'I mean, obviously there's some bad things going on in this neighborhood and, just for my personal safety, I want to know.'

It wasn't exactly the hogwash of Patrice's grandfather, but it came close. It had been obvious from the beginning that whatever happened to the Normans was aimed at them rather than me and that I wasn't in any danger. Not unless I caused trouble for myself by, oh, say, snooping around and going to Niko's office and wearing a disguise while talking with his erstwhile lover.

Now was the time to tell Narduzzi at least some of what I'd learned but, in all honesty, how could I? And it wasn't as if Mindy had broken down and confessed an affair with Niko, had she?

I decided on a sideways approach.

'Are you finding any evidence Niko was, you know, unfaithful?'

'Why do you ask?'

'Oh, well, just a sense I have. In these situations . . .'

'You've heard rumors?'

'Well, not per se.'

'What does that mean, "not per se"?'

'Well, as it happens, one of my colleagues in the writing business knew him slightly. His reputation was as a bit of a lad, but that information came from before he was married.

Still, it would be worth asking around his office, don't you think? That's where most dalliances start, isn't it?'

I was skating on extremely thin ice, and I knew it. He looked at me so sternly I was sure he was going to ask me point-blank what I knew about Mindy Goodacre. But he simply said, 'We've thought of that angle, and we're on it. Thanks anyway.'

'A lot of these rich lawyer types have country getaway places,' I said. 'Maybe they'd let the Normans hide out in, say, their hayloft. I mean, worth asking, don't you think?'

The look he gave me is pretty hard to describe, but nudging him towards Mindy relieved me of any residual guilt I may have had.

If I'd felt guilty in the first place.

TWENTY

Narduzzi left shortly afterwards, and I willed myself to concentrate on my writing. Eventually I got stuck in, wondering what Caroline's next move would be – she always surprised me. Before I was aware how much time had passed, my stomach informed me it was time to think about dinner.

I ordered restaurant delivery or carryout a lot after Marcus died. I didn't mean to, in fact I made it a point at first, for the sake of my sanity and cholesterol levels, to cook at home, but honestly, it's too much trouble for just one person.

Marcus and I had got into the habit of ordering out during the pandemic to help keep the restaurants afloat – he would go pick it up, or we'd go together, suitably protected by his-and-her masks. But with him gone – too hard, not worth it. Not fun.

Now I would eat a solitary meal on the nights I wasn't going out, which was most nights. I guess readers are supposed to envy my glamorous and successful Facebook-y life as a writer and see my solitariness as a choice, which largely it is. That's part of the mystique, carefully cultivated by my publisher. Some authors have a publicist posting constantly on their behalf about what they had for breakfast in what exotic locale with what famous person. But I'm trying to write the truth here, not a publicist's fantasy. The fact is, when you're choosy about who you hang out with and are guarded with your time, there's a limited roster of people in your life.

My blood relations are tucked away in Maine and California, some bounded by wildfires and mudslides, many living better than they deserve, surrounded as they are by stolen property. (Uncle Al on the Lost Coast, I'm looking at you.) Brief daydreams of moving to Maine are just that – brief.

I've made my own way for the most part and I'm proud of

that. I had people who supported me on the way and those people are the keepers.

But the truth is, strange as it sounds, my closest friends and family live on the written page, and I can never wait to get back to writing about them. Nothing in my real life compared with the scenery and conversations in my head as I wrote. The good people of the Dordogne, evil killers, mercy killers, children, bakers, vintners, whatever. If I didn't happen to like the way they looked, I could change the shape of their noses and their coloring or delete them altogether. I could have the villain pop into a church to pray to make the reader think he wasn't so bad after all – only to later invent a sinister reason for his frequent visits. Thinking up that sinister reason could keep me happily engaged for hours.

Of course, I could kill any of them off at will.

Part of the joy of this process is being allowed to deceive people without consequence. (*Getting to Deceive* was the title of my fifth book, by the way, if you want to look it up. It got some fine reviews from the tough crowd on Goodreads, and it sold even better than *Living a Lie*.)

In the world I created, I might throw an elegant dinner party – which I seldom did in reality. OK, I never threw fancy dinner parties. I am more in the potluck camp. But on the page, I would describe, in mouth-watering detail, people lingering over French dinners, having researched the ingredients and preparation in tax-deductible French cookbooks and restaurants. No cleanup afterward. Win/win.

My book, my rules. My make-believe world. I suppose in that regard I inherited the more useful bits of my parents' illnesses.

I missed Marcus, but I resisted all matchmaking attempts and ignored those 'How to Turn a Friend into a Lover' magazine articles. I didn't need more people in my life; I needed fewer.

The truth was, after Marcus, I just didn't trust my judgment.

The occasional look-in on my neighbors across the back, and my inserting myself into the case, had nothing to do with loneliness or aloneness. Really. It was curiosity mixed with boredom and maybe a mild case of writer's block.

That's all.

I had fed Roscoe his Trader Joe's dog food and taken my
Trader Joe's Reduced Guilt Mac and Cheese out of the microwave when someone knocked on the door downstairs. Through
the peephole, I saw Kent Haworth. Wearing, of all things, a
pulled-up hoodie over black jeans. I gasped and stepped back
from the door before my brain registered who it was.

He was late and I wasn't thrilled. I had my entire evening of
TV watching mapped out, a few crime shows queued up on the
Xfinity box. Between him and Narduzzi, this was more company
than I normally had in a month, let alone a day. But I figured it
must be important to the case or he wouldn't have driven over
here, a half-hour at best from where I thought he lived, in
Cleveland Park. A phone call would have been nice, though, after
he missed our four p.m. appointment.

'Come on in,' I said, opening the door. Surreptitiously, I
looked up and down the street to see if for some reason
Narduzzi was still lurking or had sent out a surveillance team.

And no, I don't know why I thought that. Some sixth sense
– more likely, something in Narduzzi's body language earlier –
told me he thought I was probably worth keeping an eye on. And
I don't mean because he thought I was cute. Well, I thought he
may have thought that, but under the circumstances I was, as I
have told you, one hundred percent up to things of which he
probably would not have approved.

'I was having some dinner – sorry, there's not enough to
share,' I told Kent. I brought him upstairs and sat him at the
kitchen table as I had done with Narduzzi. Roscoe, having
finished his meal, was settled into his bed to await his evening
walk. He came over to inspect Kent and found him acceptable
enough not to bite his ankles.

I thought I might as well get a nameplate for the kitchen
table; it was turning into a sort of pop-up office space with a
bring-your-dog-to-work vibe.

'But I can pour you a wine,' I said. 'Red or red, I'm afraid. That's
all I drink. What's up? Could you have phoned to say you'd be late?'

I was choosing my words carefully. 'Could you have phoned?'
was marginally more polite than 'Couldn't you have phoned?' But
I was a bit put out and more than a bit uncomfortable with having

Kent in my home at night. Given what I knew – what he had told me – of his reputation.

Accepting the glass of wine, he settled into a chair across from me and said, 'I didn't think it was safe to phone. And it looks like my instincts were right.'

I had a mouthful of Reduced Guilt so it took me a moment to ask, 'What do you mean?'

'I saw a guy leaving just as I was pulling into a visitor's spot in the courtyard round the corner from you. Boy, you have some eagle-eyed neighbors. Some woman actually followed me to make sure I was visiting someone in the complex. And not just hogging a parking spot while I went to a restaurant.'

'That was probably Marguerite. She's a self-appointed neighborhood watch maven. She maintains this sort of online crime blotter for the HOA, complete with photos of license plates. God help you if you park on any of the nearby streets beyond the allotted two hours. She keeps parking enforcement on speed dial and it's a hefty fine if they catch you. Anyway, what do you mean about your instincts?'

'The guy who was leaving was a cop who's working the case. I saw him being interviewed on TV.'

'Yes.' I debated half a second whether to tell Kent why Narduzzi had come here but vanity won out. I truly was flattered to have been noticed by the police as someone with special observational skills. 'He showed me videocam footage of a visitor to Niko and Zora's.'

He carefully set down his glass and leaned in closer. He was wearing a musky men's cologne that I promise you had zero effect on me. 'No kidding,' he said.

I took a moment to savor both my moment of glory and the wonderful low-fat sauce Trader Joe had devised for his mac and cheese. Putting down my fork and picking up my wine glass, I said, 'I wasn't really able to help, though. Grainy footage in the dark and someone dressed a bit like you, in fact. Dark clothing, hoodie pulled up to hide the face. Niko left with whoever it was.'

'Niko did? When did he come back?'

Well, crap. When *did* he come back? Did he come back at

all? 'Um. I don't know. Narduzzi didn't show me that footage
if he had it.' Why hadn't I asked about that when clearly it was
vital to the case? Was I so completely useless at this?

Peeved and taking it out on Kent, I said, 'So, now you're
finally here, is there something you couldn't just tell me over
the phone?'

'I think my phone is tapped, either because of my interest in
this case or my interest in the dozen cases that came before it.'

This took me aback, but I said, 'Do you really think you're
that special to the police? I don't know what a phone tap costs
but it must cost something.'

He picked up his glass again and sort of aimed it at me.

'You would be surprised.'

'You're just being paranoid, aren't you?'

'You know the old saying: It's not paranoia if they really are
tracking you. Anyway, what I wanted to talk about was Mindy
Goodacre of Niko's firm. And that was not a conversation I
wanted recorded. Just in case it ended up being recorded.'

'Oh?' I sat quite still. He had my full attention.

'She called me today. Apparently, she's kept the home fires
burning for me but that's not really why she called.'

Afraid he was going to say she called because she'd been
visited by a weird blonde southern woman who was clearly
in disguise and seemed way too interested in the Normans'
disappearance, I busied myself scraping the last of the Reduced
Guilt onto my fork.

But that wasn't it.

'She wants to retain me.'

'She . . . excuse me, you said she wants to retrain you? Into
what?'

'Retain, not retrain. Retain as in give me money in exchange
for my private-investigative services.'

'You're not serious.'

'Serious.'

'And you told her that was out of the question.'

'Why should it be out of the question?'

'Are you kidding? You're a little bit too close to the case, is
why. You were hired by Genevieve and her husband to look at
Niko; you're sitting here talking with me about evidence.'

'So what?'

'Did you tell her about Genevieve?'

'Should I have?'

To be honest, I wasn't sure myself. I just kept thinking, *No ethics, no problem.* How grand it must be to go through life like Kent. He looked baffled, as if I'd suggested he run for Pope.

To my mind, it couldn't be right to take money from a client and not tell her what you already knew about the case. That you were already looking into it and planning to write a book about it, no less.

Maybe the Private Eye Association of America had an ethics handbook, but I, personally, was stumped. I only knew that if they did, and Kent was a member, he'd be the last person to download it.

Then again, who was I to talk? Hadn't I just conned the poor woman into thinking I was a prospective client?

'It just seems wrong, Kent. Taking money, for one thing.'

'Why?' We were so clearly in foreign territory for him I let it drop.

'Look,' I said, 'I've got an early day tomorrow. And I haven't completed my pages for today.'

Nor did I plan to do them once he'd left. But as one writer to another, I trusted Kent to understand.

Notice how I just used the word 'trusted' and 'Kent' in the same sentence. It didn't really register. I only knew I'd had enough visitors for one day.

He drank the dregs of his wine and stood. As I got up to show him out, he came around the side of the table, moving in a little too close to me. I backed into the Corian-topped counter separating the kitchen from the breakfast nook.

'Well, if there's nothing else,' he began, his hand snaking toward my hip. I came within an inch of slapping it away, but instead used the moment to scoot out of range. If I was going to break my long fast, it was not going to be with an operator like Kent Haworth.

Was I tempted even slightly? To be honest, yes, I was. It had been a long drought and – if not for the diversion of the investigation – I might have succumbed out of pure boredom. I'm just being honest with you. Sleeping alone is not all that it is cracked up to be, and Kent Haworth was a handsome devil.

And he knew it. That, as far as I was concerned, was the entire problem.

'Not at the moment,' I said. I headed down the stairs, not waiting to see if he'd follow.

He did. I practically shoved him out the front door.

'Goodnight, Kent.'

TWENTY-ONE

The next day I took Roscoe for an early walk, planning to head straight for my office afterwards with a large almond-milk cappuccino from the Beanery. My characters Claude and Caroline had waited too long for their next scene, with too many events in my own life intervening, and I feared – not writer's block; I never got an Overlook Hotel case of writer's block where I attacked doors with axes – veering off the steady course I'd been holding throughout the latest book.

This one's working title was *Daughter's Rendezvous* – I knew the publisher would want to change it, insisting 'rendezvous' was far too difficult a word for US audiences to remember, let alone pronounce. I would wrestle by email with Delamare's marketing department for just long enough to keep my hand in and let them know how deeply I cared what they did to my product, getting completely caught up in a defense of the US public school system (which in reality I thought was going straight down the tube, to judge from nearly every encounter I'd had over the past fifteen years with any company's customer service department). In the end I'd grudgingly offer up an alternative, maybe the title I'd wanted in the first place.

Roscoe, who for some weeks had been quite taken with a German shepherd of well-earned ill repute, got away from me as I was talking with a neighbor, and I had to set down my coffee and give chase. Sadie's owner seemed quite unaware of her dog's charms and would let her off her lead at the slightest provocation. This was strictly prohibited under Section 5-7-33 of the many city ordinances on this topic (signs were posted all over the place), and if anyone thought the skirmishes over parking were bad, they should watch dog owners trying to shield AKC-registered Muffy from the unwanted attentions of a rogue mutt.

Sadie was another case entirely. Shameless and confident, if not all that attractive, at least to my eye, Sadie could have any dog she wanted, but she seemed to be developing a special bond with Roscoe, who was too smitten to realize the road ahead for him was paved with paternity testing and puppy support payments, not to mention neutering, if he didn't learn to rein in his libido.

I gave chase and the scene ended with me knee-deep in river sludge, cursing a blue streak. Sadie's owner was too busy flirting with a gray-haired neighbor I thought of as the Silver Fox to notice her dog needed a refresher course on dating etiquette at the Old Town School for Dogs.

I had Roscoe by the collar and was dragging him ashore, both of us looking like survivors of a shipwreck, when I saw Narduzzi. His arms were folded across his chest and he showed not the slightest inclination to help keep me from drowning. He was again all suit and tie and business. He carried the same briefcase as before and I wondered if there were new videos he wanted me to view.

As it turned out, there were indeed new videos for me to view.

'Hi,' I said with exaggerated cheer. I felt at a disadvantage, dripping muddy water from the knees down, my every step emitting a squish-squish noise as water gushed from my Supergas. Roscoe did not seem to understand how unwanted his attentions were towards a man wearing a suit, and I had to get him under control before he jumped all over Narduzzi. I took it as a good sign that Roscoe liked him, however. Roscoe was somewhat discerning for a dog, apart from his infatuation with Sultry Sadie, and while he had not attacked Kent, he had completely ignored his overtures.

'Hi,' he said. I could not read his expression. 'Do you have a minute?'

I looked down at myself and back up at him. 'I'm a little busy,' I said. 'For one thing I'm going to need another shower and then I have to get back to work.'

'I'll wait here,' he said, handing me another of his cards. 'Text me when you're out of the shower.'

It seemed more like a command than a suggestion, so I retrieved my paper cup of now-cold coffee and hustled Roscoe off. As we walked back toward my house, I looked over my shoulder and saw Narduzzi sitting on a park bench, staring out over the water. Sadie's owner already had him in her sights, positioning herself in front of him, likewise staring across the river towards Maryland in what I'm sure she thought of as a winsome pose.

Twenty minutes later I texted Narduzzi.

He walked upstairs with his briefcase and settled himself at my breakfast nook, precisely as if he owned the place. That was off-putting but what could I say? I offered him coffee and brusquely he shook his head. He looked tired; dark circles which I would swear had not been there the day before had formed under his eyes.

'You've been busy, haven't you, Ms Hawke.' It was not a question, and it slowly started to dawn on me that he was not here to take advantage of my keen investigative talents. Not this time.

His computer screen was open to a view of the front door of the majestic offices of Masters, Milton, and Duckett, and as I stood watching at his shoulder, a car pulled up and a striking blonde woman emerged – striking, if I do say so myself. It was Patrice, of course.

I watched the unfortunately high-quality footage as I entered the premises, tottering a bit on those heels. I really needed to practice wearing them, I thought inconsequently, my brain not having caught up to the fact Narduzzi was not here so I could help him ID the blonde from her walk. From his tone, he was well ahead of me there.

He skipped over a few frames covering the timeframe I was being straight-armed by Valentina, the front desk dragon. I soon emerged and walked out of the picture, heading in the direction of The Grind coffee shop. Now there was a little skip in my step, knowing I would soon be speaking with Mindy Goodacre and hopefully plumbing the depths of Niko Norman's character.

I'd not noticed but there was also a security camera in front of The Grind and it picked me up as I was entering moments later. I was followed, of course, by Mindy Goodacre, carrying her leather portfolio tucked under one arm. Narduzzi manipulated the dials to show me and Mindy emerging from the coffee shop and, moments later, me entering an Uber cab. Helpfully, this video also was of good quality, and the Uber's license plate practically glowed with crystal clarity.

I began to speak and he waved me to silence. He wasn't done.

No, indeed, he wasn't done. The same Uber appeared on security footage taken from the house across and down a few doors from mine on Fendall Street. The Prufrocks' house – he of the State Department, she whose pastimes were unknown, apart from childcare and online shopping. The Amazon boxes filling their steps on almost a daily basis were testament to the shopping. The nanny coming and going daily was testament to the part-time nature of her childcare responsibilities.

Anyway, the camera was clearly on some sort of time-lapse, but it caught all the highlights: me being deposited by the Uber, wearing a little less of my costume than before; a little wave at the driver as he drove off (I was still in character as a friendly southerner – no one from around here would give a friendly wave to an Uber driver); and a nice clear shot of that same license plate as he drove off. It was like a video diary of my entire day, also showing me entering the premises of my house.

I had no idea the neighbor's camera was trained on my place all the time like that. I knew, of course; I could see it. I'd just not given it any thought. But I had bigger concerns at the moment.

I left Narduzzi's side and sort of plopped down in the seat across from him.

'Would you like to tell me what you thought you were doing?'

'I just wanted to help.' It sounded lame, even to me. 'I thought I could help.'

'Why?' he asked. But his gaze was soft and mild where I'd expected to see anger. 'Do you know how many laws you've broken? No? Neither do I, to be honest. I've never had the situation come up. Normally the crooks run away from us; they can't get away fast enough, they don't just barge in—'

'I'm not a crook.'

'You and Nixon both. Look, this is the end of it. Right here and now. Or else I will go find the law to charge you with. I'll start by looking under "O" for obstructing justice.'

'OK,' I said softly.

He shut the lid of the laptop and sighed. 'You're a widow, right?'

It was no secret requiring access to a guarded database, but still it was alarming to realize he'd been checking up on me. Probably because of this Patrice caper. Otherwise I'd probably have continued in my simple role of impartial (but helpful) witness.

'So, what did she tell you? Mindy?'

'This is confidential, right?'

At that he let out a deep sigh of exasperation. 'Are you kidding me?' He shook his head. 'Of course, it's not confidential. Lives are depending on this. Just tell me what you found out.' He scoffed. '*Confidential.*'

'How did you know? I mean, did someone turn me in?' I was thinking, of course, of Valentina, who would probably like nothing better than to shop me to the police. She'd probably call the FBI while she was at it and ask about a finder's fee. I spared a moment to wonder if she weren't another of Niko's conquests.

'Of course, we've had an eye on the camera in front of that building, in case Niko turned up, for one thing. You were recognized. I recognized you.'

'Wow.' I knew it was a damned good costume, one of my best. This guy was good.

'Enough of this. Tell me what you know.'

'Coffee?'

It probably cost him an internal debate over how much more a witness would be willing to talk whilst caffeinated versus not caffeinated but finally he agreed to sharing some fresh coffee with me. My coffee from the Beanery had gone into the trash. Once we were settled again, I told him what I had learned from Mindy Goodacre. Which in truth amounted to a hill of beans, and so I said to him.

'She never said or admitted a thing, you have to understand

that,' I said. 'My takeaway from our conversation was based on my read of her body language.'

'Based on your intuition,' he said skeptically.

'Well, yes, my intuition is actually quite good, thanks. She would not have had this conversation with you or any strange male, I am absolutely certain, but she would with a sympathetic female.'

'However strange.'

That didn't seem to merit a response. I looked at him for a moment and then focused on taking a sip of my coffee.

'Sorry if it's a bit strong,' I said.

'So why the disguise?'

I'd been afraid he would ask that but there was no way around it.

'She was meeting me as a prospective client.'

'Since her expertise is family law, I'm going to guess – going way out on a limb here – you were pretending to be someone contemplating a divorce.'

There seem to be little point in denying it. He had probably verified a few things before coming to speak with me. Quite possibly he had spoken with Mindy herself, a thought that made me cringe with embarrassment. On the other hand, there seemed to be little point in my throwing myself under the bus.

'Actually, I'm fairly certain the conversation is protected by the laws concerning confidentiality between a client and her lawyer.'

'Jesus Christ,' he said. I suspected that was the strongest swear language he would use in speaking with a suspect, which suspect would be yours truly.

'All right, all right,' I said, putting up my hands in a gesture of surrender. There was zero point in provoking him, since he was well within his rights to charge me with whatever he could dream up at this point. 'That is stretching a point, I'll admit. But we were having a conversation about relationships, in a manner of speaking, and I happened to mention that Niko and his wife had disappeared. That it had all been on the news.' I was leaving out a few beats there, but the lyrics carried the gist of the conversation. 'I told her I knew he was a colleague of hers and what did she think about it? The funny thing was,' and here I leaned in, warming to my topic. 'The funny thing was, she didn't know anything about Niko and his wife disappearing. I would swear to it. Her reaction was completely unfeigned. She was, as the British say, gobsmacked.'

'Hmm. And what else?'

'Um. Well, we talked awhile and again, from her reaction, there was just no hiding something was up. I was afraid she'd leave before I could, you know, get more out of her, so I gave her a "been there, done that" sort of prompt. And while she didn't really admit the relationship, she did say something to the effect that Niko would never leave his wife. That he had told her himself he adored her and would never leave her side.'

'Is that what she actually told you?'

I waved one hand about vaguely. 'Words to that effect.'

'Would you care to tell me what put Mindy Goodacre on your super-detective's radar in the first place?'

While I felt there was no call for that sort of sarcasm, I let it pass. 'Well, I'm sort of friends with this guy who is a private detective. He and I are both writers and we belong to the same groups and attend the same events and so on. He told me he thought Niko may have played around before he was married.' I couldn't see any way around it: I had to bring Kent into this. I was rather hoping not to be asked who had told me about Kent in the first place. But if he'd asked, I would have told him. Even though it was marginally harder to explain how I'd ended up speaking with Zora's mother, I swear I would have told him.

'And after he was married?'

'Well, that's undetermined as of yet.'

'As of yet?'

'I'm sure there's lots more to learn there.'

'Jesus wept.'

He certainly was on a biblical rant. I wondered if he and his wife were religious.

'However,' I held up a forestalling hand. 'However, I will step back and let you handle things from now on. I really do apologize. And at least I did gain some potentially useful information for you.'

He sat back, crossing his arms across his chest. The gesture made his biceps press against the fabric of his suit. 'Are we going to pretend you were planning to come straight to me with this information?'

Why, yes, we are.

'As soon as I'd walked the dog this morning, yes. I'd given it some thought and realized it was exactly the sort of thing I shouldn't keep to myself. Even though – and I can't emphasize this enough – I am quite certain Mindy is blameless here. She didn't even know what had happened.' I started to mention her hay farm, but the fact I couldn't remember what I'd already told him about lawyers and their farms forestalled me. I was in deep enough as it was.

I could tell he wanted to say something more, something slightly threatening to scare me off, but he seemed at a loss for words. Whatever he was doing, I doubted he was choking back laughter. He really did look pissed off.

Since I can never stand to have anyone that angry with me, I cast about in my mind for something else I could tell him to ameliorate the situation. Having thrown Kent into the river in a manner of speaking, I was not about to do the same to Misaki, but I could see no harm in mentioning the way our thoughts had been trending in terms of the investigation, all without mentioning her of course.

'I did have a thought,' I began.

'Oh, good.'

Once again I had to fight my way past the barbed wire of his sarcasm, but I said, 'It occurred to me that a young couple like the Normans would of course have a babysitter. Have you looked into that yet? I mean, a babysitter would be right there in the house with them, at least for the child handoff, and would know a whole lot more about their relationship, at least on the surface, than I would.'

'That had occurred to us, yes,' he said. 'Look, I'm going to tell you once more. You must stop interfering.'

'I wasn't interfering. I was offering a suggestion.'

'You must stop interfering,' he repeated. 'I hope I make myself understood. I won't explain this to you again.'

I nodded meekly, genuinely contrite. It wouldn't last, but that was how I felt in the moment.

He began putting away the laptop. 'Anything else?'

I wanted to ask him so many questions, but I could think of none he might answer. It occurred to me I should probably mollify him with a bit more data coming from my side.

'Well, to be honest . . .'

'That would be nice.'

That did it for me. That really tore it. Here I was, trying to be cooperative, and he was giving me that tone.

'I was just going to say, the babysitter may be your best lead. Should I ask around and try to find out who it was?'

'Thank you for the coffee.'

Once Narduzzi had left, I retrieved a bilberry yogurt from the refrigerator and leaned against the countertop as I spooned it in, ruminating over our conversation. I supposed that in fact it had gone fairly well, since I wasn't actually sitting in a jail rather than having breakfast in my kitchen, but I was disappointed I had gotten nothing out of him. Not a lead, not a hint. The portcullis into his mind had completely closed shut on me.

He was so dismissive of the whole babysitter angle that I was tempted to drop it myself, but I had put Misaki on the case and I didn't want to let her down. I had phoned her yesterday to say I had the babysitter's name from Genevieve but, when she didn't pick up, I didn't want to leave a message like that on her machine. Then in all the excitement, I forgot. I really needed to speak with her.

I thought about texting, but my conversation with Kent had activated all my latent paranoia about wiretaps and subpoenas for evidence. At a minimum, it would be best for them to find only harmless delivery notifications from Whole Foods among my text messages. Misaki and I needed a code word for 'Mr Watson, come here. I want to see you.'

I supposed the old-fashioned way was best. I should just show up at her door and hope she was home. It was always possible that by now Narduzzi had assigned someone to watch my comings and goings, but that seemed like an extreme waste of resources. From what I knew of these investigations, they were always on a budget.

My phone buzzed as I was rinsing out the yogurt carton for the recycle bin. It was my editor, no doubt wondering what I

was doing rather than writing. Now, there was a long story that
would come in well over 100,000 words.

'Hi, Julia! What's up?'

'What's up yourself?'

I hoped she didn't have any penetrating questions, as the
novel was becoming a faint memory. I really had to get back
to it today while I still had some wits about me. I had no recol-
lection if I had left Caroline hanging from a cliff or in bed with
her paramour.

'Did you call the police like I told you?'

I also had completely forgotten our former conversation,
where she had commanded me not to keep evidence to myself
in case I got in trouble. How did she always know?

'I told him about the argument I heard between Niko and
Zora, yes.'

'Good, good. Any new developments?'

My defeat at the hands of Narduzzi fresh in my mind, a
change of topic seemed called for. 'The book is going well,
yes.'

'About the case, I meant,' she snapped. I was reminded, since
her husband died, she was a woman of few friends and fewer
social skills. This murder may have been the highlight of her
week, a reprieve from reading the shitty first draft of the next
bestseller by 'He who shall not be named', another writer in
her care. All right, I'll tell you his name. His name is James
Rugger and he is, among other authors, the bane of my existence. I'm sure you've heard of him. Comparisons are odious,
I know, but on that great spreadsheet maintained by my
publisher, James outsold me and everyone else by a zillion
copies. 'I can always google for news but you're right there on
the spot,' she added.

'I certainly am that. On the spot, I mean.'

'Well?'

Oh, God, where to start. 'As far as I know, the police are no
further ahead than they were.'

'Have they spoken with you again?'

'Well, yes, as a matter of fact. The main detective on the
case seems to think I may be helpful in solving the case, given
my profession.' This was so nearly true I didn't see any point

in mentioning he had as recently as half an hour before ordered me to mind my own business.

'Cool.'

In a way I was relieved she didn't want to talk about how the book was going, which conversation would require even more lying on my part. At the same time, and for similar reasons, I didn't want to talk about the case.

Small talk about the weather and so on with Julia was always out of the question. She functioned in a sort of Mr Spockian mode, heavily into discussions of grammar, syntax, and continuity errors, but those sorts of comments she usually saved for the review function in Word.

'And?' she prompted.

'Have we spoken since they found Niko Norman's car near the parkway?'

'No, we haven't. What's the parkway?'

I had been forgetting that – to Julia – anything outside the boundaries of New York may as well be in some remote outpost of the former Soviet empire. She had a morbid fear of flying that left her confined to New York, refusing to attend industry conventions or even go on holiday. She had last attempted train travel back in 2005 and, without a doubt, like most New Yorkers, she did not own a car. They let her get away with this because of James Rugger, see above. James was reported to love working with her and the publisher was not going to do anything to upset that golden apple cart.

I relayed what I knew about the car having been found. As much as I wanted to highlight my importance to the investigation, I felt it best not to mention the video Narduzzi had shown me. Videos plural, I should say. I was much too chastened by my recent encounter to want to talk about any videos with anyone.

'So,' I said, concluding my narrative, 'the police actually seem stumped. I'd love to help but of course I need to focus on the new book. Continue focusing on the book. Really, I've been going pretty much flat out. Just a few little holes to plug, nothing major. It'll be fine, I'm sure.'

Having sufficiently dug myself into a hole, so to speak, I decided to shut up and see what she thought about my amazing writerly progress.

Into the silence she said, 'Would you like an extension on your deadline?'

'What?'

This was an astonishing thing for a book editor to say. Deadlines were inviolate, if only on the author's side. Publishers could move deadlines into the next year on a whim if they felt like it. Authors seldom had or were given that luxury.

So such a question from any editor at any publishing house, however large or small, is simply unheard of. Once the deadline for delivery has been determined by contract, all the forces of heaven and hell cannot change it. Too many gears have been set in motion, in terms of printing and distribution and marketing and publicity and so on, for the date to be moved by so much as a month, either way.

The author has to attend a family funeral? No excuse. Birth a child? Don't care. Rebuild following an earthquake? Nope. The author must meet the agreed-upon deadline or the contract will be cancelled. Apparently murder investigations were the exception to this inflexible rule, at least in Julia's little alcohol-free world.

Who knew? All this time – who knew?

'Really?' I gasped.

'If certain conditions are met, yes. I'm sure we can work something out with your agent.'

'Sure. I mean, I'm listening.'

'This has all the elements of a true-crime story, and with you right there on the ground to investigate it. Come up with a proposal whenever the case is resolved, however it's resolved – or not – and have your agent send it to me. The only condition is, of course, I want an exclusive submission.'

This was getting to be a bit bizarre. It was as if the universe had decided to divert my career against my will. First Kent with his dubious and self-serving offer. Now Julia with an offer I knew, given her bedrock integrity beneath her gravelly exterior, was solid.

It put me in a bit of an ethical situation with regard to Kent, but I figured I'd cross that shaky bridge when I got to it.

'No guarantees,' she said, 'but if anyone can pull this off, I think you can.'

'Seriously?'

'Seriously. When you consider how often life does imitate art, this should not be a big stretch for you. You've written some really good books for us but, before the series gets stale, let's see what else you can do.'

Apart from the 'stale' bit, the woman was nearly bringing me to tears with this endorsement of my abilities. It didn't seem a good time to mention I had seriously pissed off the lead investigator already.

I simply said, 'Thank you, Julia.' Meaning it. And: 'I will certainly do . . . whatever I can do to make it work.'

Once that amazing phone call had ended, I decided it really was time to jump-start this whole investigation with a visit to Misaki. I took out the folder I had been using to make the casual observer think the HOA's mulch distribution was to be the topic of our discussions.

I made sure Roscoe had water and everything to keep him occupied, including his favorite nature channel on the TV, then I grabbed my bag, thinking: *Mulch*. That should be our code word if we could not avoid texting.

Literally as I opened my front door, there came a text from her.

I have news. Can you come here?

I texted back.

Mulch situation out of hand. Be right there.

'Where have you been? I saw that cop at your door. What's up?'

As with Julia, I had trouble knowing where to start.

'Let me in. I'll tell you everything I remember.'

And I did. We settled in her living room, which teemed with the charm of accumulated, much-loved possessions, and I did my best to encapsulate what had happened since I'd left on my, in retrospect, misguided mission to get what I could get out of Mindy Goodacre. The events of the past hours and days had somehow kaleidoscoped in my mind; I fumbled about, struggling to create a coherent narrative. When I got to the part where Narduzzi had spotted me on the security tape, Misaki gasped, which was heartening – she understood this was very bad news indeed.

'Oh my God,' she said. 'This is all my fault. I'm so sorry. What a stupid idea.'

'It's not your fault, Misaki. You are not the one in charge of stupid ideas. Generally, that's my department. Yes, it could've gone badly for me, and I have no idea why Narduzzi decided to basically let me off with a warning. I only know I can't get caught again.'

'So you're giving up the investigation.' It wasn't a question.

'Did I say that? You said you had some news. You found the babysitter, right?'

'You're sure you want to know? Maybe the less you know, the better, given . . . given, well . . .'

'Tell me,' I commanded.

She scootched forward in her seat. 'I found several things I want to tell you, actually. The real bombshell I just found out about this morning. You remember the Hubbards?'

'Sure. The elderly couple that sold their house to Niko and Zora.'

'That's just the point. They didn't really sell to the Normans.'

'What do you mean?'

'They sold to *one* Norman. Zora. Niko's name was added to the paperwork later. Initially Zora made the purchase in her name only.'

I was sitting in one of Misaki's chintz-covered chairs and began tapping my fingers against one flowery arm. Finally, I said, 'Is that all that unusual? I mean, maybe he was out of town when the deal closed and she just turned up and arranged everything herself and then later brought him in on it. How do you know about this?'

'I contacted the agent who sold the place to the Normans. I remembered who it was from the sign when the place was for sale – God knows I stared at it long enough while it was on the market. I know her; in fact, she's the same woman who sold me my place. Barb Garman.'

Everyone knew Barb Garman, or at least, knew of her. Her name was everywhere, giving the impression she bought and sold every house on the market in these parts. About ten years ago she had partnered with her son, whom everyone called Barb Junior, since no one could be bothered to remember his name. He didn't have his mother's gift for home sales, but Barb was a tough act to follow. She was indeed our local doyenne of real estate.

'She's still around? Wow.'

'Has to be eighty now.'

'Go on,' I said.

'Real-estate agents technically aren't allowed to talk about the details of their deals but there was nothing secret about this. Zora's name was on the paperwork and a few days later Niko's name was added as co-buyer. *She* had it added. Zora had.'

'OK.' I must admit I was still thinking this was a bunch of nothing and what did it matter. 'I didn't realize Zora had that kind of money, and that's interesting. I honestly thought he was the guy who brought home the groceries while she tended the home fires.'

'You have arrived at the heart of the matter,' said Misaki. 'According to the Hubbards – they say "hi", by the way, and they loved your latest book – Zora's parents paid for the house. In their daughter's name.'

'Oh.'

'It sold for $1.2 million – that's a matter of public record, of course. Not exactly chump change.'

'I guess the question may be whether they intended it to remain solely in Zora's name.'

'I'm gonna go with yes, that's exactly what they intended. They wanted to create a *feme sole* situation under the law. But it's not what happened, not how it played out.'

'It was pretty evident Genevieve didn't care for her son-in-law,' I said slowly. 'I wonder if her dislike prompted this action.'

'Once again I'm gonna go with yes. In case the marriage went south, they wanted their daughter protected, left with at least a roof over her head.'

I sat back, thinking. 'Genevieve had doubts about Niko well before Zora married him. Which this action – his name later being added as co-owner of the house she and her husband had technically bought for their daughter – would only confirm. This purchase was made before they were married, right?'

'I guess. Or around the same time. It would be easy enough

to look up the dates. But again, you've reached the heart of it. Since they were married and lived in Virginia, the house belonged to both of them. This name-addition business was basically a formality. Still, I doubt it's what her parents intended to happen when they wrote the check for such a large amount. Not being lawyers but creatives – she an art gallery owner and he an architect, according to news reports – they probably didn't realize the potential problem they were creating. Niko, a lawyer himself, surrounded by specialists in family and marital law, knew it was a loophole that needed to be plugged.'

'Her father used to be a lawyer but maybe he was a not-so-good one, which is why he gave it up for architecture. You say, "wrote a check". Are you saying they paid cash?'

'Yep. Old-Eastern-Seaboard-type money there. Somebody owned a whaling ship or two back in the day.'

'Got it. Did Barb get any sense that Zora willingly put her husband's name on the paperwork? Was there some coercion involved?'

'She didn't say anything like that and neither did the Hubbards – I doubt they'd know. As for Barb, by that point in the transaction, she had done her bit and gone off to earn her percentage somewhere else. What happened afterwards didn't really concern her.'

'It kind of sounds as if Niko was annoyed to learn he'd been left out of things.'

'Yes. Even though, as a lawyer, he'd know it didn't mean much.'

'Unless something were to happen to his wife. Then he'd have to prove he had a right to remain in the house.'

'Something like that. Not difficult to prove, of course, but I'm sure he didn't like that loose end. To be honest, in his shoes, would you? I mean, wouldn't you have felt a bit insecure knowing the marital home was only in the name of your spouse?'

'Yes. You're right. Of course, you're right. Do you have a recent newspaper? The *Gazette*, I mean, not the *Post*.'

'It's in the recycle bin. Why?'

'I'm thinking of buying a new house.'

'Really? I thought you liked it here.'

'I love it here. Can you just bring me the paper?'

'Any particular day?'

I shook my head. 'Doesn't matter.'

She went into the kitchen and in a few minutes returned with the latest *Gazette*. I turned the issue over to view the back page, which always contained a big real-estate splash of listings, glamified properties going for anywhere from half a million to $20 million or more. Barb's photo figured prominently, staged and photoshopped to highlight her best features and hide her worst, just like her property listings.

I reached for my phone and dialed her number – rather, the main number of Quinn's, the largest trader in real estate in the area. Their offices were ten blocks away as the crow flies. I listened to some classical music before reaching her extension via the automated system. There I left a voicemail message asking Barb if I could meet with her today, managing to imply I was in the market for a new property without actually saying so. I looked at Misaki as I said:

'I might bring a friend, if that's all right. You sold her her property, and she knows the kind of thing I want.' I hesitated before adding, 'She said she'd spoken with you recently.' I decided to leave it at that rather than make it crystal clear I was after something besides viewing hot properties on the market.

I rang off. Turning to Misaki, I said, 'We've been thinking: The babysitter *might* have insight into Zora's personality. But with a teenaged girl, you take your chances: anyone Zora and Niko's age are really old, in their minds, and probably beneath notice. But if anyone has insight, and superb instincts, it's a killer real-estate agent like Barb Garman. Her whole business is built on the ability to read people. Anyway, did you get anything on the babysitter?'

'Just that the Normans did use the same sitter as Mellie Broeder and Amir Deniz.'

'Our guess was right.'

'Beatrix Steppes – Trixie, for short.'

'Good work. I only got the first name from Genevieve. So, Trixie Steppes. Like a girl out of a fairy tale. Did you get a number for her?'

Misaki nodded. 'I've tried it a few times. She's not answering. Her parents say she's staying up at her aunt's place in

Connecticut, as she often does during the summer school break
– takes the train up. Mystic is a bit of a tourist destination.'

'Sure, I've been to Mystic; I went there once on a writers'
retreat. I'm not sure teenage girls think in terms of going to
tourist destinations by themselves without a posse of friends,
though. They usually travel in packs like giggling, eyeshadowed
marauders.'

Misaki shrugged. 'Apparently, she's a quiet kid, close in age
with her Aunt Lily. And she's not getting along with her parents
right now. I'm guessing about that but, talking with Mellie Broeder
and reading between the lines, I arrived at that conclusion. Mellie's
put out because now she's stuck with a sitter she's sure is sneaking
her boyfriend into the house the minute she and Amir drive away.
Their last Xfinity bill showed some movie rentals that weren't
theirs. With fitting irony, they rented *The Babysitter*. At least the
new sitter has a sense of humor.'

'That sounds innocuous. At least it wasn't porn. Or was it?'

'It's a horror flick.'

'Oh.'

'Also, they downloaded *Cabin Fever*, about a flesh-eating
virus – actually, that one doesn't sound too bad. The babysitter
one I've seen already – turns out she's part of a cult. You'd
never guess it to look at her.'

I turned to look at her. 'And all this time I thought I knew
you.'

'I love teen horror flicks, OK? It's like reliving my childhood,
but at a safe distance. Anyway, Mellie is positive the sitter is
downloading this stuff; the dates on the cable bill line up. But
the sitter tried to get Mellie's kids to say they'd done it.'

'Not good. Anyway, so Trixie Steppes is in Mystic and
not answering her phone. I don't see there's a lot we can do
about that.'

'I looked her up on Facebook. It was a long shot – teenagers
have mostly left Facebook for whatever the latest thing is. Even
Snapchat is old hat now. But there she was. Trixie Steppes of
Old Town. She's also on Instagram. Let me get my laptop and
I'll show you. Her parents are Suzie and Rocky Steppes, by the
way.'

'Rocky Steppes?'

'I know. You can't make this stuff up.'

'Could you get the aunt's coordinates from Trixie's parents?'

'Why? Do you want to send her a card?'

'I meant, her phone number.'

'Well, Suzie and Rocky were not that forthcoming. She told me the police had called, wanting to talk with their daughter, and I could tell it freaked her out. So I didn't press, beyond getting Trixie's number. I may have pretended I needed a babysitter for my grandchild.'

'We'll make a detective out of you yet.'

'Yeah. But for all I know it's not the right number – maybe she mixed up a few digits on purpose, or she told the kid to block any number she didn't recognize. Come to think of it, that's probably what I'd do if it were my kid. I'll get my laptop.'

She returned in a few moments and sat next to me on the couch. She tapped a few keys and arrived at Trixie's Facebook page.

Trixie Steppes was a pretty young woman, rounded and still mostly legs, with a pixie haircut no doubt inspired by her name. The Instagram photos and videos were identical in most cases to her Facebook postings, and the most recent images centered around her doing a catwalk for a charity to benefit victims of a rare cancer, the name of which I couldn't pronounce and could only pray I'd never have a need to say aloud.

I asked Misaki to replay one of the videos. I was struck by Trixie's sloping gait, no doubt exaggerated for effect on the catwalk, but nonetheless similar to the walk of the hooded figure in the video shown me by Detective Narduzzi. I had Misaki play the catwalk video again and again but I just couldn't be sure. It wasn't a normal walk – in other words, it didn't seem the kind of walk Trixie or anyone else would adopt in everyday life. But teenagers and their fantasies . . . perhaps she always imagined being a model, and life in high school was just practice for the big event.

'Here's what her aunt's house looks like, if you're interested,' said Misaki. She enlarged another of Trixie's photos on Facebook, revealing what looked like an old sea captain's house. The waters of the Mystic were just visible in the background. Trixie had helpfully labeled it, 'auntie's house, last winter'.

Very nice indeed. It was where I'd want to be if I were a slightly morose teen having troubles with my parents. It was, in fact, exactly the sort of bolthole I wish I'd had at that age.

My cell phone rang and I pulled it from my pocket. I'd forgotten I was expecting a call from Barb Garman of Quinn's Real Estate.

We exchanged the usual hiya chitchat, and I asked how soon she could meet me.

'I'm actually hosting an open house right now,' she said. 'You live in Old Town, right? This place is right down the river in the 22308 zip code.' She named an address on Calvert Springs Road.

'I'm familiar with the area,' I said. Outside of DC, it was the poor man's version of 90210 in California. Lawyers and government contractors might be rich, but famous actors were richer.

'Great. If you could come here? This house is priced off the charts, between you and me, even being on the river. It's absolutely gorgeous, but they'll need to come down to three-point-five mil for five bedrooms. There's no one turning up, absolute crickets, but I'm stuck here until five.'

If she gathered this was more than an expedition involving real estate, she didn't seem to care. I gathered she was so bored that whatever I had to offer was a novelty. I rang off after telling her I'd be there in half an hour.

Something about the subject of real estate had triggered a slight memory for me. Again I pulled up the website for the large cast of characters employed at MM&D. There it was: Robert Steppes, specializing in the many laws of real estate.

I turned to Misaki and said, 'You'll need to pack a bag.'

'Why? We're just going down the river.'

'I meant, pack a bag for when we get back from talking with Barb. We have a train to catch tomorrow morning. We're going to Mystic, Connecticut.'

TWENTY-TWO

T he houses in the 22308 zip code, particularly the ones sited on the river to the east of the George Washington Parkway, are where we Washingtonians host our royalty. The closer to Mount Vernon, as the saying goes, the closer to God.

I don't know if they actually say that, but it's pretty much true when it comes to the price of real estate in the area. The estate where George and Martha lived was, after all, a landmark of American history. Only in recent years had the fact it owed its existence to slavery been addressed more directly. They could hardly tear the place down, much as people may have wanted them to, but the Mount Vernon Ladies' Association launched an effort to learn from the Black Lives Matter movement, redesigning the public exhibits to reflect more of the truth. Truth being an ongoing project.

Regardless, in real-estate agent parlance, 'near Mount Vernon' was still as good as saying you could add half a million to a house's price with each passing mile, although the area closest to the estate was protected land, to the chagrin of developers. While there was a public footpath for hikers and bikers, there were no houses or other structures. It was in this general area that Niko Norman's empty car had been found.

Misaki and I looked for signs of police activity, even though we were undoubtedly too far north to see anything. The forensics guys probably had packed up and gone by now, anyway, taking all vestiges of yellow crime-scene tape with them, and towing the car to a police garage somewhere for analysis.

The area to each side of the parkway was so heavily wooded, it is certainly where I would've chosen to hide a car if I were a kidnapper. The empty car begged the question, though, of how the Normans – he or she or both of them – had gotten away from the area or been taken away. Another car had to have been involved.

Somehow, I was certain Narduzzi had already thought of that. No need for me to call the hotline with that tip.

We weren't far from the spot where Marcus had run his car off the road (a spot I always avoided looking at whenever I had to drive past) when the British woman's GPS voice announced we were nearing the turnoff to Calvert Springs Road. I activated the left-hand indicator and began to slow down; this simple maneuver seemed to enrage the guy in the car behind me, who leaned on his horn. Ignoring all the personal safety videos we had ever watched – road rage was a real thing in our area – Misaki and I both flipped the guy off as he blew past, clearly in too big a hurry to come back and shoot us both. It was one of those moments I was reminded I was not in Maine anymore, where the biggest road hazard was a moose in mating season.

The house was amazing. It didn't have the long tree-lined drive it deserved – there wasn't enough land between the parkway and the river to allow for that kind of 'English manor house' statement. But it had a stone exterior to die for, and it sat smugly on a professionally landscaped setting, looking precisely like the jewel that it was. The Potomac River was not visible from the front, but I could hear it sloshing about in the background, like a big man in a bathtub. I wondered, as I always do in such circumstances, how much work I would get done if I lived in such a place. The truth is, when I'm writing you could put me in the darkest gulag or the grandest palace and I would not be aware of either. Well, maybe the gulag would smell bad, but other than that I'd be completely content, my head in the clouds. Spending millions on housing, even though I had it to spend, thanks to Claude and Caroline, would have been a complete waste of time and money.

Barb Garman, alerted by the sound of crunchy gravel, came to meet us at the door. Misaki greeted her as an old friend, as no doubt she was, following their successful real-estate transaction. I started to introduce myself and Barb waved away the introduction. 'I know who you are. You're Old Town's famous author, aren't you? Augusta Hawke. Pleasure to meet you. I have read all of your books.'

Whether this was true or not, it certainly set us off on the right foot. Then she said, 'Why do I have a feeling you're not really in the market for a house? This has to do with the real-life mystery practically next door to you, doesn't it?'

This made me wonder many things, including how she knew where I lived. In response to my look of surprise she said, 'I've had my eye on your property for some time. If the city ever gives your place a plaque, you know you can add half a million to the price, don't you?'

Truly, in my fantasies it was twice that amount, but I just nodded. 'Probably won't happen until I die,' I said, hastily adding: 'If at all.'

'Oh, wait until you're my age to have such worries.' In fact, she looked hale and hearty, dressed in what was no doubt a collectible Chanel suit and pearls, with little Ferragamo ballet slippers on her slender feet, and generous swipes of blusher on each cheek. She was developing a bit of a dowager's hump and she was beyond fashionably thin. But she had always been one of those ladies who lunch on tiny servings of caviar, or so I imagined.

'Come on in and tell me everything,' she said, stepping back to allow us into the foyer. This spectacular chandeliered space was only surpassed in grandeur by the great room, which was at a guess thirty feet square, with a coffered ceiling and a floor-to-ceiling stone fireplace and acres of bookshelves. To one side was a little room, specially built to house a grand piano – I say 'little', all things being relative. The great room was decorated in blues and reds and beiges in 'early country squire' fashion, with flourishes here and there harking back to the Renaissance. I told myself it was ostentatious, unimaginative and over the top. I also told myself I was just jealous.

Barb had us settle onto a plush, overstuffed couch near the fireplace, and began dragging over a queen-like throne for herself. I jumped up to assist, which really seemed to annoy her.

'I can do it,' she snapped.

OK. I submerged like a whale back into the red couch, with its matching tasseled pillows, and passed a few moments wondering why office chairs couldn't be this comfortable, my eyes scanning the array of photos lining the walls. Most of them were professional shots containing various combinations of a very young child with his parents, or with sets of grandparents from one side or the other. In most of his baby photos he wore a bow tie. Adorable.

Fleetingly I thought of my abandoned manuscript, feeling almost as if Caroline were back at the house waiting impatiently for me to set her in motion again, but I reminded myself I actually had my editor's leave to pursue the current situation. I supposed before long I should let my agent in on what was happening with my career. Perhaps I would leave that for Julia. After all, this was her bright—

'She wouldn't let me take down the photos,' Barb said, following the drift of my gaze. 'The grandmother, I mean, the long, tall blonde. The incredible hulk is her husband. It's a mistake to leave personal stuff out during a showing, but you can't order people about, even when it's for their own good.'

'Especially then.'

'You were going to tell me how you fit in to this,' prompted Barb. 'Why you're here.' Misaki stood and began perusing the bookshelves, pulling out gilt-edged volumes and leafing through their pages, as fascinated as I was by the opulence. The next time I looked, she'd disappeared somewhere into the bowels of the mansion, from which squeals of 'Oh, my God!' could be heard trailing down the stairs and through the various and sundry hallways. At one point I heard her say, 'Jesus Christ! A gift-wrapping room!'

'You're quite right,' I told Barb. I assumed since she knew Misaki she didn't find her wanderings alarming. 'I live positioned so that I see the—'

'Cedar walk-in closets! His and hers. And what the fu—'

'We can hear you,' I shouted in her general direction.

'Sorry,' she shouted back.

Turning again to Barb, I started to resume my tale, but the interruptions had reminded me.

'Look . . .' I said. 'If anyone should ask, I'm here to view the house, and that's it. All right?'

'Anyone like the police, you mean?'

For a split and deeply paranoid second, I wondered if she'd been talking with Narduzzi. 'Um, yes.'

'You're not investigating, not even unofficially, right?'

'No, I am not,' I said. 'Not really.'

'You're not thinking of putting it into a book or something?'

'Not at present, even though everything I do ends up in my books, in completely unrecognizable forms. Here, in this instance, I am merely a concerned and interested civilian.'

'Me too,' she said, in a cut-to-the-chase way. 'So, you can see into the patio of the Normans. Anything happening on that patio?'

Somehow the conversation was going in the wrong direction. Barb was supposed to be answering *my* questions. But I figured, give a little to get a little.

'I gained the impression they weren't always happy with each other,' I said vaguely. Surely, Narduzzi couldn't hold such an innocuous comment against me. 'But what couple can say it's pure bliss, all day every day?'

'Half of my business is divorcing couples suddenly finding themselves needing a place to live. There's nothing you can tell me about the human condition, at least that particular facet of it.'

'Of course, you would be almost like a marriage counselor, wouldn't you?'

'Only when I can't avoid it. Some women – and men – just can't see the writing on the wall until it's too late. Now, when Zora bought their place in Kildare Place – stupid name, I've always thought – there was no sign of a problem. She was going to be a bride, and it was all lace this and satin that and who was making the cake. She really was a pretty girl. Too pretty for her own good.'

'What do you mean?'

'I mean the usual. Men, of course. You can hide that you're rich, but you can't hide that you're pretty.'

'Did her parents come with her?'

'Sure they did. It was their money.'

'And he wasn't there? Niko?'

'I never had the privilege,' she said. 'I noticed the mortgage company later put his name on the deed with hers.'

'Isn't that unusual?'

'Not really, no. It mostly happens with couples who – for

one reason or another – have a financial imbalance. Meaning, one of them has money and the other doesn't. One can qualify for the mortgage and the other can't. Or it simplifies things to let only one of them qualify. This case was unusual in that it was a cash deal and the parents were paying. Zora's parents. I've seen it all in this business, but I've not often seen it happen when the woman is days away from being a bride.'

'You might say it's rather controlling behavior on the part of Zora's parents. Not to let Niko and Zora sort out their own financing.'

'You might say that.' She had slipped into discreet real-estate agent mode, where it doesn't do to gossip about good clients. I could tell the no-gossip rule was killing her, though. It takes one to know one, after all. One good push and over she'd go. I thought a moment before trying another tack.

Scattered on a large glass coffee table between us were various sales materials concerning the house – brochures and a glossy one-page summary of the wonders of the place.

'What a gorgeous home,' I said conversationally. 'Why on earth are they selling? Don't tell me: another divorce.'

'No,' she said, evasion in her voice. 'They just found another place they like better.'

'A better place than this is hard to imagine,' I said. 'Perhaps they should see if Blenheim Palace is available.'

One photo highlighted the back yard. It had a rectangular concrete patio holding the requisite furniture and outdoor grill. It was clear from the shape and placement that was where the swimming pool had been. Clear to me, anyway, because one of the neighbors at Kildare Place had filled in their swimming pool with concrete in a similar fashion, building in its place a sort of Italianate veranda, complete with overhead fan. I thought it was a terrible waste, especially during the sweltering summers for which the area is known, but some people just don't want the hassle of the upkeep of a pool. Anyway, once done, there was almost no undoing it. The jackhammering alone would take weeks and destroy everyone's last nerve.

'There used to be a pool in back, it looks like,' I said.

She hesitated before answering. 'You're *sure* you're not a prospective buyer? Even a little bit interested?'

I shook my head. 'I could maybe swing it, but it's really too much house for me.'

'I just want to make sure. It turns people off, so even though I feel obliged to say something, it's not the first thing I bring up.'

Wondering what in the world she was talking about, I simply looked straight at her and waited for more.

Finally, she said, 'You're right – that was a swimming pool in back. They had a grandchild, a little boy. He drowned.' She waved a blue-veined hand in the general direction of the photo wall and took a deep breath. 'He drowned in the pool, last summer. He was here visiting with his parents – there's a two-bedroom apartment downstairs kept ready for them. The little boy was just at the age where he could not only walk but climb out of his crib and crawl his way up the stairs. They knew about the crib-climbing, of course, but I don't think anybody was aware how fast he was learning. What a little athlete he would have . . . Anyway, he loved swimming, even though someone still had to hold him aloft while he paddled, you know. He loved that pool. And one night . . . One night he made his way out there. One of the French doors had blown open.' She vaguely indicated the area to her left. 'He just wanted to play, you know. He'd spent all afternoon out there with his parents and grandparents and he loved it.'

I was pressing my fingers hard to my lips as I listened to this appalling story, my eyes wandering as of their own volition to the three French doors to the patio outside, where concrete filled the big hole in the ground, an attempt to bury the family's grief. And to prevent any similar disaster in the future.

It was too easy for a tragedy like that to happen. I wondered if some memory like that had prompted my neighbors to prefer a veranda to a pool.

'Can you imagine?' said Barb.

I shook my head, appalled that my offhand comment had uncovered such a horrible event. I didn't recall reading about anything like it in the news, but I wouldn't necessarily, if it had happened while I was traveling or on deadline, lost in the sort of fugue state I entered during deadlines.

'I don't know what I'd do if I lost my Greg,' she continued. 'At that or any other age.'

Greg being her son, now I was reminded of the name. He was perhaps not a match to his mother in selling real estate, but probably he was her pillar as she aged. She sat in her throne-like chair, feet together and hands folded in her lap, her curly hair dyed an unapologetic red, looking for all the world like a twenty-first-century Elizabeth I.

The whole familial thing was putting me in mind of Zora's child, Harry. Was there anything a parent wouldn't do to protect her child from harm? I wondered exactly what had prompted Zora to make sure Harry was safely in the care of his grand-parents. Did she sense he was in danger? Or did there simply emerge a last-minute need to free herself from childcare for the day? I still found it hard to believe she would just leave him and abscond permanently, unless she'd found herself and her husband embroiled in something completely nefarious.

Something dangerous. What was I even thinking? That she and Niko had fallen victim to some drug cartel? That kind of thing, as they always say when things go wrong, just doesn't happen in Old Town. At least not that often. There were gangs in the West End but, for the most part, they didn't venture east for a night out. Unless the drug trade was going better than I thought, they probably couldn't afford it.

Zora didn't seem to have given her mother any indication that Harry would be with her for longer than a day. But why the excuse of the phony doctor's appointment?

Maybe it spoke to her relationship with her parents. I still thought their intervention in her real-estate matters – not to mention, in her marriage – was a bit over the top, even for millionaires used to having their own way. She was a grown woman, after all.

'You won't repeat any of that,' said Barb. 'It's water under the— oh, God. I mean, it's history now and it needs to stay in the past. The new owners won't want that kind of atmosphere hanging over the house, and certainly the present owners just want to get away from the memories.'

I was waving my hand during this little speech as if to say, Don't even think about it. 'Of course, I won't say a word.'

Misaki came into the room just then, still agog. 'There's a two-bedroom apartment downstairs,' she said.

'Yeah, I know,' I said.

'With a bath, a kitchenette, and a little sitting room with a fireplace. It's completely private to the rest of the house. A burglar could live there for weeks with no one noticing. Like something out of *Parasite*. It's amazing. You should have a look while we're here.'

'We should go,' I said, freeing myself from the plush embrace of the sofa. It was disorienting to stand, as if I expected the air surrounding me to be as soft and cushiony, as supportive. I staggered a bit. The shock of Barb's revelation had probably done something to my blood sugar.

Misaki was quick to catch the shift in mood in the room. 'I'll meet you at the car then.'

'Join you in a minute,' I said.

As I heard the door close behind her, I said to Barb, 'Again, no worries. It's not my business anyway, and I'll stay out of it. I wonder if you will be hearing from Zora's parents. The longer this goes on, the more the question is going to be what happens to their house.'

She shrugged. 'That's a question for the legal brains to haggle over. I'm sure the child gets the house, perhaps in trust to the grandparents until he reaches maturity. But we're forgetting Niko has an interest in this, too. Do you know anything about his family?'

'No, and it's a very good question. He may have been alone in the world apart from Zora and Harry. I haven't heard that he has any relatives hounding the police for answers as to his whereabouts.'

'You're speaking of him as if he is in the past tense,' she pointed out.

'I know. He may very well be out there alive in the world, and so may she. Let's hope so, at any rate.'

'Good luck finding out,' she said. 'Do me a favor and let me know what you learn. And do spread the word about how gorgeous this place is. I'm tired of sitting alone out here all day.'

I left her to her queenlike solitude, thumbing through one of her expensively printed brochures as if looking for typos. I had a feeling there would not be a lot of takers for the mansion on Calvert Springs Road.

TWENTY-THREE

'That house,' said Misaki, fastening her seat belt as I climbed into the driver's seat. 'It speaks to how the rich are different, doesn't it? I mean, she can't afford to pay someone to wrap gifts for her? She needs a whole room to wrap gifts in? With little built-in rods to hold the rolls of paper, like in a department store, and built-in shelves of transparent drawers full of ribbons of all colors? Or maybe she pays someone to come to the house and wrap the gifts. Who gives that many presents anyway, except maybe at Christmas?'

I turned on the engine. 'I guess it falls into the category of harmless hobby. It could be worse. She could be a gun collector.'

I navigated the car towards the exit.

'There's no pool,' Misaki continued. 'No tennis court either.'

'Too busy wrapping presents to play tennis,' I said.

It seemed cruel of me to let her prattle on about that ridiculous house. I was very much aware I had just promised not to say a word about the drowning, so I was feeling torn. I'd just sworn an oath to practically a complete stranger, and Misaki was my friend. But it didn't seem like a promise I should break immediately, before the car had even cleared the short drive. I changed the subject.

'When we get home, I'll get the train-ticket reservations sorted and find us a place to stay. I hope we don't have too much trouble; it's a popular time in that part of the world. We—' Just then my phone rang. I'd left it on the Jeep's console. It was Kent.

'I was wondering what happened to him,' I said to Misaki. 'Maybe he heard something from his police source. I'll call him after we get back.'

My agent also rang as I was driving. It's illegal (at long last) to use a cell phone while driving in Virginia, so I sent her to voicemail. Perhaps Holly had spoken with my editor and was wondering what was up and was I crazy. I doubted very much she'd be keen on my taking a leave of absence from a successful series for a hypothetical true-crime book. After all, at this point there was no solution to the crime; I could only write pages of questions that remained unanswered.

Besides, there was the pesky matter of a signed contract for the series and the already deposited advance on royalties, which I didn't particularly want to return.

I dropped Misaki off at the corner of Fendall and Federal before deploying the garage door opener and driving the Jeep inside. This maneuver always required nerves of steel. More than once, I had driven the wheelie bins straight into the drywall and had to have the wall repaired at $400 per episode. I really needed to widen the space by taking down the sagging shelves on the left, which mainly served to hold cardboard boxes of my author copies. After so many books, I was fast outgrowing the limited storage area. For all I knew, those boxes contained only mildewed, ruined tomes of yesteryear. It was high time I had a look.

Despite my need for more storage, the Petit Trianon down the road held little appeal. I liked being in the center of things in Old Town, within walking distance to everything. At least in theory. I liked knowing all the restaurants and art exhibits were right outside my door, even if I didn't take nearly enough advantage of them.

Would working on a true-crime book get me out of the house more often? Question answered: It already had. I had exited the world of make-believe and was by necessity out in the real world, asking questions and generally poking my nose in. And I liked that. Surely my agent would understand. Why I hesitated to simply tell her flat out what I wanted to do was that she might worry I was upsetting a stable applecart filled with golden delicious apples, to stretch a metaphor. I liked Holly Wilkes – she was young and ambitious and smart and hardworking, and I didn't want to go out of my way to tick her off.

As I was pulling into the garage, the twin Ryan boys emerged from next door, each carrying plastic bats and balls, no doubt on their way to the nearby children's playground. By the time I came out of the garage, their mother had joined them.

'Hi, Mollie.'

'Hi.' She aimed a smile in my general direction in her slightly distracted way. With three kids – twin five-year-olds and a thirteen-year-old girl – I'd be distracted, too. She always looked as if she'd applied her makeup under the flickering lights of a Motel Six bathroom.

'Quite a lot of excitement we've had lately,' I commented neutrally, as if remarking on the weather. Nonetheless, she glanced nervously down at the boys in case the next words out of my mouth were 'murder' and 'kidnapping'. This was another of the weird artifacts of being a crime writer. No one entirely trusted you not to lose your shit at any given moment. I nodded to show my understanding of the need for discretion.

'The police came to see me,' piped up one of the boys. I could never tell the twins apart and had given up trying. Bright red hair, bright blue eyes, matching bright yellow polo shirts.

'They did,' Mollie agreed. 'Peter here asked Detective Narduzzi and Sergeant Bernolak to show ID before he'd talk to them.'

I laughed, thinking how much Narduzzi would have loved that. Mollie's chest inflated with maternal pride.

'Peter, that was exactly the right thing to do,' I said. I leaned over, hands on knees, in that awkward posture we adopt when we talk to children, as if they were tiny imbeciles. 'Were you able to help the police?'

Yes, I was reduced to this. I was interrogating a five-year-old to find out what he knew. After all, the back of the Ryan house directly overlooked the Normans'. I was not going to let this opportunity pass me by.

Paul hung back shyly behind his brother. It was clear Peter was to be the spokesperson for their little brotherhood of two.

'I asked him where was the cat and he didn't know,' said Peter contemptuously, vastly disappointed, as any taxpayer might be. 'Police should know.'

'Cat?' I said mildly.

'The people had a cat.' *Obviously*. 'Who is feeding the cat?'

Fucked if I knew. I looked at his mother.

'The Normans had a cat,' she said. 'We could see it from our window out the back, you know. Peter is worried about it. I told him the police would take it somewhere safe.'

Peter shook his head vehemently at this naïve faith of his
mother's.

'I saw the cat, after. It was dark.'

I took a moment to try to process this, the way a five-year-
old would process such a situation. It was not a far stretch for
me: I remembered with stunning clarity being five years old
and my frustration with adults who simply could not or would
not listen and understand what I was trying to say.

'The cat was dark?' I asked. He shook his head.

'Not all of it.'

'It was a calico,' his mother offered.

'Didn't mean the *cat*.'

Again I struggled to keep up, and clearly he wasn't going to
help me. I looked behind him at his brother Paul. He looked
so terrified, I quickly withdrew my gaze. What was it with these
two? What were they trying to tell me?

'You mean it was dark outside.'

Peter's *Duh!* went unsaid, possibly because his mother was
there and without question he had been taught to be polite to
adults. With the possible exception of the police.

'You saw the cat outside, in the dark, after the people were
gone,' I said.

He nodded.

I straightened up to look at his mother. This was inching
dangerously close to a full-on discussion of a police case, and
Mollie looked suitably concerned.

'We should go,' she said. 'I like to get them exercised well
before dinner so they have time to clean up. Bye now.'

She sort of bundled them off. Peter and Paul trailed behind
her, their heads together in what I was sure was a familiar
configuration. Only Paul – or was it Peter? – stole a glance
back at me over his shoulder.

Thoughtfully – full of thought – I let myself into the house.

Upstairs in the living room, I flung my purse on a chair and
went to get some iced tea from the fridge. The heat of the day
had crept up on me; I thought about taking a shower before I
began packing my bag for the next day.

First I had to get the train tickets and things sorted. And I needed to walk Roscoe. And give his sitter a call, speaking of sitters. Chelsea, a local bartender, usually sat with him when I was gone. If she wasn't available at this late notice, I'd have to bundle him off to the kennel. Another chore added to my list.

I decided to call Kent as Roscoe and I headed out of the house to the dog park.

'It took you long enough,' he said in greeting.

'You're the one who's all worried about the phones being tapped.' *Which is absurd, by the way*, I didn't add, because I was no longer sure it was.

'I know. I don't have time to meet in person. We'll have to take the risk.'

'What? You have something?'

'I finally got in touch with . . . you know. The woman I told you about. The one who might know something.'

'The Irish one?'

He shushed me. 'Keep your voice down.'

'We're on the phone, for God's sake. Anyway, what about her? Does she know something? Does she have a name yet?'

'Sure, it's, um . . . It's better you don't know her name. Anyway, she says they found a footprint on the marble floor of the entryway of the house in question. A shoeprint.'

'With you so far.'

'A two-dimensional print. Not latent, but visible.'

'Got it.'

'OK. Are you ready? You're gonna love this. The shoeprint is from a male – going by the size and make – and it's not a match for anything in the closet of the people's place.'

'For God sake, Kent, just speak in plain English, will you?'

'The footprint is from a Nike sneaker and – wait for it, this is so great—'

'*Kent.*'

'It's too large to be a shoe belonging to Niko. They did analysis of the dirt left by the person in the house who should not have been in the house, if you follow. The shoeprint, made by dirt on the shoe, has plant matter in it. And they're working to compare the plant matter with the plants in the area where the car was found.'

'You're kidding. So they may have evidence of someone tied to the dumpsite being in the house. This could mean whoever it was scouted out the dumpsite before coming to the house or he returned from the dumpsite for some reason and walked around the house. Maybe looking for something. What do you think?'

'I think you're thinking the way I'm thinking about the matter.'

'If you don't quit talking like that, I'm going to hang up.'

'I was just getting ready to hang up anyway, so I don't care.'

'Anything else?'

'They're also looking at some unique wear patterns on the shoeprint.'

'OK. Great. Any fingerprints in the house that didn't belong there?'

'None that couldn't be accounted for – at least, so far. I'll let you know when she gets back to me with more. And you, what are you finding out?'

What was I finding? Damn all, really. I had talked to a real-estate agent and been told an absolutely tragic story about an accidental drowning that would haunt me probably for the rest of my life. I had learned the name of the Normans' babysitter and was headed out on a probably fruitless trek to Mystic, Connecticut, to see if I could find her somehow and talk to her in person. The only thing I had that resembled a lead was a missing cat.

'Ask your friend about the cat.'

'What cat?'

'The Normans apparently had a cat. It's gone missing.'

'What's your source for this information?'

This was, I supposed, where I must tell him, in the spirit of full disclosure, that my source was a rather know-it-all five-year-old. Somehow I didn't feel that would carry much weight.

'The neighbors. The neighbors say they had a cat. I never saw it. It must've hung out in a different room.'

'Come to think of it, there's a cat tree thing in one corner of their living room. I saw it on the crime-scene photos. From what I recall, you wouldn't have been able to see it from your place.'

'Wait a minute. You've seen the crime-scene photos?'

'Sure I have.' A beat. 'Maybe you should keep that under your hat.'

'I wish you could untell me that you've seen those photos. Do you have any idea how much trouble Bernadette or whatever would be in if that got out?'

If it were possible to hear someone shrug over the phone, I would swear he was shrugging. Too bad for her if she got sent down the river. I was also concerned that a loose cannon like this woman was allowed near a crime scene. But I sure as heck wasn't going to call Narduzzi and let him in on this. That was one twist of the pretzel too many.

'And you . . . you could lose your PI license over this.'

The pause went on long enough that I added, 'You do have a PI license, don't you?'

'Of course, I do,' he said, his voice ringing with self-righteousness. 'It would be illegal for me to operate without one.'

I did not want to explore the hierarchy of illegalities as stored in Kent's mind. I just did not.

'OK. I mean, not OK. I'm agreeing to nothing. I know nothing about nothing, OK? Especially photos. But I wonder where the cat went to?'

'I doubt it matters. Look, I've gotta run. Let me know if you hear anything.'

And he was gone, leaving me staring at my phone. Roscoe meanwhile was urging me to walk faster. He did not fool me for a minute. He was hoping his little girlfriend would show up. I should say his big German shepherd of a girlfriend, Sadie. But I had things to do, things to ponder, things to pack.

'You've seen the cat, haven't you?'

He did this endearing thing where he cocked his head, trying to understand.

'That's why you've been barking at odd hours. You've seen the cat.'

TWENTY-FOUR

The next day, Misaki and I took an Uber to the Old Town station to catch the train to Mystic, which was scheduled to leave at the ridiculous hour of 5.48 a.m.

'There was no train later in the day?' Misaki wanted to know. 'Really?'

'There was but it would get us there at nine thirty at night – too late to do any exploring. Plus, we'd be tired. We need daylight and energy for this investigation.

'Experts say sleep deprivation leads to mistakes. At this rate we'll probably solve the wrong crime.'

'We'll sleep on the train. Come on. If I'm interpreting that garbled racket over the loudspeaker correctly, we'll be boarding soon.'

Luckily, I'd been able to leave Roscoe with Chelsea, who'd be staying over in the guest room. Among my other last-minute instructions, it occurred to me to ask her to feed the cat if it showed up.

'Since when do you have a cat?'

'I don't, not really. There might be one at large in the neighborhood. If you see a calico in my patio, give it some of my canned tuna. Roscoe has taken to barking lately and I wonder if it's the cat he's been seeing.'

While packing things in my shoulder bag, I'd come across the notebook I'd begun with Misaki at the Beanery. I'd been so full of hope that morning, so confident the list would expand to contain a myriad of clues which would solve the case of the missing Normans. I dug out a pen and added 'Cat' to the list. Now I had:

- Babysitter (Mellie Broeder, Amir Deniz – and others?)
- Niko (Masters, Milton, & Duckett)
- Zora's parents
- Cat

After careful thought, I amended the last item to read:

- Cat (calico)

If the cat had a name, I was one hundred percent sure it didn't matter.

I also found this notation:

- Confirm Prufrock's name; how to reach her?

Which had led nowhere. She and her husband had not been in the neighborhood since the Normans' disappearance, but the neighbor who occasionally took in their mail had emailed me her cell number. I'd called and left a message, suggesting I was looking for a babysitter's services: no response. It was a long shot, anyway; I thought Angelique Prufrock could safely be eliminated from our inquiries.

Some train of thought led me to think of Valentina, who 'greeted' visitors at Niko's office. She was a little young for Niko but would that stop him? Besides, I didn't like her, and I wanted her to be involved somehow. Even as I realized that wasn't a very good reason, I added her name: Valentina Pavlova.

We hadn't got too far, I thought, apart from my establishing Prufrock's name was Angelique, not Angela. Anyway, the worst case would be that Misaki and I would have a nice trip to a beautiful part of the world, leaving the crime solving to the professionals. Which of course was as it should be. Just ask Narduzzi.

The Mystic Outdoor Art Festival happened to be running during our stay, which had mightily complicated my search for reservations in a quaint B&B. I'd finally landed on a small mom-and-pop outfit, which had raised its rates for the festival, but the woman I spoke with on the phone was perfectly nice and promised the price included breakfast. It wasn't as if I had a lot of choice at that point, so I gave her my credit-card number. How Misaki was going to feel about being surrounded by arts and crafts was anybody's guess – actually, she would probably hate it – but we weren't there for the photo frames made of yarn and popsicle sticks. I just hoped we could find Trixie if there was a big crowd.

Misaki and I boarded and found two facing seats. We could have driven to Mystic in slightly less time, but that would involve travel on I-95, a hair-raising proposition I avoided on any day, in any weather. Besides, I like train travel, the illusion of freedom it offers as I hand off my travel woes to Amtrak. Let them worry about running out of gas or whatever these things ran on. A bonus was no airline rules about carry-on bags that wouldn't fit in the magically ever-shrinking overhead compartments.

I retrieved my laptop before stowing my bag in the train's overhead. I planned to work on a scene where Caroline was literally up a tree fighting off drug-dealing brigands. Her superior in name only, Claude, was of course nowhere to be seen, off somewhere having a celebratory dinner with his family, oblivious to the danger he'd put Caroline in.

Misaki likewise pulled out her iPad, on which she appeared to be reading a book by a competitor of mine – and weren't they all? I decided to say nothing. It wasn't exactly her fault I didn't have a new book out just yet.

The whole up-a-tree tree situation with Caroline did remind me to tell Misaki about the Normans' cat.

'So it appears to be missing,' I said, rounding off my narrative. 'I had wondered why Roscoe was barking so much. Also wondering if I should be walking him more often to dissipate his nervous energy before someone called Animal Control. I think he was alerting on the Normans' cat.'

Misaki looked unimpressed. 'It's what cats do,' she said. 'They wander off and come back when they think you're appropriately contrite and have upped your food game to lobster thermidor. Especially if it's a male cat.'

'It's a calico, so more likely a female,' I said.

'Whatever. Do you think it's important?'

'I think it's odd. Genevieve never mentioned a cat. Wouldn't Genevieve ask the police about it? Wouldn't she take it in, much like she took in the child?'

'Well, those are two different things, really. I like cats, but it still wouldn't be my first concern ahead of my grandkid.'

'Of course not. But there's something odd,' I insisted. 'The cops must know there's a missing cat – OK, maybe they wouldn't care, but why would Genevieve not mention it?'

'She doesn't know there was a cat?'

'Yeah, or maybe the cops told her not to mention it. It might be the kind of clue they leave out on purpose to weed out false confessions. If someone confesses and claims there was no cat in the house and, especially, no cat hair or cat paraphernalia like that cat tree, they can eliminate him or her.'

'Right.'

'It could have something to do with forensics, as well,' I added. 'You can't be in a room where a calico's been and not emerge with cat hair clinging to your clothing.'

'OK, that all makes sense. Maybe it just escaped out the front door, especially if there was some kind of ruckus. Do you really think it's important?'

'If it just escaped, no, but if it was taken, why and by whom?'

'That's trickier,' said Misaki. 'Have you ever tried to steal a cat? Get it to go in a carrier? And again, why? Why would a kidnapper or abductor stop and fuck about with the cat?'

'Beats me,' I said. 'Anyway, it seems to like my patio. It – or *something* – seems to like my patio. So I've told Chelsea to feed it if it comes round. Try to keep it in the neighborhood until we can figure out what's going on.'

She looked at me. 'You're really into this, aren't you?'

'Yeah, I have to admit. I was getting in a bit of a rut, you know? You can't keep writing the same old stuff, sitting at home by yourself day after day.'

'How's it going with the Desperados? Are you still meeting up with them?'

'My grief group?' I nodded. 'Yes, every month. The last time the topic was the dear departed's eating habits.'

'That sounds kind of gross.'

'The topic overall was the pandemic, for those whose husbands were still around during lockdown. Apparently, some of the men's eating habits were the last straw, and their widows use those memories to build an iron cage against their grief. One of them said her husband shoveled food in his mouth like a man with a backhoe. I thought that was pretty funny: I knew exactly what she meant.'

I remembered Genevieve Garnier saying something similar when I spoke with her, that she wanted to push her husband's face in his granola bowl because the sound was more than she could bear some mornings.

'Also, there was the husband who chewed with his mouth open.'

'Deal breaker,' said Misaki. 'Honestly, didn't she share a meal with him before they married? What was it – an arranged marriage?'

'You overlook a lot. It's hard to explain.'

'*That* you don't overlook.'

The backhoe eater had died suddenly of a heart attack. The open-mouth chewer had been a suicide.

'One woman swears her husband could practically unhinge his jaw to eat large mouthfuls. He died on the beltway – lost control of the car while wolfing down a Big Mac.'

'Like a snake swallowing live poultry.'

'That's actually a myth they can do that – the unhinged thing. Anyway, did your ex have no flaws?'

'Oh, yes. But I didn't need a grief group to help me learn to despise him. Divorce is different.'

'I'll bet,' I said. 'Anyway, overall the Desperados are making progress, if in fits and starts – a bit of backsliding only to be expected, like in an AA group. At this point, even the ones who have moved on are afraid to quit in case they regress.'

'How long have you been going now? Two years?'

'Closer to three. I started right after Marcus died. A grief counselor sent by the police after his accident turned me onto it, and it really has been a lifesaver. It's been the same group for the past year now. Initially we let in newcomers, but at some point that stopped. Eight grieving women seems more than enough. Buying boxes of facial tissues would get to be too expensive otherwise, even though we take turns hosting, like a book club. Sometimes lately we laugh more than we cry, but some of these women have been through hell.'

'Worse than you?'

'I'd say so. Yeah. I try not to be judgy, even though you have to wonder why they put up with what they put up with – I mean, sometimes they suspected what was going on but the state of denial was total. One woman found out via the autopsy on her husband after he killed himself that he had had a vasectomy she knew nothing about. They'd been trying for years to have a child and she couldn't figure out what was wrong.'

'Wow. Now, to give her credit, that would be hard to guess.'

'We're trying to encourage her to learn to hate his guts. But hatred takes a long time to harden. And personally I don't know when forgiveness arrives.'

'Speaking from experience,' said Misaki, 'it takes years. And I only went through a prolonged divorce.'

'One of the women – I'll call her Alice; the group is supposed to be anonymous – Alice always says it's not a question of forgiveness, it is a question of how often she was going to let the same person hurt her again. Words to that effect. Because he will come back – the person who hurts us – only in a shape and form we won't recognize. He'll be tall where the other person was short, round where the other was thin, that kind of thing, but the same *type* of person will come back. Always, according to, erm, Alice.'

I could picture her clearly, the woman whose real name was Iris, a woman always so fastidiously dressed it was impossible to picture her in the throes of passion or any other throes. But it was obvious she had been desperately in love with her husband.

'Your mind wants to be ready,' I concluded. 'To be prepared. It doesn't want you to forget, and that's a good thing. I agree with her.'

Still, I wondered if this was why I still couldn't bring myself to erase Marcus's messages on our landline's answering machine. Did I want to remember? Or was I afraid I'd forget?

'A bit of a stumbling block to dating but, yeah, I get it,' said Misaki. 'I get why people would feel that way. Also, if someone does something unforgivable, those people can't walk around expecting to be forgiven. But they do, especially the narcissists. So, yeah. The push–pull brain gymnastics. Love slash hate.'

'Forget what religion teaches. It's self-defense, and self-defense is a good thing.'

Quietly she said, 'You miss him. Marcus.'

I nodded and looked away, as if something had appeared out the window that didn't look like row after row of people living in poverty. 'Like crazy, yeah. He was always just there. And one day he wasn't. It's not just that I miss him when the garage-door opener doesn't work, stuff like that. For that I can call a handyman. It's more having someone to talk to at night. Heck, even someone to watch TV with, someone to shout at the screen with.'

'Try Match.com.'

'No.' After a pause I said, 'Everyone hates being alone. Me, I'm not afraid of dying alone. I'm afraid of living alone. And sometimes . . .' I couldn't say the thought aloud. Sometimes the only thing keeping me going was my writing. Not just sometimes, all the time.

'Just remember his annoying habits. Didn't Marcus have any annoying habits?'

'Besides cheating on me, you mean? I don't know. You'd have to ask his girlfriend.'

I'd forgotten to turn off my ringer for the quiet railcar. A call came in and reflexively I sent it to voicemail.

When I listened to the recording, it turned out to be from Angelique Prufrock. Knock me down with a feather. I signaled Misaki and took my conversation into the noisy car.

'Hey!' Angelique answered right away. 'You need a babysitter for your grandchild, is that it?' I hadn't actually said that, but I let her assume, given my advanced age, that's what my babysitter query was about. 'Congratulations,' she added.

I felt increasingly uneasy about the subterfuge, but I let her carry on down the wrong path, gushing about the wonderfulness of babies in general. After all, it was entirely possible my stepson and his wife would produce a child any day now. The chances I would need a babysitter for it, though, approached zero.

'You said in your message you were wondering about Trixie. Look, I can only tell you, I used her once and I will never use her again. I wouldn't have her in my house, to be honest.'

I pulled the phone away from my face to stare at the screen. This was not what I had been expecting. Trixie had been described as a quiet girl, superior to the rogue sitter who streamed expensive movies with her boyfriend. Resettling the phone against my ear, I relayed this impression to Angelique.

'Still waters,' she said. 'Trixie went through my underwear drawer while we were out with friends, can you believe it? It completely creeped me out. It was like having the Golden State Killer in the house.'

'You're sure?'

'I am. And furthermore, there's a bra missing; I paid around $150 for that thing in Paris. I looked for it for ages before I realized what she must've done. So anyway, if you want a recommendation for a good sitter, I'll shoot you a text with a couple of names.'

I allowed her to think she was being helpful, and that I was eternally grateful for those names and for her time. Which I was. I felt awful that I used to call her Princess Prufrock, now she was being so nice about the grandchild and all.

'Sorry I took so long to call you,' she said. 'I cover Wall Street for the *Journal* and it's been crazy, as I'm sure you know.'

So that's what she was doing all this time. I really should have given her more credit and I was duly abashed. I thanked her profusely for her time, apologizing for the interruption, before I rang off. Whatever kind of brain it took to write for the *Wall Street Journal*, it was the kind of brain I didn't have.

Putting away the phone, I noticed I'd missed an earlier call from Kent. I rang him back.

'I tried you earlier,' he said. 'Where are you?'

'Nowhere I can talk,' I said. 'But I've got no news, anyway. Do you have something for me?'

'Yeah. Remember the plant matter I told you about – the stuff they found in the shoeprint? It's checking out. Forensics are nearly certain that whoever was standing in the entryway also had visited the place where the car was found abandoned.'

'They could run the tests that fast? That's terrific. Even better, you're no longer talking like you're in a spy movie. I could actually follow your meaning there.'

'I keep forgetting. Anyway, they're working flat out to get any kind of result. Shannon says all other cases are being pushed aside; all hands are on deck for this one.'

'You're really going to have to sort out this woman's name. Seriously, Kent. You just can't—'

'Do you want to hear this or not? What they've found is moss or lichen or something – don't ask; there's a Latin name for it – but whatever it is, it's extremely rare in this area, so the fact they found a match is a big, big deal to the case. It's nearly proof positive – once they catch the guy.'

'But they're no nearer knowing whose shoeprint it was.'

'It doesn't sound like it. The whole investigation must otherwise be dead in the water if they're that excited about moss. Even unassailable evidence is meaningless without a suspect.'

'And there's no suspect in sight.' I sighed. 'The shoeprint suggests he had help. Or she did. Or they did. If Zora and Niko did this together, with a third party helping, I can't even guess at a motive.'

'*Cherchez* the money, I always say. But where is he? Where is *she*?'

'What did your friend say about the cat?'

'Crap,' he said. There was a pause and I could picture him smacking his forehead. 'I actually forgot to ask her. We got sort of busy. It doesn't matter, does it? Cats do cats.'

It was getting harder to believe anyone would hire Kent as an investigator. 'I guess it doesn't matter,' I said. 'Just a loose end. Look, speaking of which, I gotta go work on my book now. Talk about loose ends! *Really*, I mean it. I'm so far behind.'

'Me, too,' he said. 'The writing life, eh? And to think people envy us.'

'Crazy, I know. They say the neon lights are bright. Anyway, thanks for keeping me in the loop. Call when you know something. And for heaven's sake, find out this policewoman's name.'

'It's kind of awkward to ask now.'

'Goodbye, Kent.'

TWENTY-FIVE

I did manage to get some writing done – during the next hours, the manuscript grew by four pages, all of them usable. I also started a new Word document of notes about the Norman case. *Just* in case editor Julia came up with an enticing offer.

Before I knew it, Amtrak's Northeast Regional was crossing the Mystic River, squealing and squawking its way towards the shingle-style station, delayed by over an hour. Misaki and I decided to believe Google's estimate of a ten-minute walk to our inn rather than hope to nab an Uber. The crowds leaving the train suggested there might be a wait.

'Captain's Log, Stardate 1654.8,' said Misaki, as we tugged our wheelies past colonial houses and storefronts. 'Crew's attempts to escape the bonds of Old Town's twee planetoid atmosphere failed.' Her wheelie caught on a cobblestone and she paused to wrench it free. 'Crew now facing starvation. Requesting permission to return to home planet immediately. Jones Out.'

'Stop,' I said. 'I agree Mystic looks like Old Town repotted, but we're not here to sightsee. Didn't you say they have good seafood restaurants?'

'No, I said somewhere this close to the sea should have good seafood. It was a random hypothetical remark. Let's offload our bags at the hotel and get something to eat. No matter how many food-like items Amtrak packs into one of those cheese trays, it's still not food.'

'Food next,' I promised. 'We'll get our room sorted first. The woman on the phone was nice enough, but she did make it clear that this weekend especially the place was in high demand so we needed to be on time.'

'Why "in high demand"?'

Somehow I had forgotten to fill her in on this. 'They're having their annual arts-and-crafts festival this weekend.'

She stopped dead center of the sidewalk, causing a small collision of holidaymakers behind her.

'Arts and crafts? You mean displays of overpriced, poorly executed paintings, and crafts that look like something my grandmother made in the nursing home when she was ninety and losing her eyesight?'

'It's a very famous festival, Misaki. I'm sure it won't be as bad as all that. Besides, remember we are not here for the festival. We are here on a mission. A very important mission to save lives.'

'Captain's Log, Supplemental. The mutinous crew is invoking the name of Captain Bligh, which even the Federation will have to admit is a fair comparison.'

'It'll be fine. Promise.'

'The first stall you stop at selling glazed pottery, I'm on the next train out of here.'

'Promise,' I repeated.

We arrived at the Whale's Inn and were greeted by the 'pop' side of the mom-and-pop business, a man who introduced himself as Elias Biddlecombe. In keeping with the overall nautical theme of his life, Elias had cultivated a sea-captain's beard. The entire place likewise was naval-themed, blue-and-white stripes and anchors wherever you looked, with the occasional red accent pillow and dozens of miniature ships in bottles in case you entirely missed the point you were near the ocean. Misaki grumbled all the way up the rickety wooden stairs to a double bedroom overlooking the river, turning her back on the stunning view as she unpacked. My diagnosis was low blood sugar. Marcus used to get that way, too, and was impossible to live with until he was fed.

'OK,' I said, 'our first port of call is dinner. What does your guidebook recommend?'

'"Port of call". That's it. I'm bailing now.'

'Sorry. The inn's motif does get into the blood.'

'It doesn't get into mine,' she said. 'This is a complete waste of time. We'll find the babysitter kid – *maybe*; did you see the mob out there? – and she'll tell us the Normans were good tippers who never hassled her about her friends coming over to raid the liquor cabinet while they were gone.'

She pulled out her phone and punched some coordinates into a GPS app.

'The Wayward Oyster Restaurant and Bar. *Christ*. What does that even mean? Oysters don't move, do they? I hope we survive long enough to write a review. It's three blocks away and at least it's got four-stars-and-a-smidge ratings. Come on, you can comb your hair later.'

'What's wrong with my hair?'

'Come *on*.'

I knew better than to argue. I reorganized a bobby pin or two as I walked behind her.

It was all comfortingly familiar, just like being with Marcus when his blood sugar crashed.

The Wayward Oyster ranged along the Mystic River, and we were lucky enough to be seated at a table overlooking the water just as the sun was setting. This view seemed to satisfy Misaki as making the entire trip worthwhile. Especially once the drinks and appetizers and a breadbasket arrived.

The food was basic and wholesome, the seafood lightly seasoned and broiled. We only had to ignore the shortcomings of the server, a young man destined for greater things, perhaps a stint of community service. Once our meals arrived, with a clatter of plates and silverware, silence reigned while we dug in. It was fortunately not the type of place that went in for local bands playing loudly in too small a place.

Over coffee, Misaki and I began to map out a strategy.

'I would call Trixie's parents again, hoping for a little guidance,' I said, 'but I'm sure it will absolutely freak them out to think we're here looking for their daughter. Worse, what if they say something to Narduzzi?'

'Our cover story, should he ask, is going to have to be we've developed a sudden passion for arts-and-crafts fairs. You can probably pull this off better than I can.'

'I can indeed. I'll have you know at one point I became somewhat of an expert at latch hooking. I have many fine rugs to show for it. Well, I would have, but I donated them all. I like to think I helped the Red Cross build a hospital somewhere, some war-torn place without water or air conditioning.'

'Latch hooking? What, like occupational therapy?'

'In a manner of speaking, yes. It was either that or take up smoking. Lesser of two evils.'

'For sure.'

'All part of the grieving process. Anyway, it taught me an appreciation for things like embroidery and needlepoint. The patience required is incredible.'

'Not to mention the eyesight. Anyway, where do we start? Mystic, from the map, is split in two by the river. Groton, where we are, is more the tourist draw.'

'Should we each take a side of the river?'

'I think we should stick together on the touristy side.'

'OK,' I said. 'Don't forget, the downtown will be a mob scene. We have to brave it, but talk about a needle in a haystack.'

'I don't know. A teenage girl? Arts and crafts? Will there really be anything to grab her attention?'

'There will be food, like hot dogs and corn on the cob. Maybe if we just stake out the food vendors, we'll see her. And shopping, although maybe not the kind of shopping she'd be interested in. Reproduction candlesticks and real chamber pots.'

'You are stereotyping. Not all teens are shallow consumers with headphones.'

'Hmm. You remember what she looks like?'

'Pixie haircut, pretty. Yes, generally, I do. But in among the tourists . . .' Misaki looked doubtful. 'Funny thing is, they look like the same tourists we left behind in Old Town.'

I looked around the restaurant. 'They do, don't they?'

'It's like they followed us here. I could swear the guy in the red Hawaiian shirt was on the train with us.'

'Maybe they're paid actors who roam from historic village to historic village to make places look popular. Anyway, there's also an aquarium and a living seaport museum. And an arts center.'

'I would have gone for the arts center at her age,' said Misaki.

'I'd have gone for the food. Jeez. Maybe this wasn't such a great idea. She could be anywhere.'

Misaki drained her coffee. Putting down the cup, she said, 'Don't you worry. If she's here, we'll find her. At least we know what the aunt's house looks like, from the Facebook photo.'

'Thank you,' I said. It seemed as though her blood-sugar levels were back where they belonged. She was beaming.

'For what?' she asked innocently, Stardate tantrums forgotten.

'For believing. For letting me drag you up here when I know you have things to do. It's just that I've exhausted all the narrow investigative avenues allowed me by Narduzzi. He'd be within his rights to come down on me like a ton of bricks after warning me to stay out of it. But an innocent trip to an historic village with a friend I can probably explain away.'

'I didn't actually say I'd lie to the police for you,' Misaki pointed out. 'Even though I probably would. Kind of depending.'

'At least we can say – if only to ourselves – we've tried everything we could to find Niko and Zora. That baby needs its parents.'

'If I can help with that, you know I'm in.'

TWENTY-SIX

The next morning, we got an early start. I hadn't been expecting much from the Whale's Inn's complimentary breakfast, nor did I need anything after the size of the meal at the Wayward Oyster the night before, but it was a surprisingly tempting array of home-baked bread and pastries, fresh-cut fruit, and aromatic coffee served buffet-style in the small dining area. Ladder-back chairs, possibly antique, surrounded individual round tables, the tops made of ships' wheels encased in acrylic; I suspected the fine hand of the innkeeper in their creation.

I filled my plate as I waited for Misaki to finish dressing, telling myself I needed fuel for the day ahead. Who knew when or if we could break for lunch, after all?

'So, what brings you here?'

It was Elias, our innkeeper, pulling out a chair and sitting down opposite me.

'We're here for the arts and crafts. My friend and I just love events like this.'

'Most years I buy a booth to sell my carved whales,' he said. 'Not this year. Too busy. Ever since they lifted the pandemic restrictions, we've been run off our feet, me and the wife. You were lucky to get a last-minute cancellation.'

'So I'm gathering,' I said. 'The crowds were pretty thick when we arrived and the festival hasn't even opened yet.'

'More than two miles of arts and crafts,' he assured me. 'Hundreds of artists. Folk come from all over.'

'Two miles? My friend will be so excited. I hope there's pottery.'

'Like they invented it, yes – lots of pottery. You're from Virginia, right?'

'Northern Virginia,' I agreed, nodding. 'Out of Maine.' I made the 'Northern' distinction because there were certain stereotypes assigned to the region to the south of Old Town.

Northern Virginia was as liberal blue politically as most of the southern regions were conservative red, with precious little purple to separate them. There had long been talk of breaking the state into two legislative pieces, if only for economic reasons – the north trended wealthy; the south had many areas of poverty – much as there was debate in California whether to divide itself into northern and southern parts.

'We get a lot of visitors from your part of the world,' said Elias. 'The train makes it an easy connection. Tell your friends.' He produced a book of matches from his pocket and handed them to me. The cover featured an etching of a whale over his name and website: 'Elias Biddlecombe, Fine Carving and Engraving. BiddleBestCarvings.com'.

'Hmm,' I said. In truth I wanted to focus on my meal, but he was a friendly guy and I liked him. Just then Misaki emerged from upstairs and he offered up his seat. 'No rest for the wicked,' he said. 'Enjoy your stay.'

Couples and families began to emerge from down the stairs and from the hallway leading to the back of the inn. Once Misaki and I finished breakfast we sailed forth (sorry) into the bright sunny day, the humidity offset by cool breezes off the water. I imagined the area would have its share of storms, but be somewhat protected by its tucked-away inland location and by Mason's Island at its base. On maps the island looked like a cork that had floated loose from the mainland.

We made our way to the downtown area, dodging little display tables being set out by shop owners to attract passersby. It was only ten o'clock, but clusters of people were starting to emerge from the various inns in town. There was no parking to be had. Once you got away from the bascule bridge which linked the two parts of Mystic and carried car and foot traffic into Main Street, diversions had been put in place to discourage cars and encourage walking.

This main street was extraordinarily wide – big enough for a landing strip – and had been given over to the festival. The crowds were suntanned and happy, ready to spend money, probably already anticipating lunch in one of the historic downtown restaurants. There were signs for a Children's Art Park, and indeed many families seemed headed that way.

It was soon obvious this was not going to be the pokey homegrown affair of our imaginations. Tented tables had been set out with displays of handmade jewelry and all manner of nautical-themed decorations for sale. Photography was big, as were pottery and woodwork. Our host had a lot of competition in the carved-whale arena.

I was tempted by the pottery at one booth, my hands itching to hold a beautiful, blue-glazed pitcher, but simultaneously I could feel Misaki's judgment, her eyes boring into my back.

'I haven't touched anything,' I told her.

'Keep moving. Eyes straight ahead if they're not in search of a teenager with a pixie haircut.'

'OK, OK.' We were kept to a snail's pace by the milling crowd. I hadn't quite believed Elias when he told me it was two miles of goods on offer, but that began to feel like a conservative estimate. I did indeed keep my eyes open for our quarry, but while there were dozens of girls of approximately the right age, many of them being dragged about by their families, none of them matched the girl slinking her way down a runway in the Facebook photos.

I recalled Angelique's reservations about Trixie. It certainly painted a different picture in my mind, one I didn't particularly like. On the positive side, I was gathering she was a rather sophisticated young woman, and perhaps she would have picked up on any undercurrents in the Norman household. The business with the missing bra was a bit creepy, but it did indicate a certain avid interest in people's sex lives, which knowledge might prove helpful.

At any rate, we'd come too far to give up now. Our train left the next day, creating at least in my own mind a deadline for our return. There were other trains, of course, but it was difficult to see what we might accomplish by adding another day to our trip.

We walked and walked and craned our necks and looked and looked. There were vendors selling wonderful carnival-style foods, including roasted corn, for which I quickly developed a craving. After a couple of hours, I talked Misaki into taking a little break for some bottled water so I could try some of the corn. It was slathered in salted butter, absolutely delicious, and before long much of it had dripped on my white T-shirt. 'Damn,' I said, fruitlessly dabbing at the stain with a paper napkin. 'I'll have to go back and change.'

'I think we should split up anyway. This is not a place where you find unchaperoned teenage girls,' Misaki declared. 'Across the bridge there is some kind of mall. How about if we branch out and meet around three back at the inn? You stay on this side, but maybe get away from the festival. Try the coffee shops.'

I could certainly see her point of view. There were few unsupervised teenagers at the festival; it was all young families and young or retired couples. There weren't even groups of teenagers traveling in sniggering or braying packs.

'I'll see you at three at the inn,' I said. 'Text if you have any luck.'

Back at the inn, I ran upstairs to change my shirt. Room service hadn't yet started, so I didn't interrupt anyone or even see anyone until I reached the front door of the inn.

'There's no problem, is there?' It was Elias. He had a way of appearing without notice, despite the fact that every floorboard I trod on in the place creaked like something from a horror film. I supposed from living there so long he knew which boards to avoid.

'I spilled food on my shirt,' I said laughing. 'Hard to believe I was even hungry after that wonderful breakfast. Be sure and tell Mrs Biddlecombe. I assume it's her cooking.'

'It is,' he said beaming. 'I'll tell her.'

I had pretty much checked out of the conversation, and was scrolling around my phone in that impolite way we have all started to behave in society, when I came across the photo of Trixie's aunt's house which I had saved in my photos app. I looked up and saw Elias watching me. Partly out of embarrassment at my rudeness I said, 'I wonder if you would recognize a house if I showed you the photo?'

'Might do,' he said. 'A house around here? I've lived here most of my life so, yes, let me have a look.'

After a mere glance he said, 'It's the old Morrison place on the river. They order takeout from us occasionally. We offer that service at night, during the slow periods anyway. Like you said, Mrs Biddlecombe is a wonderful cook. Lately the orders out there have doubled. I reckon she has guests.'

'Guests,' I repeated. And that would be Trixie.

I showed him the Facebook modeling photo and asked if he'd ever seen her.

He shook his head 'no'. But at that point I thought he might be getting a bit suspicious of my interest. What I would want with a teenage girl was anyone's guess – some messy custody battle may have flashed through his mind, a battle of the type Niko was supposed to specialize in. An innkeeper sees all sorts, and I couldn't but applaud his caution, if that was what it was. Certainly a strange woman cropping up asking about a young girl might be a bit irregular. I decided not to press it. Surely someone else would know the location of the Morrison house.

I said my goodbyes and practically flew out the door. I had already decided to try the nearby grocery store, another mom-and-pop affair, pretending I was lost. They gave me directions out of town, telling me it was a half-hour walk at best.

'Good thing you're wearing sneakers,' said the woman. 'It's not that easy to get to.'

On leaving the store, the first thing I did was text Misaki. *Eureka!* ☺

She didn't reply but I didn't stay to wait on her. I texted her where I was headed and started walking.

My phone rang as I was crossing the street towards the harbor. It was Chelsea. Eyes swiveling left and right as I walked, I answered.

'Is Roscoe OK?'

'Roscoe is grand. You asked me to call if I saw a cat.'

'A calico cat. Yes. You saw one?'

'I did. Roscoe spotted it first, of course. It dropped into your patio from the top of the wall, and stood about, mewling like a lost soul. I did what you said and got out the tuna for it. I only gave it half the can on a saucer, I didn't want to make it sick with too much.'

'Good. Good thinking. Besides, you'll want the rest for when it comes back – if you can sort of train it to keep coming back, that would be great. Then, if you can throw a blanket over it or something and bring it inside. Do not attempt to capture it without a blanket. It will scratch your eyes out, probably. Best to keep it away from Roscoe of course.'

'No worries. It's a sweet little girl, just hungry and scared. You can tell she's someone's pet. Once I've fed her a couple more times, I know she'll be mine. Cats are fickle, you know.'

'No worse than people,' I said, thinking of Kent. And Marcus. 'Anyway, great news. If you do manage to get it inside, I'll tell Narduzzi.'

Who will want to know how come I know so much about the cat. Darn it. Easy to say the Normans' cat sort of fell into my life, harder to explain how I knew it had potential value for his forensics team.

'Who's Narduzzi?'

'Never mind. The cat is sort of a witness to a crime, that's all.'

'Whatever,' she said.

Spoken like a true bartender. Chelsea had heard it all.

TWENTY-SEVEN

I had to rely on the grocery-store owner's directions rather than use the GPS on my phone. Around these parts, apparently, 'old Morrison place' was the only address one needed, no street name or number required. Also around these parts, so strongly reminiscent of Maine, 'old' could mean centuries old. I imagined even the postal service and UPS had adapted.

'What kind of house is it?' I'd asked the 'mom' of the store. 'I mean, what size?'

'I don't know, do I? I'm not an architect. It looks like all the other houses round here. It's got shingles.'

I was holding up the checkout line by that point, but I was confident she had pointed me just enough in the right direction that I'd have no trouble.

Of course, I got lost a few times along the way and, whenever I was still in a somewhat habited area, I would pop into a shop or a gas station to recalibrate my route. The grocery-store woman had proven to be somewhat vague, if not downright unreliable. She had said to keep the water to my right, which basically meant I should head east, then turn right after the yacht club but before I reached Stonington Road. I never did find the yacht club but eventually I ran smack against Stonington Road, which meant I had to backtrack.

But this was not a simple shoreline, of course – Mystic and surrounds was full of inlets and outlets and harbors and God knew what else, the water threading its way in wherever it saw an opening. Where a road or path might logically lead off towards the kind of solid ground where a person might decide to build a house became increasingly difficult to determine. I quickly reached an area where there was zero human habitation. This told me I was on the right track, but it also told me I had no idea where the Morrison place might be.

I thought about going back and . . . what? Look for Misaki so we could get lost together?

She rang me about five minutes later, wanting to know where I was. Busy freeing myself from some snakelike undergrowth twining round my ankle, it was a question I could not answer.

'I'm lost, actually,' I said. 'I'm looking for something called the old Morrison place. It's the aunt's house, according to our innkeeper.'

'What street is it on?'

'I wish I knew.'

'Are you somewhere I can meet you?'

'I'm not anywhere anyone can ever meet me, actually. It has to be nearby. It's not like there are hundreds of houses and I'm looking for one lousy house. You saw the photo. It's one of those sea captain's houses. Remote. With shingles. It's supposed to be right on the water, on a sort of hill. I've been up and down a few hills by now.'

'Do you have Find a Friend on your phone?'

'I told you I'm not going in for Match.com or any of that stuff.'

'It's a phone app. A GPS-type thing. So that I can see where you are if you give me permission.'

'I have to download it?'

'Yes, you have to download it.'

'I'll try. I'll call you back.'

Opening the App Store was one thing. Downloading the app was another. Minutes passed, the little round downloading symbol moving agonizingly slowly after several dramatic pauses and burps and hesitations. Just when I thought it had stalled out for good: success. I opened the app and was asked for a ton of information I didn't really have time to deal with or think was anyone's business, but I punched it all in, anyway.

Finally, after four tries, it told me it was satisfied with my password, which I am sorry to have to tell you was obscene because by that point I was losing it. Then a series of steps demanded I do this, that, and the other, including click on a link in my email so the thing would know it was me. Who else the fuck would it be? I wondered. I was just remote enough I could get a signal, but it wasn't strong enough for this nonsense. The email was what finally broke me. I tried a few times and gave up.

I called Misaki to tell her it would have to be a solo mission.

'But I'm good,' I assured her. 'If I can't find the place, I'll just backtrack. I have some sense of where I am now.' I looked around. 'I know I've seen these bushes before.'

'Look,' she said. 'Text me if you find the house. Meanwhile, I'll ask around. Other people must know where it is.'

'Just don't believe anyone if they tell you it's an easy walk. Signing off now. Hawke out.'

My Fitbit was probably maxing out in terms of number of steps walked for the day. Possibly my device was being reported as stolen to the people behind the phone app which I used to sync my fitness data, for surely this account had not logged such a trek since its owner had got lost in Rome.

Our lives were so much ruled like this now. I'd forgotten to even worry about the possibility the Russians, for example, were somewhere taking an avid interest in my physical fitness. But all of us were on some big digital spreadsheet in the sky and there was no escape. Even my stepson, who lived off the grid near Vancouver and would rather be impaled than open a Facebook account, was unable to escape the need for a bank account and a team of financial specialists to manage his trust fund, which he'd inherited when his grandfather passed. I avoided any conversation with him suggesting that this was no one's idea of eking out a living off the grid. Pointing out the incongruities of his life, as I saw it, would have added another brick to the wall growing between us.

Estrangement is too harsh a word, perhaps. I would have liked to have been a part of his life but he never encouraged it, by the simple expedient of never returning my texts or phone messages or thanking me for remembering his birthday. My involvement ended when Marcus ended, I got that. Taking the hint, I left him and his wife alone to prepare for the next global disaster. Indeed, the happiest I had known either of them to be was at the start of the pandemic when their opting-out of civilization looked as if it were about to pay off.

I realized I was growing cranky from exhaustion and frustration. I wished I had thought to grab an apple from the breakfast buffet. But I was so confident Misaki and I would have a nice lunch somewhere. Possibly even with Trixie, pumping her for information.

The rather simple and straightforward walk promised by the woman at the grocery store had not materialized, and at some point I realized I was walking in circles. I stopped and listened for an indicator: the sound of traffic, the sound of waves crashing, the sound of the bridge being raised or lowered over the Mystic River, a dog barking, a garbage truck rumbling by. Nothing. I was at the foot of another slight rise in the landscape which could possibly lead to a site for someone centuries ago to have built a house. Or could possibly lead to some desolate space overlooking the water. I'd found a few of those today. It was time to decide – once more into the breach, or head back the way I thought I had come. Using what sunlight shone through the trees as a measure, I could at least know I was heading westward towards civilization.

I had entered a forested area heavily overgrown with under-brush, and I decided to plunge through, do or die. It was possibly the most arduous part of my walking day. But I noticed that some of the underbrush had been broken. Possibly by a human being, possibly by an animal – a large animal – breaking through. I could also hear water – running water, as of a stream, and it was very near. Water always meant civilization nearby, didn't it? I was exhausting my limited scouting and tracking skills, but this was the first sign I'd really seen of something alive apart from myself. So I lurched ahead, grateful to be wearing jeans and not the shorts I'd considered that morning.

I fought against brambles and long grass and soon was rewarded not only by a narrow stream, but by the sight of a roof against the sky. The roof of a house I sincerely hoped was the Morrison place. With renewed enthusiasm I plunged through the untended wilderness, now following the trail of the water. There was no smoke coming from the chimney to indicate anyone was home. But of course, at that time of year and time of day, no one would be lighting a fire.

I could smell success and elatedly I quickened my steps, walking practically straight uphill now, as if I were on a climbing machine at the gym. If there was a road leading to the house, I had approached from the wrong side to use it.

Now I could see a neatly kept yard with an old-fashioned clothesline. Pairs of jeans and shirts lifted in a light summer wind. It was impossible to tell if the clothing was men's or women's. One of the shirts moved and began walking towards the house. Wait. *wait.* I was dehydrated but not hallucinating. It was a large male figure. And it looked like Niko Norman and it walked like Niko Norman.

Because it was Niko Norman.

TWENTY-EIGHT

He hadn't spotted me; I was sure of it. Nonetheless I quickly took cover behind some bushes. It was all I could do not to gasp in shock. Or call out to him, good old neighbor that I was. It was taking my brain a while to catch up. We were not back in Old Town. We were in Connecticut on a rocky outcrop of land where Niko had no business being. Not while all the police forces in the mid-Atlantic states were looking for him, if not all the forces in the entire world. Technically, of course, I had no business being there either, but at least I had a terrific excuse. I wonder what his terrific excuse was, but every instinct told me to shut up and stay hidden.

And go get help.

I was just about to act on this very good suggestion from my brain, doing an awkward maneuver of moving backwards while still on my haunches, like a retreating sumo wrestler. I did this all the while completely forgetting I was on an incline.

Learn from me. If you find yourself in such a situation, it is not going to end well if you are so busy keeping your eye on your quarry, in case he emerges again from the house, that you forget to glance over your shoulder to see where you're going. But I was rewarded when Niko indeed came out of the house again. I pulled my phone out of my pocket. I wanted to call Misaki but didn't dare risk it. By the same token, explaining any of this to the police with a call that might be overheard was out of the question.

I texted her:

I found Niko.

I was about to expound on this when a female emerged from the house. Had she seen me from one of the upstairs windows?

I did a quick dive for cover, and as I did so I lost my footing. My phone flipped out of my hand, landed in the stream, and sank without a trace beneath the water.

This would have been a good time to get the hell out of there but I had to know. The woman kept her back turned but surely it was Trixie? From that gliding walk, from her posture.

She never looked in my direction. Apparently, my camouflage as a harmless woodland creature was working. She said something to Niko and they both laughed.

But what was Niko doing here? With an empty-headed and possibly sex-crazed teenager, no less.

Perhaps I had just answered my own question.

Who better to help you with a nefarious plan, though? Someone young and malleable he could bend to his will, someone whose aunt owned a remote cottage, perfect to use as a hideaway. I briefly stopped to wonder how long this unholy union would last. The silly romantic girl and a man I was coming to think had a streak of ruthlessness a mile wide.

I couldn't get a good look without blowing my cover, but it occurred to me: it might even be Zora. If I were going on the run, the first thing I would do would be to cut my hair. Even the sacrifice of those long, gorgeous locks would seem worth it if she were facing a prison term for any of this. Although what the charge would be was anyone's guess. The police couldn't even get her for filing a false report, although they probably could get both of them for wasting police time and resources.

I couldn't be one hundred percent certain it was Zora. The short stature, the curvy build were the same. I had to get closer to find out what was going on. But did I dare risk it?

Together they took the laundry off the line and went back inside. It was the break I needed to get closer to the house without thrashing about too much, alerting them I was there.

My head was still spinning with the possibilities. I had been so certain Zora would never leave her child, even in the capable hands of her mother. If this person was Zora, none of this matched what I thought I knew of her, which I now realized wasn't much. But surely her plan was to retrieve the child at some point. What Niko's plan was was anyone's guess.

Was Genevieve in on it? I would have bet against it; nothing in her behavior suggested anything except a woman frantic to find her daughter.

And Trixie? How did the babysitter fit into this? Even a

light-fingered babysitter, as I had been told she was? It was a large step from petty pilfering – I wouldn't even go so far as to call it theft – to involvement in an abduction or kidnapping scheme.

Maybe she was in the house – if she was here at all. Misaki and I had no one's word she was with her aunt except her mother's word, and she too clearly was reluctant to talk about her daughter at all. It wouldn't be a stretch to think she might have misled us, never dreaming we'd come up here to have a look for ourselves. I was beginning to suspect everyone, and that was starting to look like a good strategy.

A car was parked by the side of the house. It wasn't a car I recognized, and I assumed it belonged to the occupant of the house, who I still assumed was Aunt Lily. I had again made up my mind to go for help when the pair reemerged. A cheeping sound indicated one of them had unlocked the doors of the car.

I decided I really needed to get a closer look at the license plate. Softly, softly, I crept towards the house, going as fast as I could manage, afraid they would drive out of sight before I could get there. My foot slipped on the slimy bank and caught in a gnarled tree root.

My ankle gave out, an event I unwittingly broadcast with a startled cry and a splash as I landed in the water.

Niko heard it.

His head swiveled in the direction of the sound. He had been carrying a shopping bag and he dropped it, running to investigate, shouting at the woman to stay put.

There was no escape. I tried my weight on the foot and it wouldn't hold for a second. The pain was agonizing, even though I suspected it wasn't broken – I hadn't heard anything like a 'snap' as it went. It was probably just a bad sprain, but no matter; either way I wasn't running or walking anywhere. I would have to throw myself on their mercy.

Niko, coming closer, sliding down the hill to the river, obviously recognized me. I could see the moment when his face hardened. He came splashing through the water to where I'd fallen to drag me to shore.

I tried on a smile – worth a try. 'Niko!' I said delightedly. 'What are you—'

'Come on,' was all he said, twisting my arm up behind my back. Again I cried out in pain, a sound he ignored as if it were noise coming from a TV. He began forcing me towards the house, a failed attempt at a frog-march. The pain, excruciating now, made me land on one knee, nearly dislocating my arm. I hoped Trixie – or Zora – was taking notes on how this guy treated women.

'Goddammit,' he said, throwing me over his shoulder caveman style, pretty much the way you'd carry a toddler having a tantrum. He headed towards the house, saying something to the woman as he passed. I couldn't catch what it was, nor could I see her from my upside-down angle. I only had a view of her feet, shod in pricey sneakers like the ones Trixie wore in her more casual Facebook pics.

There was no escaping the conclusion: somehow Trixie was in this up to her neck.

She held open the screen door to allow him to enter with his burden – me. We crossed a room, probably a kitchen, the floor of which was covered in linoleum which had seen better days. It was red with those black-and-gray speckles, a style last popular in the fifties.

I was desperately trying to notice everything I could about my surroundings so I could report this incident at a future time. It never crossed my mind I might not get that chance. The mind wants you to survive and plans accordingly, even when things are looking very bad indeed.

Someone – I couldn't tell who it was, but I assumed Trixie – now held open a door at the other side of the kitchen. I could see a set of wooden steps leading down to a stone-lined cellar and I braced myself for an ungainly descent, my knees held tightly at Niko's shoulders. I grabbed at the wooden handrail and realized what a mistake that was as soon as my hands came away with splinters. Another shriek of pain.

My attempt at resistance seeming to anger him, he sped up the entire process by simply throwing me down the stairs.

I hit my head on a wide wooden baluster on the way down.

And I passed out before I reached the bottom.

TWENTY-NINE

When I came to it was dark, although there was no way to tell if that meant it was midnight or just that any windows were covered. I felt something moist on my face and I was sure it was Roscoe trying to wake me up. I reached out to pet him and felt a human arm.

'Don't talk.' It was a woman's voice I didn't recognize.

I tried opening one eye just to see if it worked well enough to bother trying both eyes. But I couldn't believe either one of them.

'Zora?'

This time I was sure. With frightened eyes, hair disheveled, the remnants of her dark makeup a streaky mess. It was Zora; I was in no doubt. Her long, dark tresses had been lopped off, for what reasons I could only guess. She was mopping at my face with a rough washcloth.

I pushed it away. Everything hurt. Even my eyelashes hurt.

'What the hell? Zora? Do you have any idea how many people are looking for you?'

She signaled me to keep my voice down.

'How's Harry?' she whispered. 'How's my baby?'

'He's with your mother. He's fine.'

There was in fact a source of light from somewhere; it seemed to come from the door through which I had so recently been tossed. In that light I could see the gleam of tears in her eyes. They conveyed what remained of her mascara down her face.

'Here,' I said, handing her the washcloth. 'You need this more than I do.' As I offered the cloth, I could see there was a dark stain of blood on it, so I quickly withdrew the offer.

'What did they do? Did they kidnap you?' Silly question, of course they did.

'He was already married.'

I didn't have to guess whom she meant but numbly I whispered, 'Niko?'

She nodded mutely, resuming her gentle ministrations. I seemed to have an open wound on my forehead. Which would explain the blinding headache and the problem I was having processing simple information. Such as, my neighbor Niko of Kildare Place was probably a stone-cold killer, in addition to his lesser faults, like being a philanderer and a mulch hog.

'How do you know?' I asked her.

'I can hear them talking at night in the kitchen. I listen at the door. He was already married to her when we met. Already married when he and I got together. And planning—'

We heard the shuffle of feet upstairs. Both of us held our breath in case someone opened the door and came down the stairs. A long minute passed and whoever it was could be heard walking away, going further inside the house.

She seemed to understand from experience this meant we could not be overheard. In a somewhat louder whisper, she said, 'The day he kidnapped me – crazy word for it but that's what he did – it was the anniversary of the day we met. He suggested a romantic picnic at "our" spot down GW Parkway. Things hadn't been great between us for some time, but I was happy he was making such an obvious effort. Not just happy, thrilled to pieces. That's how stupid I was. It was in the park we first met, at a party. He crashed the party or maybe I encouraged him to. It really was love at first sight. At least I thought it was.'

'What happened? He lured you to the spot and then . . .'

'And then, I don't know. I don't know what happened. I woke up down here. Where are we?'

'We're in Mystic. Maybe just outside the boundary; I'm not sure.'

'Mystic? Where is that?'

'Connecticut. Beautiful little town, a tourist resort along the shore. So, I gather you've never been here before.'

'No.'

'Is your husband from here?'

'You mean the man pretending to be my husband.'

'Yeah, I guess that's what I mean.'

'I don't have the first clue where he's from, but he never mentioned Mystic.' She shook her head.

None of this second-wife business could involve Trixie, unless she'd been a child bride. Absurd and impossible. How had she been roped into this? Had she been roped?

'We have to figure a way out of here. I've tried everything but in the dark . . . There's a half-bath down here but it's windowless.' I heard a rattling sound and for the first time I realized she was wearing handcuffs, her hands in front of her.

'Jesus Christ. He put handcuffs on you?'

She was better at staying on topic than I was. But then she'd had more time to get over being terrified and frantic about the situation. Hearing that the baby was all right seemed to be all she needed to keep going.

'The other windows, the two in this room, are boarded up,' she said. 'I've tried everything. The only way out of here is up the stairs and through the kitchen.'

'OK. The first thing we do is get those effing things off you. Help me find something.'

The cellar was full of junk and boxes of books and board games like Monopoly and Scrabble and jigsaw puzzles, but from where I was, I could spy no handy tool kit. I had to drag myself around the room rather than stand, leaving a trail of gunk like a snail from my plunge into the water; the ankle throbbed with an alarming intensity, and I only could hope Niko hadn't managed to actually break it throwing me down the stairs.

The puzzles looked like they'd be fun, if I were up for leisure activities. Some were no doubt pandemic purchases, used to while away the time in lockdown. There was a complicated-looking Monet of a thousand pieces, a Van Gogh – the view of the courtyard of the Arles hospital, where he had stayed. Munch's *The Scream*. Given ordinary time I'd have explored the book titles as a key to the homeowner's personality. But needs must. I moved – or rather, dragged – on.

There was a free-standing cabinet with clothing and blankets, a large trunk, an empty crate. She'd made a makeshift bed on the floor in one corner, or someone had thoughtfully provided it for her.

It was an appalling situation, different from anything she had been used to in her young life, and it told me more than anything else Niko had no plans for keeping her around. The miracle was she was still alive.

I couldn't think of a nice way to ask her why that was so; I blurted it out.

'They didn't kill you outright. That means . . . what? What do you think?'

'I've thought about that – a lot. He may have some half-baked plan for a ransom demand. Actually, given it's Niko, the plan will be fully baked. He's smart.'

'The demand would be to your parents?'

'Yes. They're well off. And I know they'd do anything to rescue me. Pay any amount.' She shook her head. 'I can't believe he's done this. You have no idea . . . they helped him in a thousand ways, not just financially. I knew they didn't like him, but they never let it show, especially not once the baby arrived. They did everything they could to make it work for all of us. *I* did everything I could to make it work. I had no idea – none – what he was up to.' She hung her head. 'None.'

'Did he ever hit you?' I asked.

The look on her face before she turned her head away gave me my answer. That was the 'talent' of the abuser, to make his target feel ashamed.

Her silence only added fuel to my determination to free us both.

I began quietly rootling around, looking for a tool, a rock, a brick, a hammer – something I could use to force those damn things off her. All I could find was a croquet mallet and a flashlight. I tried the flashlight switch and was rewarded with a dim, flickering light. The batteries weren't strong, but at least it was something.

I wondered why I hadn't received the same treatment as Zora and then realized they probably had only one pair of cuffs. They hadn't been expecting visitors they'd have to imprison.

I sat back, frustrated. Not only was there nothing heavy enough to do the job of smashing the chain open, but I was afraid of making the kind of racket that was sure to attract attention from upstairs.

It was then I remembered: my character Caroline had been

in a similar fix once with some bad guys, drug lords who were the bane of her existence.

I fumbled around in my hair until I found a bobby pin and I pulled it free, holding the little piece of metal in front of me with – no doubt – a crazed look in my eyes.

'Your hair looks fine. You could use a conditioner, is all. What are you doing?'

I unfolded the pin, working in the semidarkness, until by the feel of it I had managed to flatten the bend in the center. I put one plastic tip in my mouth, gnawing and pulling at it with my teeth until it came off. I spit it out.

I bent the very tip of the end to a ninety-degree angle. Then I motioned Zora to scoot close to me and hold out her wrists. I stuck the flashlight down the front of my T-shirt, into my bra – as I angled towards her, the light was aimed at her hands.

Locating the lock as much by feel as by sight, I inserted the bended tip. Then I bent the main piece backwards until the end was in a 'Z' shape, giving me leverage as I poked about, willing the internal mechanism to jar loose as I plucked away at it blindly. It was a frustrating few minutes, and I found myself wishing I had actually practiced the technique before I had my series character use it. However, I'd been reliably informed through my research that this method would work – with a bit of patience.

Exactly what I didn't have.

Luckily, Zora was a docile type, practically bovine. Exactly the type I imagined Niko preyed upon. I don't know how I had come to think differently, but no doubt after some time living with Niko, her fighting instincts had been aroused. Motherhood probably finished the course she needed to take to start standing up to her husband.

Never suspecting, by the sound of things, what he had in store for her. Despite her looks, despite the fact they had more than sufficient money for their needs and beyond, despite – or because of – his wealthy in-laws, Niko wanted more, or other, or whatever was most unattainable. Whatever carried the most risk. I'd have bet he was a killer attorney in the courtroom. I would say a take-no-hostages type, except that was exactly what he had done here.

During a breather in my lock-picking, I asked Zora how she had been treated – apart from being held captive in a cellar against her will. I was trying to figure out what the end game was here.

'I'm turning the flashlight off for a moment,' I said. 'I want to save the batteries as long as possible. Just try not to move or you'll dislodge the hairpin.'

'OK.'

'Does he have a gun?' I asked. 'Does she?'

She shook her head. 'Not that I saw. I just woke up – you know, like this. There was no need for them to threaten me with a gun. I had already decided to do whatever they said. What choice did I have?'

'Did he say what was going on?'

'I mostly dealt with her. And she wasn't at all talkative.'

'Is she behind this, do you think? Or is he the . . . what we'll call the brains of the outfit?'

'I think it's him. But she has no problem with it.'

I tried to shift into a comfortable position on the cold cellar floor. I must have grimaced.

'When I get out of these things, let me look at that,' she said. 'It's your foot, right?'

'Ankle.' I turned the flashlight back on, resettled it against my chest, and resumed fiddling with the lock. I could almost feel it start to give; my heart rose. 'Did they feed you?'

'They'd leave food at the top of the stairs. It's OK food, whatever is left over from what they'd had that night, I'd guess. She'd throw bottled water downstairs whenever she thought about it, which wasn't often enough. Whatever they were feeding me was sometimes too salty – she's a terrible cook.'

She seemed pleased with that lack of talent in her husband's choice of criminal companion. As if kidnapping her and planning to do God-knew-what with her weren't the more worrying trait.

'Speaking of food, your cat is fine. Dining in style.'

'I didn't dare ask. I thought the poor thing was locked inside with no one there.'

'Oh, there have been plenty of people in your house, believe me. The police would have fed her if all else failed, but my dog sitter is on the case now.'

'That's one mercy anyway.'

From her language, I was starting to suspect some kind of religious inclination. If it had been me, I would have been cursing a blue streak, probably threatening revenge. She didn't seem resigned to the situation, anything but that, but she was relying on some inner strength I hadn't credited her with. Niko had seen her as an easy, soft target. But maybe Niko had been wrong.

Let's hope he was. I was going to have to count on her to hold it together. We had to get out of this place, and it was going to take both of us on our best game.

'He ever mention the name Lily?' I asked. I was starting to perspire a bit. The cellar wasn't warm but it was clammy. Plus, I was terrified I'd have to give up and leave her here, figure out some way to save myself, then bring back reinforcements in the form of the local police. By which time . . .

I couldn't think about that.

'No. Who is Lily?'

'She owns this place. Trixie is her niece.'

She wasn't expecting that. 'You mean, our babysitter? Trixie?'

'Yeah.'

She shook her head. 'My god. She's just a kid.'

'But you know her. If she's here, if she's involved in this somehow . . . Couldn't you – you know, work on her? Soften her up? Make her see this is wrong?

Again she shook her head. 'No chance. The door opens; she throws or sets the food down; the door closes. It's dark in here; her figure is only backlit. She doesn't stay to chat.'

I told her what I thought was going on, from what little I knew myself, ending with, 'Trixie may be innocent. She may have been coerced into this for some reason.'

'Innocent isn't a word I'd use to describe Trixie,' said Zora.

'Wise beyond her years, is she?'

'You could call it that. Maybe she was just acting as a go-between? I told Niko I didn't want her in the house again after the last time. But that was months ago.'

'That sounds familiar. Did she steal from you too?'

'Huh? No. It was just a feeling I had. I thought she was sly. I'd catch her looking at me and she wasn't even embarrassed

to be caught staring; the sly look never left her face. It was
creepy, that's all. What do you mean, steal from me too?'

'My neighbor across the way claims she stole from her.
Lingerie.'

'Ugh. Anyway, he didn't argue. He seemed baffled but he
didn't argue. I assumed he was worried I thought she was too
attractive to have around. And maybe there was a bit of that
too.'

'It's not like there's no precedent. Never have a beautiful
woman working in your house, dependent on making sure the
"master" of the house is well tended to. It's bound to end badly.'

The light from the flashlight shifted and shimmered with my
every move. I was beginning to wonder if I could somehow
attach the thing to my forehead, but just then I heard and felt
the little click which told me I had released the catch. The
opposite lock was ten times easier since I was now ten times
better at picking locks. The cuffs fell away with a soft clatter
of metal. I hoped if anyone could hear the sound, they'd just
assume she was rattling around down here like the prisoner of
Zenda. I don't think anything epitomized Niko's evil so much
as his treating Zora, his own wife and the mother of his child,
like this. I supposed it was a small mercy he hadn't killed her
outright, but her usefulness as a hostage hung by a thread, I
imagined. I further imagined he wouldn't hesitate to get rid of
his liability.

And I assumed that, like a true lawyer, that was exactly the
way he thought of her. A potential liability.

And now me.

Zora wasted no time, scrambling quietly around the room,
sorting quietly through the various sporting equipment and
abandoned home improvement projects. I thought longingly of
my townhouse overlooking the back yard of my neighbor with
his many half-finished schemes.

And that odd memory somehow strengthened my resolve. I
would get out of this. I would get us both out of this and
I would see my home again. And I would ask my neighbor
what he was doing back there.

And I would offer to help him.

She came back carrying the croquet mallet, a roll of duct

tape, an old ski parka, and a folded blanket. 'I'm going to stabilize your ankle,' she said. 'You're going to have to keep your weight off it. But obviously we're going to have to get out of here.'

'You know how to do that? The ankle, I mean?'

'I should; I'm a nurse. I quit when Harry came along; I wanted to stay home with him. But marketing from home, I missed being around people. I was planning to go back to work at the hospital when . . . you know.'

When Niko made his move. I wondered if her career plans might have precipitated his actions somehow. Once she was working outside the house, he would have to build his scheme around her schedule. So long as she was at home with the baby, she was easy to find. Maybe even a bit easier to con, too, since her world was narrowed so much between just him and the child. The perfect little nuclear family.

She was always exactly where she said she would be.

I was mildly ashamed I didn't know this basic fact about my neighbor's choice of career. How could I live for years so near so many people and know nothing about them? Not even bother to ask?

I resolved to be nosier – correction: more inquisitive, more neighborly, more caring and involved – when and if I got out of here. Like Scrooge, I vowed to keep Christmas all the year.

She instructed me to lie down, adding, 'You can use the mallet as a crutch once I get you up and running.'

THIRTY

She set to work by tucking the ski jacket beneath the length of my ankle and lower leg, following this by setting the blanket on top. Although she was being extremely gentle, the pain was extremely great. She had to wrap the duct tape around in several places, of course, all of which necessitated my foot being lifted off the ground. I tried to help as much as I could rather than have my limb be just a dead weight.

'Do you think Trixie helped with the actual abduction? Or was she just up here waiting at the house?' I asked her.

'She may have been waiting at the park. I remember another car was there by the side of the dirt road as we turned to go deeper into the woods. The only people who use that road are the National Park Service Police, and they've had so many cutbacks that few of them are ever around. It's a remote area, tucked between the river footpath and the highway. There's an enormous tree canopy, tons of forested land. I remember wondering who else could have found our romantic little place? Our little secret hideaway? I was annoyed by that. Anyway, I didn't recognize the car but it had to be Trixie, now I put it together. Or now, I'm guessing, her aunt? What I don't know is if they put me in the trunk or in the back seat.'

'I'm going to guess the trunk. And they drove you all the way here. Which cannot have been pleasant.' I was thinking if they took the expected route, they'd have had to cross a toll booth or two, maybe pull over to a rest stop. There would be photographs. If we ever got to the point of proving who and what they were.

'I must really have been drugged. He gave me something. There was wine. Yes. There was wine – he'd shown up with a picnic basket. A bunch of expensive stuff he'd bought at Balducci's. I was desperately pleased by that. It seemed like a real turning point in our relationship, you know?'

Well, it certainly was that.

'He put something in the wine. That must have been it because he didn't drink any. He said he had to work on a case later in the day and needed to keep a clear head. And he made a little joke about how he had to be in top form, for me and for the client.'

I was trying to sort out what Niko's long game would be. He had abandoned his car in the woods near Dyke Marsh. Probably his plan was to reappear a few days later, dazed and disoriented, claiming to have been kidnapped with Zora, who was still being held for ransom by thugs. He didn't know where he'd been; he'd been drugged and blindfolded. He'd escaped. And so on and so on. Obviously, there were parts of the story I didn't know and possibly would never know, but I'm sure those were the broad outlines. Then he'd go to work on Zora's parents, making sure they paid the ransom, that the police didn't talk them out of paying. He probably knew to the penny how much he could ask for.

Not that it would take a lot of convincing for them to pay. They loved their daughter, and the more time I spent with her the more I could see why.

Or maybe, if Niko were especially cunning and patient, he would simply wait the seven years required in most states to have Zora declared dead, to collect the insurance, to inherit the house, to inherit whatever savings she may have had.

Would that have been enough? For a man like Niko?

Somehow, I doubted it. More than enough would never be enough.

Whatever happened, I'd be willing to bet Zora's body would be in the Atlantic Ocean by then. Niko would get the cash, and he and his wife – after a suitable pause – would 'marry' for the second time and disappear – for good this time.

Or maybe not. This taste of success might be all Niko needed to make him believe he could do it all over again. He just needed to find another pliable rich target. Such laughs!

Finally, Zora sat back, satisfied with her work.

'That will do for now,' she said. 'We have to get you to a hospital. I don't dare try to set a fracture here. But before you know it, you'll be up playing tennis.'

I was sure this was the feel-good spiel she gave all her

patients. She was even smiling, for the first time since I'd been thrown so unceremoniously into her life. She was optimistic by nature and, because she was, I was gaining hope as well.

We could do this.

But do what exactly?

She said, 'Our best chance is when she opens that door. It's locked, of course, and there's not a thing we can do until it's unlocked. We must attack her, disable her – I don't know what. Or how.' She paused and added, 'I may have to run for help by myself and leave you behind. I'm so sorry. I don't see how you can run on that, even using the mallet as a crutch.'

'Slowly, that's how. If he's still in the house, and I'm assuming he is, he will come running unless we can grab her very quietly, without alarming him that something's wrong; that she's been gone too long or something.'

Just then we heard voices, his and hers, coming from under the door at the top of the stairs. I grabbed the flashlight. It wasn't especially large or heavy, but it was what I had for a weapon to hold in my right hand.

I looked at her. We didn't dare speak. The voices were near enough now to be quite clear. And what we heard was this: 'Now we have to get rid of the other one, too.' It is the strangest thing, hearing your fate discussed like that. Completely chilling and completely terrifying: Niko, a man I barely knew, deciding my awful fate. My disposal was just another chore, like picking up the dry cleaning on his way home.

'It's going to be easier after all to just bury them both here,' he continued. 'It'll be too hard to drag two bodies up the stairs and down to the boat, especially without being seen pulling out, even as remote as it is. We don't dare chance it. That old dirt cellar, though – it might make for some hard digging.' He paused. Something might have shown in her face, as if the enormity of this was sinking in. 'Are you sure you're up for this? Because if you're not . . .' What sounded like tender concern for his companion's welfare managed to convey a threat. Was the threat that three bodies were no bigger a deal than two?

I looked around wildly for a weapon for Zora to use. She was doing the same. There was a set of dust-covered golf clubs in a back corner near the bathroom. I motioned to her to grab one. She came back with what looked like a nine-iron. Good thinking. She must have played golf to know the wooden clubs had too much give in the swing.

We could hear them, their footsteps, leaving the kitchen. They had probably come to get a drink or something and were going back into the living area. I didn't realize how loaded with adrenaline I'd been until it drained from my body. I wanted to collapse, and collapsing was a luxury. I did sit down at the bottom of the steps.

'What time does she bring your next meal? Is there a schedule?'

'Not so you'd notice. Of course, I've lost my sense of time down here, but I think she's been pretty regular with the meals, twice a day, breakfast, which is usually just bread, and dinner. And the bottled water, of course. In between times I do get hungry.'

'Me too.' I was wishing I hadn't brought up the subject because in fact I couldn't remember how long it had been since the buttered-corn fiasco. And suddenly I was hungry. I patted my pockets but all I found were those matches given to me by Elias.

Elias. Was there any chance he would notice I'd been gone too long? I'd shown him that photo, which he recognized as the Morrison place. But would he do anything about it? Why would he?

Would he say something to Misaki if she came back to the inn asking after me?

She might find the Morrison house in much the same way I had, but what would happen if she came to the door looking for me? Would they grab her too?

'Is there a bucket or a pail or something down here?' I asked Zora. 'If so, fill it with water and bring it here.'

'There's a plastic wastebasket.'

'OK. Also, some kind of metal container – anything that won't melt.'

I was realizing that to sit there waiting for them to show up and feed us or kill us put all the initiative and the timing on them, when what was needed was for us to control the timing. To set an ambush. To lie in wait for our prey.

She looked baffled but she said, 'In the bathroom there's this metal box holding the towels. I'll go get it.'

'Good,' I said. 'It doesn't have to be watertight. Is there any ammonia in there? Any kind of cleaning product? Rubbing alcohol?' I was desperately searching my 'What Would Caroline Do?' database. Hours of research on the web, much of it discarded, the rest distilled into perhaps a sentence or paragraph of the finished novel.

'There might be some bleach.'

'Bleach is always good. Any aerosol cans? Hair spray? Pretty much anything with a propellent.'

'You're not thinking of cleaning the place, are you?' But she got it: she was smiling again.

I smiled back. 'Only in a manner of speaking. Bring whatever you find. The more toxic the better. Oh, and see if there are any cotton balls, or some cotton wool. Or makeup remover pads. Anything like that.'

'What are we doing?'

'We're building a tinder nest.'

THIRTY-ONE

Zora brought out a nice assortment of household chemicals, nearly all labeled with warnings about avoiding contact with the eyes. She had to make two trips – like most seldom-visited parts of houses, the space over the years had become a repository for overflow purchases and stuff no longer used but deemed too good to throw out. There were some nice spray bottles of toxins to clean the house with. I shook them to make sure there were some contents left inside. The fullest ones I set to one side.

I turned my attention to the flammables.

'There's a Monopoly game over by the cabinet, and Chinese checkers and Scrabble board sets,' I told her. 'Bring me those. Maybe a couple of paperbacks. The romance novels would be good.'

She seemed to have accepted that she was taking orders from a deranged person, but she quibbled over the romance novels.

'I like romance novels,' she said.

I bet she did. And look how well that was turning out.

'This is not a literary judgment. They use the cheapest paper possible to produce those. Well, also the mystery novels, but I'm not burning mystery novels. Unless maybe there's a James Patterson?'

She actually started unpacking one of the boxes looking for a Patterson.

'I was kidding. Come on. Hurry up.'

What I planned carried several risks – if what I was doing could even be dignified by the word 'plan' – but I was gambling on our warders not wanting to burn the house down with all of us in it. I placed little value on Zora as a hostage, although my sense was that he would keep her until the last. I should say, keep her alive – he might need to provide proof of life at any moment.

My sense also, most definitely, was that I was expendable.

And because of the ankle, a very easy target. But he probably thought he'd completely incapacitated me already, if not killed me outright. I doubted either way it altered his plans, beyond having to bury us both in the cellar.

'First thing,' I said, 'they need to believe they've killed me. So I will need to remain exactly where he saw me last, sprawled out at the bottom of the stairs. They can't be allowed to see the splint on my ankle, so you'll need to cover me with a blanket – maybe make it look like you're trying to show respect to my dead body. Or just not have to look at it.'

She nodded solemnly. She seemed to be catching on to the fact that dead bodies were very much a potential outcome of this scenario.

'You'll have to stand by at the top of the stairs and get ready to deck him with the golf iron.'

She looked up the stairs to the small landing. 'There's not going to be enough room for me to get a good swing in.'

I could see she was right. It would be close combat, and he'd be able to grab her arm well before she could clobber him.

'Is there a baseball bat? Cricket bat?'

'Maybe a cricket bat; let me go look.'

A faint rustle of wooden and metal objects came from the corner nearest the bathroom. I held my breath: Every sound seemed amplified.

The danger was so real and so close. This had to work. I had absolutely no promise to give her or myself that it would. It was still better than sitting here waiting to die at the hands of this thug and his deluded partner.

She came back empty-handed except for a hair dryer. 'If I hold it by the electrical cord, I can maybe whomp him with this?'

I shook my head. 'Not heavy enough. It's mostly plastic. We're going to have to go with the sprays.'

We tested each of the cans, discarding those that showed the slightest inclination to clog and not emit a steady stream of product. Then I told her exactly what I wanted her to do. She listened carefully, eyes wide, like a child being told to memorize an address. I made her repeat it, which she did, almost word for word. The beauty of Zora was that childlike quality. I wanted to make sure her child got to enjoy the full advantage of it.

'Remember,' I said, wrapping up my instructions. 'This is for Harry.'

I couldn't shout directions from the bottom of the steps, so I lay there mutely as she set the trap, waving my arms about and pointing as necessary, prepared to draw the blanket over my head at a moment's notice.

I wanted to draw Niko, thinking we needed to immobilize the bigger, more physically robust threat first. Whatever drew him into our lair needed to be loud and threatening. Not that he was above sending someone else to do his job, but that was the chance I had to take.

Once he was under control, we could deal more easily with her.

'What time do you think it is?' I whispered. 'Without the flashlight I can't see my watch.'

'Judging by my stomach, dinner is about an hour away.'

'OK, we need to do this before she's in there messing about in the kitchen. We need to get him first. Can you hear them out there?'

She pressed her ear against the door and whispered down the stairs, 'Yes.'

'You have everything ready?'

'Yes.'

'Let's do it. I don't know about you, but I want out of here.'

The explosion was all I could have hoped for. It was particularly satisfying because my character Caroline had used a similar technique in my tenth or eleventh book – after so many, I couldn't be sure. But she had become increasingly cunning, adept at circumventing her boss where necessary, which was often, and foiling the bad guys by fair means and foul. I was extremely proud of her, even though she was me in a strange, strange way.

I had helped Zora line the metal pan from the bathroom with shredded bits of cotton wool, toilet paper, and a paperback romance novel called *Passion's Proud Promise*. On top of the

tinder nest we sprinkled Scrabble board pieces and fanned
Monopoly money about strategically to capture the flames. In
the middle of this sat the batteries from the flashlight, nestled
like two eggs.

Next I had Zora pour a combination of bleach and rubbing
alcohol onto two washcloths from the bathroom. This I
had learned, via my research for book twelve, would produce
chloroform, but the exact ratio was difficult to judge and
obviously I wasn't going to test it on my own face. It was merely
one of our backup measures. I placed one washcloth next to
me on the floor, loosely wrapped in a fold of blanket, as far away
from my face as I could manage; Zora had the other tucked into
her back pocket to use on him if she got the chance.

But since that would require getting close enough to
overpower him physically, her first weapons of choice were
the aerosol spray cans, of which she had a nearly endless
supply.

The fire took careful tending, and of course the danger
was that Zora would get caught in the blast as the chemicals
inside the battery exploded from the heat. A bucket of water
stood at the ready about halfway down the steps.

Once the tinder caught and the kindling began to heat up, she
stepped down the staircase, shielding her eyes from the explosion.
The flames were substantial and the explosion when it came was
actually quite wonderful. Do not try this at home, kids.

In no time at all we heard footsteps running towards the
kitchen above. Zora, God bless her, now stood braced at
the top of the stairs to one side with her spray, avoiding the
flames. The door flew open and, as I'd hoped, there was Niko.

'What in hell is going on?' He stepped over the threshold,
bent, I would imagine, on revenge.

'You've killed her!' cried Zora.

I heard her improvising, strictly against my instructions,
as I lay still under the blanket with my own cans of hairspray
and deodorant, a croquet mallet and a golf club.

'You have got to get her out of here,' Zora went on, her voice
an ill-controlled shriek of shredded nerves. Nerves and some
unsuspected acting chops. 'I won't be stuck down here with a
dead body, Niko! Enough is enough.'

It worked. After all, she knew how the guy ticked over better than I did. He didn't even notice the cuffs were gone. It was the one stupid thing she could say that would distract him for the second she needed to begin to pull the aerosol can out from behind her and aim it at him.

'You stupid little b—' he began.

By this point Zora had stepped back down the steps and was about two yards from the landing. He flung himself at her.

And lost his footing on the Chinese checkers marbles strewn on the landing. For good measure, she'd sprayed them with Lysol to make them slick.

'For Harry!' she shouted as she brought out another spray can and aimed it into his face. Judging by the color it emitted, a luminescent blue, she had chosen to use the spray paint.

She gave Niko a mighty shove down the stairs. He grabbed blindly at the handrail and she executed a nice judo-style kick with her foot to dislodge his hand from it.

He fell ass over teakettle and almost landed on top of me.

My disguise as a dead person no longer needed, I threw off my blanket and managed to drag myself close enough to be ready to unleash the full fury of my croquet mallet on his head once his body came to a halt.

Which I did. For good measure I sprayed deodorant in his eyes. *Couldn't hurt.* He groaned and started thrashing around and I whacked him again, this time, I hoped, between the eyes. It was still dark, with only the flames from the small fire to see by, but the luminescent paint on his face helped.

As satisfying as all this was, there was no time to savor the moment. We had the woman to deal with almost immediately. I looked up the stairs and saw, silhouetted against the light from the kitchen, a female form. I felt immensely exposed in the sudden light.

'What have you done to Niko?'

There was no easy answer to that so we just stared her down, breathing heavily from our exertions. I took a moment to reassess because something in her appearance seemed off to me.

'I think he's dead,' I said finally. 'I may have killed him.' I wanted her to come closer so I could use one of my sprays on her. She didn't seem to have a weapon and I wanted to keep it that way.

The backlit figure, sidestepping the marbles, inched her way down the steps, her entire focus on Niko and whether he was breathing.

At least, I thought, I'll finally get a closer look.

Because whoever it was, I of course knew now it was not Zora. She and Niko had not teamed together in some elaborate hoax to con her parents into paying ransom money.

And even peering through darkness against the glare from the kitchen, I didn't think it was Trixie, either.

This must be Aunt Lily. The same haircut, the same bone structure, the same way of carrying herself, but this woman was a slightly older model, perhaps thirty or a bit more, just losing the slightly rounded edges of youth.

Otherwise, Trixie's aunt was a lookalike for her niece. God only knew where Trixie was. Probably safe at home, pretending to babysit as she rifled through her clients' wardrobes. Her parents likely had lied about her whereabouts to protect her.

Lily sped down the stairs so quickly, I was afraid Zora couldn't catch her with the spray. But Zora had a backup plan: Now standing beside the stairs, she stuck out a golf iron, holding it tightly by the handle and using it as a tripwire to catch Aunt Lily's ankle.

Lily fell on top of her lover. Which seemed entirely fitting.

We tied them both up. He got the handcuffs, she got a dish-towel binding that Zora brought from the kitchen, along with a knife. Best we could do.

They were both still out but I didn't count on that lasting long. We had to get out of there. And with a mutual nod, that's what we did.

THIRTY-TWO

reedom! It was so blessed and sweet. Zora ran from that house like the hounds of hell were after her, not even caring where she was going. I did my best to keep up, using the mallet as a crutch. We needed to put as much space between us and those two as we could. I was convinced Niko would come after us, and when he did there would be no talking him out of his plans for us. Not that there ever was a hope of that.

Neither of us had a phone, of course, or I would have dialed 911 right there. But in the absence of technology, we simply ran.

We ran right into Kent Haworth.

'Jesus Christ,' I said.

'Not quite,' he said, his handsome face with its Hemingway beard grinning ear to ear. 'Just me.'

'What in hell are you doing here? Never mind, explain later. You have to call for help *now*.'

He pulled out his phone. 'What's this about? I'll have to tell them something.'

'The short story is I found Niko and Zora.' I waved my hand to indicate the area behind me. Zora hung back, waiting to see what was up. I motioned her forward. 'It's a long story. What are you doing here?'

'I followed you, obviously. You and your friend.'

'Why didn't you just come with us?'

'Because I knew you wouldn't want me with you. You ladies were on a mission all to yourselves to solve the case and you didn't want any interference.'

This was so close to the truth I didn't bother arguing. Something that had bothered me about our last phone conversation suddenly came clear in my mind. I remembered him using expressions like 'all hands on deck' and 'dead in the water' and maybe 'watertight'. His subconscious mind was telegraphing

all these nautical expressions because it knew he was headed
for a seaport town. It was probably a writer's trick of mind; I'd
been doing much the same thing.

He looked down at his phone. '*Damn*,' he said. 'There's no
signal. Stay here.'

'Who is this guy?' Zora whispered, watching him walk away.

'Just an old friend. Well, not really a friend; it's sort of a
business relationship. He was helping me find you. Your parents
hired him a long time ago.'

'What?' she looked genuinely shocked. Whether she felt
betrayed or simply astonished, it was impossible to tell.

'They wanted him to look into your husband. I guess we
have to stop calling him that now.'

'It takes a while to undo that thinking. Believe me. Why
didn't you know this Kent guy was following you?'

That was a very good question.

'I'll ask him when he gets back.'

She seemed to have made up her mind about something.
'There has to be a phone in the house. I'm going back. You
wait here. One of those two may have left their cell phones out,
at least, if there's no landline. And even if their phones are
locked, you can always dial emergency.'

'I really don't think it's a good idea to go back in there, Zora.
They may have come to by now.'

'I'll be careful.'

'I'd go with you but I can't walk much more on this thing.'

'No. One of us has to wait for your friend anyway.'

'He's not my friend,' I said to her retreating back.

She ran quickly, hoofing her way back up the incline, atop
which the house commanded a view of the river and the ocean
beyond.

Minutes passed before I heard a distant rustling in the leaves.
It was Kent, out of breath.

'There's a road not far from here. I caught a signal, and the
police are on their way, but I told them to meet us there on
the Old Post Road.'

'How far? On this ankle, I'm not sure I can make it.'

'Yeah, OK. Where did the girl go?'

'Zora? She went back in the house.'

'Is she crazy? They're still in there, right?'

'Last I saw. Are you seriously leaving me here?'

But he'd already left.

Minutes passed and I started to wonder what was taking Zora so long. Had she not found a phone? Worse, had she found Niko or Lily, released from their captivity, despite the trouble we'd taken to immobilize them?

What was taking the police so long, for that matter? And what would happen if we weren't out there waiting for them, as promised? They'd probably write it off as a hoax and head back to town.

Someone with two good legs needed to head into Mystic for help. I wasn't eligible and Zora seemed the best option. I wanted to get her to safety since she had been the target all along. As for me, I didn't particularly want to be left here alone without any kind of protection. Kent wouldn't have been my first choice for that, but he was what I had for the moment.

I was terrified that Niko, especially, would come to, and that would be nothing but trouble. Aunt Lily would be a handful on her own, but it was Niko I was afraid of.

Just then Kent came running back down the hill.

'Where's Zora?'

'Don't worry about her.'

It was then I saw the gun in his hand.

'What's that for?' I asked. But somehow I knew.

'What do you think? You just had to stick your nose in, didn't you?'

'Kent, come on. You know the kind of day I've had? Put that away.'

Why was I so surprised? Kent had not shown a shred of decency the entire time I'd known him. That he should be mixed up in this should have only seemed logical. Tell that to my brain, though, which was still scrambling. It was getting harder to tell who to trust.

'Where is Zora?' I repeated.

I had a distant relative who had surrendered to Alzheimer's disease not long before, but before she left us she spent the last ten years of her life repeating the same questions over and over and over. Talking to her on the phone, which I did as often as

I could until it became utterly pointless, was an exercise in torment and sorrow. I would answer her questions repeatedly, and finally start trying to say goodbye. This elicited another round of 'Where do you live?' and we'd start over. This was what passed for conversation, and I supposed it was no worse or more pointless than other conversations I'd had.

My own brain seemed stuck on, 'Where is Zora?' but as my shock began to recede I added, 'You haven't hurt her, have you?' I hadn't heard a gunshot, but there were other ways, and I was certain the true-crime writer slash PI before me knew all of them.

My hand around the handle of the mallet was starting to perspire. I spent a split-second debating whether to lift the thing over my head like a hatchet or simply brace myself against the pain and whack it against his hand, the hand holding the gun, as hard as I could. This was the route I chose, and I did succeed in making him drop it. We were scrimmaging for the weapon when it hit the ground, a scrimmage I was bound to lose, when suddenly Zora appeared behind him. He heard or sensed her arrival and, distracted, turned towards her.

In his confusion he didn't stop to realize it wasn't Zora but Lily, who had somehow managed to escape the dishtowel we'd used to bind her. I suspected I hadn't been ruthless enough with the bindings, and with her small wrists she'd been able to wriggle out of them.

Even as she said, 'Kent, no!' his gun went off and he shot Lily through the chest.

All that PI target practice had paid off. It was the sort of wound you may not recover from.

There was a rustle of movement in the undergrowth and two policemen emerged from the trees, on the run, guns drawn. They were mere seconds too late to stop Kent from killing but they would later make reliable witnesses to murder.

THIRTY-THREE

'When did you know?' Narduzzi demanded. It was the next day and he, Misaki, Zora, and I were at the Whale's Inn with the little sitting room off the breakfast area all to ourselves. Elias had insisted on getting his wife to provide tea and cookies when he saw the state everyone was in. He also organized a spare room for Narduzzi once he learned he was here on official police business. He seemed entirely thrilled by all of this. Perhaps carving wooden whales had its limits in the adventure department.

'Something made Zora suspicious,' I said, looking at her, 'and she'd gone back into the house on a pretext, to use the landline. Right?'

'What made you suspicious?' he asked Zora.

She shrugged. 'What kind of PI doesn't think to use the phones in a nearby house instead of trekking all over the place looking for a signal? It was like something out of a bad mystery novel.'

'I thought you only read romance,' I said.

'Same thing,' she insisted. 'Romance is the biggest mystery. Anyway, it was only common sense to run for the nearest phone and, for a so-called expert, the guy wasn't using common sense.'

'I guess I also grew suspicious of our rescuer when he was gone too long looking for a signal,' I said. 'But to be honest, I never held Kent in high regard, so I wasn't as tuned in to suspecting him as you apparently were, Zora.'

Too late had I questioned his use of pronouns. He'd asked if they were still in the house. How had he know there was more than one person involved?

'Maybe I've just had more practice with liars,' she said. 'Look, are you sure you're going to be able to implicate her, too?' she asked Narduzzi. 'This Lily person? There's so much of what happened I can't remember.'

'They'll be able to tell if Lily's car was used to transport you. It's extra evidence, even if we didn't have a cellar full of evidence in that house. They'll examine the wheel arches and the footwells. They may be able to pinpoint where her car had been, using pollen analysis alone – even determine when it was in the area where Niko ditched his car. They'll also examine her shoes and his. Don't worry: they've got her cold. Or they soon will.'

I remembered Kent's talking about the size of those footprints and then I also remembered: this was *Kent*. Probably not one word he'd told me had been the unvarnished truth.

Zora nodded. 'Look, my parents will be here any minute. They're flying up to extract me from the situation – they're getting a few lawyers involved – and they're bringing Harry. I'm sure you understand.' I didn't think it was my imagination that at the mention of lawyers, her eyes flitted over to meet Narduzzi's gaze. She wasn't in any trouble, I was sure, but there was a lot of explaining to do.

Narduzzi turned to me as she left.

'It turns out you both were right to suspect Kent,' he said. 'We think he was hired by Niko to sanitize the investigation Kent ran on Niko before his marriage, an investigation instigated by Zora's skeptical parents. Niko paid him far more money than they did for a clean bill of health. The fact he was a bigamist meant of course he could never inherit from Zora, just for a start. Even with his name on the deed to the house, and so on. If he was found out, it was all over. Kent's report to the parents failed to mention either Niko's marriage to Lily or the fact his law degree was bogus.'

'For real?' said Misaki. 'He did pretty well without a degree.'

'Smart people think they don't need the credentials,' said Narduzzi. 'Up to a point, he was right. Niko is a complete charlatan and Kent has been in on the plot all along. He followed you and Misaki up here, knowing you were up to something. He was probably on the same train as you.'

'The police must've received more than a few calls by the time this was over,' said Misaki. 'I called them in probably just as everything was going down. I told them, Augusta,' she turned to me, 'that you had been supposed to meet me but were not answering your phone. And the last I heard you were off looking for the kidnapped couple who were all over the news. It was such a crazy story, I don't know why they believed me.'

In the end it was a scene of complete chaos up there at the Morrison place and the police took everyone into custody until it could get sorted. Everyone looked like a bad guy. Everyone turned on everyone. With Lily incapacitated, possibly dying, I was willing to bet Niko would blame her for everything. It would be interesting to see how far he got away with it. But there was little question in my mind they'd nail him.

Still, not until that morning had Zora and I been told we were free to go.

'The Mystic Police called our office to confirm what you'd told them,' said Narduzzi. 'As soon as I heard the names, I knew I had to get up here on the double. I already had a man trailing you. But when you two split up he had to make a choice, and he decided to follow Misaki.'

'You had us followed?'

'You didn't notice a guy in a Hawaiian shirt?'

I turned to Misaki. 'As a matter of fact, we did.' Then I turned to him. 'It's a wonder there was a seat left on that train. You didn't trust me.'

'Can you give me one reason why I should have trusted you?' he asked.

'Let me think about it. I'm sure I can come up with something.'

'I'm sure you can.'

Misaki left to pack for our return trip. I stood to join her, and Narduzzi motioned for me to sit down. He wasn't done with me yet.

'Look, before you say anything, I told you about the babysitter and you didn't follow up. I told you twice, in fact – I distinctly remember. So this is on you.'

'What do you mean, on me? The babysitter had nothing to do with it. They used her aunt's house as a hideaway, that's all.'

'Far from *all*,' I said. 'It was the key to the whole case, admit it. The fact that Aunt Lily's niece Trixie had been the Normans' babysitter was a situation arranged by Niko. Even though she

was a lousy babysitter and didn't last long on at least two jobs
I know of. I'll leave it to your team of experts to figure out
how or why she was living in the neighborhood at all. But
Trixie's father is a lawyer in Niko's firm, and that might have
been a lead to follow up, don't you think? If you hadn't been
so busy trailing me, you might have gone to the website for
the firm and seen the guy's name there. How many lawyers in
DC named Robert "Rocky" Steppes can there be?'

'OK. I'm going to give you that one. Would you like to
address tampering with a witness?'

'Tampering with a witness? What witness? You mean the
cat?'

'I mean the boy, of course. The twin who lives next door to
you.'

'Peter? He's five years old!'

'Precisely.'

'Precisely what? I mean, WTF? He can't even tie his own
shoes yet. How is he a witness?'

'I had told you very clearly to stay out of this.'

'A small child was worried about a cat he'd grown attached
to. What did you want me to do? Ignore him?'

'Never mind.'

He looked at me. Somehow I knew there was something
weighing on his mind – something more than my appetite for
lawbreaking. What he said next surprised me.

'Kenneth Branagh calls it "the corrosive power of lust". I don't
know in what context he said that. I must've read some interview
with him somewhere. But I think it's a perfect expression. "The
corrosive power of lust".'

'You are thinking of Niko and Lily, of course.'

'No. Not just of them.'

'I'm sorry. I don't follow.'

'I looked you up. Actually, I looked up your husband,
Marcus. I read . . . um . . . I read about his accident.'

'Yes?'

'I read that the police investigators determined he'd been
coming from Calvert Springs Road. The night he had his
accident.'

'Then you know more about it than I do. No one ever

mentioned where he'd been to me. Only where he'd ended up.'

'There are cameras along that parkway, and the avenues leading off it, because it's such a common place for speeders and drug dealers and anything else going. You know how it is. On a completely open road like that, people think they can do what they want and not get caught. Anyway, there was camera footage showing him, showing his car, leaving a specific property on Calvert Springs. One of our guys went to interview the woman at that address. You see . . . the car had to have come from that house. You know the setup; you've seen it. Your husband's car could only have come from that house. Anyway, there was this woman living there alone.'

'Did she happen to play bridge, this woman?'

'Hmm?'

'Never mind. Go on.'

'As I say, she was living there alone. She and her husband had split after a family tragedy.'

'A child drowned.'

'I thought you knew – I mean, I thought you knew who she was. Why else would you go there for an open house? I thought – I guess I thought you were just using the open house as a ruse to see inside the place.'

'How pathetic of me but no – I had no idea. I mean I knew my husband was unfaithful, but I didn't know who the woman was. I didn't know anything about her, and I didn't really care to know. But hold on a minute. You were following me even then?'

'I assigned Sergeant Bernolak to keep an eye out. I didn't think you'd be able to resist a mystery.'

I returned home the next day, taking the time on the train ride back to think things through. I had just skipped from my fictional world into an even stranger world. And something in me wanted to turn the experience into a story. A true-crime story. With Kent Haworth soon to be languishing in federal prison and unable to profit from his crime, I figured there'd be an opening in the field.

I decided to give my agent a call first thing when I got home and see what my editor could talk her into.

Actually, that ended up being the second thing I did.

The first thing I did when I got home was delete all but one special message from Marcus on the answering machine. I wanted to free up space for any new friends to leave a message.